One of Our Spaceships is Missing

Other books by Chris Gerrib

The Pirates Trilogy:

The Mars Run

Pirates of Mars

The Night Watch

One of Our Spaceships is Missing

Chris Gerrib

Space Wizard Science Fantasy
Raleigh, NC
www.spacewizardsciencefantasy.com

Publisher's Note: This is a work of fiction. Names, characters, places, and incidents are a product of the author's imagination. Locales and public names are sometimes used for atmospheric purposes. Any resemblance to actual people, living or dead, or to businesses, companies, events, institutions, or locales is completely coincidental.

Cover art by MoorBooks
Editing by Heather Tracy
Book Layout © 2015 BookDesignTemplates.com

One of Our Spaceships is Missing/Chris Gerrib.— 1st ed.
ISBN 978-1-7350768-4-3

Author's website: privatemarsrocket.net

For My Parents.
They are not big readers, but they supported me.

CONTENTS

Chapter 1

ValuTrip Cardinal

Victoria

Victoria settled behind the piano in what most passengers misnamed as the First-Class lounge of the in-system spaceship ValuTrip *Cardinal*. The lounge was open to everyone, although only first-class passengers got their first drink of the night "free" from the bar—given how much more the first-class passengers were paying for the same food and only marginally larger cabins, that "free" drink came very dearly indeed. She stretched her fingers.

"Hi there, good looking."

"Hi there yourself," Victoria replied, glancing up from her music display. "Well, Hank," Victoria said, putting her hands on her hips, "I like that dress." The dress in question was a spaghetti-strap number made of two pieces of material, black and white, connected by white lacing. The lacing started at the top of Hank's cleavage and ran diagonally down her chest, becoming a side slit at her right hip. It was an interesting way to tastefully expose a lot of olive-colored skin.

"I'm glad you like it," Hank replied. "I had to send down for my stored bag to get it."

"It was worth it," Victoria said. *I hope you tipped the guy who had to go get your bag for you*, she mentally added, then wondered why she cared. *It's not like that SOB will be able to spend any money after tonight.*

"So, what are you doing after your set?" Hank asked.

"You, hopefully," Victoria replied. She smiled—it was the line she'd used every night since they'd hooked up.

"If you can catch me," Hank said.

Yeah, not like you ran from me very fast. Victoria felt her face flush and looked away. *The woman was* very *talented in bed.* "Be a dear, Hank," Victoria said. "A glass of wine for a working stiff?"

Hank set her glass of beer down on the small bar which wrapped around the piano—an act that highlighted the cast on her right wrist. "Coming right up. Wouldn't want you to get dehydrated."

Victoria unabashedly admired Hank's ass as the woman sashayed to the bar. "Not what you think of when you think Navy," she whispered to herself. Commander Henrietta "Hank" Solis, United States Navy, Retired (at age forty-five!), had treated herself to a long tourist visit to Mars and was now returning home to take a job with "the VA," whatever that was. Victoria had hooked up with her on the first night out, and now, five days later, they had a regular thing. *Pity you're never going to see Earth again.* She chuckled. *I'm getting soft in my old age.*

Victoria adjusted her microphone and noticed her boss, Jack Otarski, buttering up one of the passengers. He frowned on crewmembers having relationships with passengers. He frowned a lot, as crew members hooked up on the regular.

Hank returned, her dress emphasizing her lack of a bra. "She was out of pinot noir, so I got a red zin."

"That works," Victoria said. Helen, the bartender, probably had plenty of pinot. Switching to zin was a signal that something was not going to plan, which was just wonderful. *I've spent two fucking years working on this plan and I'll be damned if this doesn't go off.* Victoria was especially pissed given the event was supposed to have happened last night. They were already twenty-four hours behind schedule. She noticed her boss checking his old-fashioned wristwatch, so she launched into her first song, a mid-tempo ballad which had been a respectable hit twenty years ago. *No point in getting him wound up until after we've pulled off tonight's activities.* The audience was of an age to remember the song, and the opening bars produced smiles. *It is nice to be appreciated.*

***

Fortunately, thanks to some long-forgotten union functionary at the International Spacefarer's Union, solo performers were guaranteed a ten-minute break every hour. Her boss Otarski would have her on a clock, but she'd get her ten minutes.

At her first break, ostensibly to "powder her nose" but really to find out what tonight's fucking hiccup was, Victoria went toward the toilets at one corner of the lounge. They were tastefully hidden from the rest of the lounge by a metal and glass divider. Also hidden behind the divider was a fiberglass door with fake wood grain discreetly labeled "Crew Only." She used her access band to open the door and stepped into a hallway. Unlike the passenger lounge with nice but generic wallpaper and wood-grained fiberglass trim, the hallway was painted metal with harsh industrial lighting.

Bruno was waiting for her in the hallway, his green hair clashing with his pale skin and the red overalls of the ship's repair department. His hair wasn't a dye job—his grandmother had had her hair gen-moded and he'd inherited the coloring from her. "What's the malfunction now?" Victoria asked.

"And good evening to you too, your Highness."

"Your Grace. I'm a Grand Duke, not a Royal. My oldest sister got that title."

"Whatever, Vicky."

"Point, please. Get to it."

"Don't have the keys."

Victoria bit back a curse. Bruno was an odd duck, especially for a crook, and surprisingly offended by profanity. Given that he looked big enough to wrestle elephants and that she needed him, offending him now was not an option. "Why not?"

"Tomas missed the lift."

"You told me Tomas was a super-duper pickpocket."

"He is. He missed."

"Well, tell him to try again. And don't miss."

"If he does?"

She glared at Bruno. "Then you need to go sit on Davidoff. This does not, I repeat, *does not*, work without those keys." The keys in question were physical pieces of metal, needed because they allowed one to bypass the regular electronic security elements. On a spaceship, there were places that needed to be accessible no matter what. Her people needed to get to more than one of those places.

"I'm on it."

"Thank you." Victoria tapped Bruno on the arm, avoiding wincing at his greasy coverall. "If you end up having to get forceful with Davidoff, keep it quiet and try to keep her alive. We may need her."

"Those two things may be in conflict with each other."

"The highest priority is quiet. Alive is nice, but secondary." She gestured down the hall. "Now, if you'll excuse me, I do, in fact, need to take a leak before my next set."

Bruno gestured toward the unisex single-occupancy toilet down the hall. "By my leave, your Grace."

No, it's by my *leave, you dolt.* She nodded and stepped around him.

Once ensconced in the toilet, Victoria indulged herself by whispering, "I am surrounded by fucking incompetent asswipes who can't pour shitty water out of a boot with instructions on the God-damned heel." She shuddered. *Which cocksucker of a God did I offend to deserve this?*

On finishing her business, Victoria took a minute to look at herself in the mirror under the glare of the industrial lights in the toilet, which was tiny enough that she could have washed her hands while on the throne. *Ha. Throne. Fitting.*

Victoria was listed on the ship's books as Stevens. It was actually her legal name, taken from her husband before she'd taken his life. Her real name was Hakken, and her older sister was, after the untimely death of their parents, Queen of Ganymede and Red Queen of Luna. The United Nations of Earth, back when that was a thing, had kicked them off of Luna and the Martians, those stick-up-their-ass do-gooders, had kicked them off of Ganymede. The Martians—who controlled access out of the Solar System at the time—had also flat-out blocked them from leaving.

The family had ended up on Mercury, rich in dignity but merely well-off in money. Under the free-wheeling Syndication of Mercury, the Hakkens could call themselves whatever they wanted and run their domes with a free hand as long as the uranium flowed. Her great-grandfather and grandfather had both been much more interested in politics and the "proper conduct of aristocracy" than in mining. Uranium had not flowed while money had, including the money to get Victoria a Master of Music History degree from the Royal Welsh College of Music and Drama.

Victoria reached into the pocket of her dress and produced a tube of lipstick. She uncapped her lipstick and started to touch up her lips.

Her parents, desperate for money, had concocted a plan to marry her and her sisters off to rich off-worlders looking for a title. Then they'd died in that unfortunate shuttle crash. Now, the family's fortunes rested on the success of this plan. There was a long list of people on Mercury who would gladly divide up the family properties if this mission didn't pay out. *I can't let them down. I won't let them down.* She capped her lipstick. *Let's go do this.*

Kelly

Kelly Rack stood at the door to the first-class lounge, leading three fellow Martians. She rotated her head, trying to relieve the soreness in her neck. The ship ran on one Gee, which was useful since that was what the gravity was like on Earth, but that was three times what she was used to. It was amazing how heavy stuff was, like your head.

They were all exchange students, heading from Mars to Earth, and besides the unpleasant encounter with gravity they had been having unpleasant encounters with American liquor laws. Specifically, they had discovered that in America, one had to be twenty-one Earth-years old to buy booze. Since a Martian year, a Mear, was 1.8 Earth years long, that meant one had to be eleven and two-thirds Mears old. Kelly, the youngest of the group, was nine and a half Mears old, and given her lack of stature, looked younger.

"You sure she's gonna sell to us?"

Kelly looked at the boy. Spider, they called him. He was from Franklin City South High School while Kelly had attended City North. They'd seen each other at the orientation for outbounds, but not really hung out. Even on this tin can they'd not been around each other much.

This expedition, however, had been Pete Gliese's idea. Pete of the cute ass. *Stop that. You have a girlfriend.* Kelly glanced at the bar and away from Pete. *Well, I think I have a girlfriend.* Leah had been very vocal in her disapproval of Kelly going to Earth for a half-Mear.

"We doing this or not?" Spider asked.

"I am," said their fourth, Zola, a cute brunette with dreads. "Not that it's going to work."

"You're sure she's a Martian?" Kelly said, pointing out the bartender. Spider nodded.

"So?" Zola said. "Works for the USians."

"We won't know until we try," Kelly said. *Why'd you come if you didn't think this would work?* "Attack, troopers, attack."

Kelly felt like a momma duck being trailed by her baby ducks as they walked to the bar. She noticed a woman with warm, amber-colored skin playing the piano. Hot, but just at the ragged edge of too old for her. An olive-skinned woman—definitely too old but still very attractive—was in a two-tone dress at the piano bar, giving the singer the lust-eyes. *I guess the hottie's got her a benefriend. Shame I'm taken—either one of them looks like they could be fun.* She glanced over her shoulder. *So could Pete. Damn—maybe I should drop Leah.*

There were only two free seats at the bar and Kelly—having designated herself as leader—grabbed one of them. Spider, surprisingly forthright for such a mousy fellow, grabbed the other.

"What can I do for you?" the bartender asked in her heavy Olympian accent.

"I'll try the ship's red," Kelly said.

"You've been watching too many old videos," the bartender said with a smile.

"You don't have grow rooms on this tin can?" Spider asked.

"We got'em," the bartender allowed. "Been a long time since anybody used them to grow grapes for wine. If you're in for a red, I got a special on the cabernet."

"That works," Kelly said. She gestured behind her. "For the group."

The bartender winked. "Coming right up."

Chapter 2

ValuTrip Cardinal

Victoria

Victoria finished her song to a smattering of applause. She glanced over at the group of Martian exchange students who apparently thought they were pulling a fast one on Helen. *That cocksucker. I told Frank Malan no kids on this boat.* She cued up another song, one which had just charted on Mars, in honor of her underaged guests. *Oh well, can't do anything about it now.*

***

Hank had wanted to go dancing, so after her final set Victoria had taken her girl by the hand and gone to the dance bar. The Martian kids she'd seen at her bar were there as well, having been discreetly run out by her boss. Almost immediately after they arrived, Hank allowed herself to be dragged out on the floor by a dreadlocked Martian girl. The girl, clearly a bit tipsy, was trying and mostly succeeding to teach Hank the moves to the hot new Martian dance.

Let them have their moment of fun. It will be the last for a long time. The hell of it, was that the "new" dance was actually a revival of a dance craze from the first decade of the 21st century, as were the low-rider jeans all the kids were wearing.

The DJ got tired of catering to the young and put on an older song—quite possibly one which the kids were conceived to. Hank, a pleasant sheen of sweat on her brow, came back to the table. "You ready to go?"

"I thought you wanted to dance?" Victoria said.

"I did." She winked. "Now let's dance under the covers."

Victoria appreciated that the American Navy was as direct as other navies when it came to sex. She looked past Hank to see Ted Beale waving at her from across the room.

Guy was as subtle as a moose in heat. "You go on—I gotta say hi to one of my fans."

"Don't be long," Hank said, faking a pout.

"I won't."

As Hank left, Victoria crossed the dance floor and settled onto a low, rounded stool at Ted's table. "Talk to me," she said.

"We have keys," Ted replied.

"About fucking time," Victoria replied.

"Exactly what Bruno said."

"I didn't think he would say shit if he had a mouth full of it."

"He will," Ted said. "He just doesn't like ladies to cuss." Ted ran a finger down her bare arm. "Or show off too much skin."

"What the actual fuck?" Victoria said, jerking her arm away.

"Hey," Ted said, hand held up defensively. "I'm merely reporting." He shrugged. "Guy's from some nutso religious sect or group or whatever."

"Yet he's willing to do this."

"I think as far as he's concerned we're all heathens and whatever happens to us is God's punishment for heathen-ness."

Victoria was not sure 'heathen-ness' was a word but decided not to argue the point. "Where are we on the timeline?"

"Everything is moved back one hour." Ted pointed his chin at the door. "So, you probably got time to bang that hot piece of ass."

"Then I shall."

***

She managed to get the best stateroom on the ship, Victoria thought, lounging on that stateroom's bed with a satisfied grin on her face. *After tonight, I shall have to move in.* Crew quarters on the *Cardinal* were spartan and tight, and everybody had a roommate assigned by the company. Only a couple of the senior officers had singles, and those also doubled as their offices.

Hank's stateroom, on the other hand, was large—as spaceship cabins went—having room for a built-in couch and a chair in a little sitting area which was separate from the wood-grained fiberglass desk. Beside her, Hank stirred in her sleep, causing the sheet to slide off her very firm ass. *Maybe I should just keep her.*

Victoria's access band beeped quietly. She silenced it and slid out of the bed. She picked up her dress from the heap of clothing on the floor and pulled it on, then went looking for her shoes. The room was dim, lit with just a nightlight, so it took a minute to find her black shoes on the dark gray carpet. It hadn't helped that they had both been in a hurry to get their clothing off when they hit the door.

Shoes on, Victoria opened the door to find Ted Beale standing there. "This isn't your cabin," Victoria said in a low voice. The time was quickly coming to go loud, but it had not arrived yet.

"Problem," Ted said.

"Step back," Victoria said. She stepped out into the passageway and eased the door closed behind her. "And keep your voice down. Now what?"

"Zoren's a bust."

"Who's Zoren?" Hank said.

Victoria turned around to see Hank peeking around the door and apparently using it to shield her nakedness. "Long story," Victoria said.

"What does she know?" Ted asked, the stress obvious in his voice.

"I didn't mean to wake you," Victoria said to Hank, wishing Ted would shut the fuck up.

"On the ship I kept getting woken up in the middle of the night for reports," she replied. "Became a light sleeper." She looked at Ted. "Isn't your cabin on the other end of the corridor?"

"He was just going there," Victoria said. She looked sternly at Ted. "Weren't you?"

He really wasn't. It was more like he'd grown roots. He was also pale, and a thin sheen of sweat had popped on his upper lip. *It is so hard to find good fucking help.*

"He doesn't look so good," Hank said. "Maybe I should call somebody?"

"No!" Ted said, entirely too forcefully.

Victoria turned to fully face Hank. "Thanks dear, but I got this."

"Got what? Let me call..."

Victoria pushed the door as hard as she could at Hank, knocking the other woman back into the cabin. She followed that up by barreling into the cabin and throwing a left jab at Hank's nose. It landed solidly and Hank's head bounced against the wall to the cabin's bathroom. Hank fell back into the main part of the cabin with Victoria on her heels.

Hank was clearly surprised but swung a haymaker at Victoria, catching her on her right side. Victoria replied with another jab and an undercut, catching Hank in the stomach, doubling her up. She put Hank in a chokehold. "Stop fighting or it's lights out," she growled into Hank's ear.

The other woman tried to flip Victoria over, but Victoria tripped her and they landed on the bed with Victoria on top of Hank. "Have it your way," Victoria said and choked the woman into unconsciousness.

Once Hank stopped moving, Victoria rolled off of the bed. Ted had at least had the sense to step into the cabin and close the door behind him. "The other cabins will call Security," he said.

"If they didn't hear us earlier," Victoria said, "they won't now." She pushed a strand of hair out of her eyes. "Got some tape?"

"No."

Of course not. Why would you have something of use? "I think she had a roll in the bathroom."

Kelly

Kelly stood at the door to her cabin with Pete—he of the superb ass—next to her. Too close, really—his smell was heady and slightly intoxicating. *Or is that the booze talking?*

"If you've got a roommate we could go to my cabin," Pete said. "Ship had a last-minute cancellation and I'm a solo." He held up a hand. "Just to hang out."

Well, that's not wasting any time. She sighed. *Hanging out alone might lead me to do something I regret.* "Actually, I was solo too." Apparently more than one person had bailed on the idea of going to Earth. "But no, that's okay," Kelly said. She forced herself to take a step back, the weakness in her knees not entirely due to the ship's higher gravity. "I've got a girlfriend back on Mars." *Well, I think I do.*

"She's millions of kilometers away." He made a show of looking at the time readout on his access band. "Oh, just got a couple dozen kilometers farther while we talked."

"Just because she's not here doesn't make it okay."

"What she doesn't know won't hurt her."

Now that was an old line. "Not true."

"Ah, come on, you're killing me here!"

Kelly smiled. "As my drill sergeant said, you'll figure something out to entertain yourself. Goodnight."

"Wow," Pete said, miming being slapped. "Nice brushback."

"Sorry," Kelly said, sticking her tongue out at him.

Pete looked bashful, which made him even cuter. "Can't blame a guy for trying."

She thumped him on the chest, trying to look angry. "There's trying, and there's hitting them on the head with a club and dragging them back to the cave."

"Sorry," Pete said, still bashful and cute.

Kelly stood on her tiptoes and planted a quick kiss on his cheek. "Stop looking like a damn sad puppy dog or I'll forget myself."

"That's part of my master plan," Pete said, chuckling and smiling.

"Yeah, you meant to do that," Kelly replied. "Good night," she said into his chest as she hugged him.

"Sleep well, Little Bit," he replied.

She gave him a playful poke. "Enough with the short jokes!"

"Sorry," he said with a wicked smile. "Breakfast tomorrow?" he asked hopefully.

"If you can dodge Mrs. Hacker," Kelly said, referring to their Earth-based chaperone. Their days were spent in the ship's conference rooms, attending orientation for their arrival on Earth.

Kelly stepped inside and shut her cabin door, then leaned against it. The cabin steward had tied a towel in the shape of a monkey, and it was swinging from a hanger in the middle of her tiny room. "Wanna party, Miss Monkey?" she said. She giggled, and tossed the towel-monkey toward the tiny green built-in couch. The inhabited area of the ship was spun to create gravity, and as a result the flight path had a noticeable curve to it.

"If my curve ball had been that good on Mars I'd have made the varsity team," she said. She undressed for bed, noting that pretty much everything hurt. She'd been told the pain would go away once her body adjusted, but so far that hadn't happened. At least the engines had stopped. When they were running, the thrust made it seem like you were standing on a sloping hill.

***

Kelly jerked out of bed, sending her pillow flying. A loud, pulsating alarm was sounding "ah-oo-gah," and a strobe light was flashing in her room. The alarm stopped, and a woman's voice came over the public address system. "Bravo Bravo, Bravo Bravo. Please proceed immediately to your emergency stations. Bravo Bravo, Bravo Bravo, please proceed immediately to your emergency stations."

The voice was way too calm for the horn that preceded, then followed it. Artificial or pre-recorded, Kelly decided. She glanced at the clock in her room. *Three-twenty AM!* "God help them if this is a drill!"

She rolled out of bed, her heart pounding, and trotted to the bathroom for a quick pee, then scrambled into last night's clothes. She opened the door to see one of the cabin stewards pounding on doors. "This is no drill!" the woman said in her unfamiliar but presumably Earthling accent. The deck curved up away from Kelly and so made the woman appear to be uphill.

"What's a 'Bravo'?" Kelly asked.

"Fire!" the woman replied. Kelly felt a lump in her stomach. "I'll get this side," Kelly said, pointing over her shoulder with her thumb. "We need to get them out now— smoke can kill quick." She moved down the corridor, pounding on the half-dozen cabin doors between her and the staircase to the ship's theater, her emergency station. The last door she knocked on was opened by a woman wearing nothing but a bra and a glazed expression on her face.

"You'll surely want some clothes," Kelly told her with a smirk. The woman clapped a hand on her exposed area and closed the door with the other one. "At least I'm not hung-over," Kelly said under her breath as the alarm blared. They'd only been able to get two drinks before getting cut off at the bar, and that was hours ago. *Well, I was only able to get two. That Zola chick drank like a fish. I hope she's able to function.*

When they'd done the drill, just before leaving Phobos, the lobby area had been full of crew members in yellow hi-visibility vests in the lobby, smiling and directing traffic. Now it was just passengers, many still dressed for sleeping. The lump in her stomach moved to her throat. *Maybe this was the real deal.* But where was the smoke? Even a little fire, like the trash can fire in the school dome last Mear, had left the pressure dome reeking of smoke for days.

The ship's theater was up one level and anti-spinward from her cabin, on the main passenger level. Kelly reached that level and turned left from the stairs, wondering why, if there was a fire, none of the pressure doors were closed. In the domes on Mars, the first thing you did was try to prevent the fire from spreading. Kelly couldn't imagine it would be different on a spaceship. *Except a spaceship is smaller and you can't just suit up and go to another dome.* For that matter, why hadn't anybody turned up the lights? They were still at the dimmer "go to bed, people" evening setting.

Kelly saw Pete stepping up from a side staircase into her level. He was dressed, but his hair was wild. He paused and let her catch up. There was now a stream of people moving in the same direction.

"Damn lousy time for a drill," he growled.

"Bravo's code for fire," Kelly explained, "and does this feel like a drill to you?"

"Why is the ventilation running?"

Kelly hadn't noticed that it was running but killing ventilation in event of a fire was something she'd been taught in first grade. *Are these Earthlings that stupid?*

The theater lobby had a small bar/refreshment stand in the middle, now shuttered for the night. They followed the crowd around the stand and came face to face with a group of crewmembers being directed from a side door by a pair of figures dressed in black, including black face-covering knit caps. They were armed with riot gear, including stun sticks.

"Shit!" Pete exclaimed. "Pirates!"

Pirates? What the fuck—did we somehow get sent back in time?

"Shut up, kid," an older passenger next to them growled. "What's going on?" the man asked of the nearest figure.

"Get inside!" the figure said, pointing at the theater.

He the boss?

Things seemed to move terribly fast. Pete stepped around the arguing passenger and delivered a sharp blow to the gunman's chin. The guy he hit staggered back. Pete started to press his attack, but the other gunman brought up a short black stick and pressed it to Pete's chest. Nothing happened.

"Check the batteries?" Pete asked, grabbing for the stick.

Stickman jerked it away from Pete and swung it like a club, catching Pete on the jaw. He stepped back and Stickman swung at him again. Pete tried to duck but instead took the hit on the side of his head just above the ear. Pete collapsed like a puppet whose strings had been cut. "That's enough of that shit," Stickman said.

The dude Pete hit took the opportunity to kick Pete in the ribs as he lay on the floor. Stickman grabbed him. "We got people to move."

"You," Kicker said, pointing at Kelly and a couple of other passengers. "Carry him, now!"

Kelly and another passenger grabbed Pete's limp and very damn heavy body, and started to lug him into the ship's theater. Once inside the door, a third gunperson—the masks and clothes made it hard to tell gender—directed them to drop Pete on a chair. They did so and were hustled away. Kelly noticed some guards directing people on the theater floor, and about a dozen people with rifles were placed strategically on the stage and upper balcony. *If the people in the balcony start shooting, it will be a bloodbath.*

They were directed into the folding theater chairs and made to fill up all the rows—she ended up in a row just three back from the stage. Other than the barked orders of the guards, the theater was quiet. Most people were still in nightclothes, but a few uniformed crew members were visible. They were intermixed with passengers, and clearly as confused and scared as everybody else.

Kelly looked down at the access band on her wrist. The little blue light which indicated that the device was working was off. She pressed the home button to call up the time display, but nothing happened. As she sat there, she noticed other passengers trying their bands with the same lack of result.

They sat for maybe thirty minutes, while passengers and crew came in. First, it was a steady stream, then stragglers, then finally small groups or individuals—most being marched in at gunpoint by one or more guards.

Eventually one of the guards, a large white man with a beard and shaved head, stepped out onto the center of the stage. He was the first person Kelly had seen who was not masked. "People of the good ship ValuTrip *Cardinal*," he said, his voice booming through the amplification system of the theater, "may I have your attention."

He waited for a few seconds, although since none of the passengers were talking, Kelly wasn't sure why he bothered. He began again. "People of the good ship *Cardinal*. Good morning. You may address me as Commander Zero or just Commander. Although a few of you have been, shall we say, difficult, most of you have been cooperative. I hope for your sake that cooperation continues."

"Some of you have asked what is going on." He smiled. "Well, let me tell you exactly what is happening. My associates and I have taken control of this vessel."

Okay, now I have been sucked back in time. Kelly felt the beginnings of a hysterical giggle and she clamped a hand over her mouth. Pirates were something that happened to people in bad videos of the old days and history lessons of before Mars became independent, not now. Given the number of gasps and moans, a lot of the people in the room were having similar thoughts.

"As I said," Commander Zero said in his amplified voice, "my associates and I have taken control of this vessel. That, from your perspective, is the bad news." Another grin, this one more wolfish. "The good news, from both our perspectives, is this: All we want is money. The ValuTrip corporation is well-capitalized and has quite substantial insurance coverage. It's the shipping company's money, not yours. When we get that money, you get to continue on your journey."

He pitched his voice again, sounding almost friendly. "So, do what you're told, and you get to go home or wherever you're going with minimal delay. Fight us and you die." He held out his hands to the crowd. "The choice is yours."

"You won't get away with this!" somebody yelled from the audience. Somebody else yelled, "Bullshit!"

Commander Zero sighed theatrically. "There is always somebody in the crowd who needs a more direct lesson. Observe and learn." He waved at somebody behind him on stage.

Two crew members, with their hands bound behind them, wearing the light blue shirts that signified they were ship security, were marched on stage by a group of masked goons.

Without a further word from Commander Zero, the goons forced the two security officers to their knees. Another goon pulled out a pistol and shot one officer in the back of the head. The other officer tried to get up, but the goon shot him as well. Blood, brains and bones splattered onto the stage. Something hit Kelly's head and she reflexively brushed it off. It was bloody and white.

Oh fuck—that's a piece of skull! She clamped her hand harder over her mouth, trying not to puke. The echo of the shots rang in the room, then the thud as the lifeless bodies hit the stage floor. Kelly smelled blood and gunpowder.

"They both elected to resist," Commander Zero said. "They lost the election. Does anybody else care to resist?"

The room was silent except for the sound of somebody retching. Commander Zero let them sit for a long minute. Kelly gulped. Obedience was the only choice.

"Good," Commander Zero eventually said. "Now, although we wish to make this operation as painless as possible, for everybody's safety and security, a few minor changes are required to our normal routines. I think—I *hope*—that having seen what happens to those who don't cooperate, everybody here *will* cooperate."

After another one of his wolfish smiles and dramatic pauses, Commander Zero said, "Here's your first test. Stand up, take off all your clothes, and pass them down the aisles. Do it now!"

At least in boot camp they pretended it was for a shower and we were just all girls, Kelly thought, standing up to do as she was told. She realized that she was sweating profusely—a sweat that had nothing to do with the temperature. She felt like she was watching herself in a video.

After the execution of the two security officers, there was no resistance, but a lot of visible embarrassment. Kelly felt her face redden, but she refused to try and cover herself with her hands. *Let them gawk. I'm sure some of them are having parties in their pants already. If they wanted us dead, we'd be dead,* she decided. The coldness she felt wasn't entirely due to her lack of clothing.

***

I wonder if they're just going to let those bodies lie on the stage and rot. They had been sitting in the theater for some time. It felt like forever but was probably only a couple of hours. *Damn glad I stopped and peed.* It was about the only level of dignity Kelly had left. Many of her fellow passengers did not even have that, judging from the smell.

This will definitely be the experience of a lifetime. Even before she was approved as an exchange student, nearly everybody had told her to finish high school and see Earth. *It looks like I'll be lucky to see tomorrow.*

One of the masked goons stood at the end of the row. "Everybody in this row, on your feet!" His voice sounded masculine although he wasn't very big. His nonlethal weapon more than compensated. Kelly stood up and overbalanced, nearly falling into the seat in front of her. She caught herself just in time.

"We're under thrust," Kelly said, earning her a growl from the guard. When the ship's engines were firing, the thrust mixed with the centrifugal force of the spun passenger section made everything seem to be on a slight incline. Since everything was visually the same, it was a disorienting effect.

Under the man's command the row of people filed out into the passageway.

Once there, Kelly saw a table set up with folded sets of clothing—the kind of cheap cloth crap you gave to prison inmates. She was marched in front of a table and one of the guards asked her name, then checked her off on an electronic tablet.

"Extra small," the goon behind the table said.

"Where's Pete?" Kelly asked.

"Who?" the goon asked as another female in the prison garb handed Kelly a pile of clothing.

"The man I came in with. He got hit by a guard."

"He's in bad shape, kid," the female handing out clothing said. "I don't..."

"Move along!" the goon said.

Kelly followed the line of people out of the theater. There was no opportunity to put any of the clothing on—the group was marched barefoot and bare-assed back to the lower promenade deck, where the bulk of the staterooms were.

"Go to your staterooms, and do not leave unless told otherwise," the leading goon said. Kelly did so, noting in passing that the lock to her stateroom had been disabled. She wondered if they could lock her in or not. Inside she found that her cabin had been efficiently stripped, with all her personal stuff removed. Even the bed had been stripped, although a pile of presumably clean linen had been deposited there.

Kelly had just gotten dressed when the door flew open and an older woman—naked and carrying clothes—was pushed into the cabin. "This is your room now, bitch," the goon pushing the woman growled.

The woman had fallen to her knees, and Kelly moved to help her up, noting her left wrist and forearm were in a cast. There was a fresh bruise on her face and another on her side.

She looked familiar, and clearly took care of herself. Had she been a decade younger Kelly would have hit on her. Well, that and not having a girl back home. "I guess I'm your new roomie," the woman said. "Wonder what happened to your old one."

"Didn't have a roomie," Kelly said. "Kelly Rack. You are?"

"Henrietta Solis," she replied in what sounded like an Earth accent. She stood up slowly. "Friends call me Hank."

"You're an Earthling?"

The woman stopped unfolding her clothes and glanced up. "We prefer Terran, but yes."

"Sorry. What brings you here?" Kelly asked. "I mean this cabin?" Kelly felt her face flush, not entirely out of embarrassment over the faux pas. It was a stupid question. *The pirates brought her.* Kelly realized it was the first time she'd used the word "pirate" to describe her captors. *Pete called them pirates.*

"Apparently first class is now the Home for Wayward Hijackers," Hank replied in a flat voice. "So, they moved me."

Kelly suddenly felt dizzy and sat down on the bed.

"You okay?" Hank asked. She walked over and touched Kelly's head. "You're bleeding."

No, I'm not okay. We've been hijacked. "Just tired and hungry," Kelly said, forcing herself to be factual. She touched her head and her hand came back with a bright red spot. "Not my blood. Also not used to this gravity."

"You sure?"

"It's from the ship cop. I was in a front row."

"Good," Hank replied. "I mean good you're not hurt." She stepped away and pulled on her shirt. After an awkward silence, she asked, "So, is that a Martian accent I hear?"

"Yes, ma'am," Kelly replied. "Franklin City."

"You can knock off the ma'am. Just Hank is fine."

"Force of habit."

"Unusual habit," Hank said, unfolding her pants. The tiny cabin only had one metal chair with padded arms. Kelly was sitting on the bed—a single bed that folded up into a couch. "Where'd you get that habit at?"

"State militia," Kelly said. "I got out of boot camp a month ago."

"Martian months, I assume?"

"There are other kinds of months?" Kelly replied, hazarding a joke.

Hank smiled, a smile that didn't make it to her eyes. "Yes, my greener friend. Earth months only have thirty days in them."

It was still weird. Kelly ignored the derogatory nickname 'greener' for 'little green men.' Most Earthlings didn't know what the context for the phrase was.

"You sure you're not bleeding?" Hank asked.

"Yes."

Hank walked over and ran her hand through Kelly's hair. "Well, you are bleeding. Looks like a small cut though. Stay put."

Hank, still wearing just a shirt, which could kind of work as a really short minidress, stepped into the toilet. She returned with two handfuls of tissue paper. "Best I could do." She used one handful, wet, to wipe the cut and handed Kelly the other handful. "Hold this over the cut. It's small, but head wounds bleed like a son-of-a-bitch."

"Thanks." Kelly did as instructed, while Hank put on her pants. "You look familiar."

"Small ship."

"Were you in the first-class lounge last night? Making googly eyes at the piano player?"

"I was. Made more than googly eyes at her." Hank touched the bruise on her face and winced. "Then she gave me this."

"Why?"

"Cause she's one of the fucking hijackers, the bitch," Hank replied. She rotated her arm. "Then left me tied up in my cabin."

"The crew's in on this?"

"Well, at least one of them is." Hank sat down on the bed next to her. "What was your MOS in boot?"

"MOS?"

"Military Occupational Specialty," Hank replied. "What you trained to do."

"I'm non-drilling, so I didn't take a specialist course," Kelly said. She looked at Hank. "You know an awful lot about military for a Blue-girl."

"I'm ex-military." She leaned in and offered her hand. "US Navy, Retired. Formerly in command of the Deepwater Combat Ship *USS Priti Shah*." Kelly shook it, and Hank asked, "Non-drilling?"

"It means I just went to boot camp and wasn't assigned to a unit afterward."

"Oh."

"US," Kelly said. "That's in North America, right? And were you Fleet or Marine?"

"Yes, the United States of America is in North America, and it's a wet-water organization, not space-based like yours. I was Surface Warfare."

"Oh." If the US Navy was like the Martian Navy, that meant Hank was a captain, either First or Second Class. Kelly leaned back against the metal wall of the cabin. "That's where I'm going." *Or was going,* she added mentally. "North America. Darien, Illinois, to be exact."

"How ironic," Hank said. "My brother lives in Westmont. It's the next town over. We grew up there."

"I'm finishing high school there," Kelly said, surprised at how normal the conversation seemed. "What happened to your wrist?"

Hank glanced at the cast. "Fell while out hiking. If it had been on Earth, I'd probably been dead."

Any sense of normality ended when all three of the small video monitors in the room turned on, playing at high volume. The video was of a red-headed man with a full beard, wearing the black utility uniform of the goons who'd taken the ship.

"Listen up, prisoners," he said. "We're going to let you eat. Here's the process."

***

"That was awful," Kelly said. They were back in their room, and Hank was working to drop the fold-out bunk bed above the main bed. The meal had been sandwiches and fruit, handed out as they marched through the dining area.

"Not exactly up to their usual standards," Hank said, her back to Kelly. "At least we're not on cleaning detail."

After food, a bunch of people had been diverted to the auditorium and told they were going to 'clean up the mess you made of it.' There had been another announcement during the meal that, starting later today, everybody was going to be on a work detail. "Idle hands do the Devil's work," Hank had said under her breath.

"Is that from the Bible?" Kelly asked.

"I think so," Hank replied. "But in general, if you let people sit around and do nothing they get up to all kinds of shit."

"Wonder where they are taking us?" Kelly said as Hank completed her task. The bed proved to be already made.

"I for one don't want to be around to find out," Hank replied.

"It's not like you can just get off and walk home," Kelly replied.

Hank stopped and laid her hand on Kelly's shoulder. Hank wasn't that tall but was taller than Kelly. "I intend to fight these fuckers."

"With what, Captain?"

"Commander," Hank corrected. "And with everything I have, Private."

Kelly snorted. "Which is nothing."

"I've got a brain, don't I?"

"So do they. Plus guns." Kelly gave her a confused look. "Remember that blood on me? Those cops decided to resist and died." *And Pete too. Is he dead or what?* "Why? Just to save the insurance company some money?"

"We'll have to be smarter than they were. Didn't they teach you if captured to resist?"

Kelly had a vague recollection of a lecture in which resistance had been discussed. She'd been so tired at the time that she'd slept standing up.

"What part of this are you not understanding? A friend of mine resisted. He got the shit stomped out of him. Two cops resisted. They got executed." Kelly gestured at her shirt. "These people didn't just cook this up yesterday. They're pros and have a plan."

"I'm sorry," Hank said perfunctorily. "But you can't just roll over and die."

"If they wanted us dead, we'd be dead," Kelly said with more force than she felt. "They want money, and I intend to live. The way I see for that to happen is for me to keep my head down and do as I am told. Consider it boot camp take two."

Hank's look got even darker. "Miss Rack. Can I at least count on you to not blab to the guards?"

"Captain—"

"Commander," Hank corrected.

"Commander," Kelly replied. "I have no intention of talking to the guards about anything."

Chapter 3

Kansas City

Ray

Ray Volk's phone rang. He blinked at the light of morning seeping around the corners of the drapes, then glanced at his bedmate, a man sleeping face down on top of the covers. *What's his name? Ed, or was it Earl?*

"Ray Volk," he said into the phone, which he kept in audio-only. No point in flashing his caller.

"Good morning, Special Agent Volk," came the reply. It was his boss, and she was preternaturally perky in the mornings.

"Special Agent in Charge Fetterer," Ray said. "To what do I owe this call?" Ray slid out of bed and headed to the kitchen, glad yet again that he left his phone on audio only.

"Have you seen the news today?" Fetterer asked.

"Afraid not," Ray replied.

"One of our spaceships is missing."

"What is this, the 21st century?" Ray asked while pressing the button to start the coffeemaker. "How do spaceships go missing?"

"Good question. And no, your calendar isn't broken."

"Here's another good question," Ray asked. "Why are you calling me about this?"

"The missing ship was nominally based in and operated out of KCK."

KCK was what locals called Kansas City, Kansas. Ray lived in KCMO, for Kansas City, Missouri. "Which answers why it's in our office." The FBI routinely helped the National Transportation Safety Board (NTSB) on crash investigations, partially as legal muscle and partially to preserve a legal chain of custody for evidence in case the crash wasn't an accident. "But that doesn't answer the question of why me? I don't usually work crash investigations."

"Klinger went into labor last night," she said. "Early, but that happens with twins."

"So, I'm crash-and-smash now."

"Do you know anybody else on desk duty?"

No, I do not. "Just because I shot somebody..."

"You would think after a second time you'd remember the rules."

Ray could hear the irritation in her voice. He also knew that the rules were four weeks desk duty, but he decided not to call out that fact. "Where do you need me?"

"The Crowne Plaza downtown."

"Because?"

"The ship left from Mars. Mars has designated somebody as liaison, and you're available to pick him up."

"Now I'm an overpaid taxi driver." Ray glanced at the time readout on the coffeemaker. "Do I have time to get some coffee?"

"If you're quick, yes. I'll send the detailed who-what-where to your handheld."

"Thanks, boss."

"Oh, and Ray?"

"Yes, ma'am?"

"Don't fuck this up." She sighed heavily. "And for God's sake, don't shoot anybody."

"I won't."

Ray broke the connection. *Technically in the last shooting the suspect had a gun, which justified my response.* Alas, the gun had been a cheap fake. It wasn't helping that Ray had been in two prior gunfights, two more than most cops ever experienced. The news media was portraying him as some sort of goon who shot first and asked questions later.

Coffee in hand, he walked back to the bedroom and stopped at the door, looking at the man he'd brought home. He was definitely not Steve, Ray's ex-husband. Ray winced at the thought—the divorce had been surprisingly ugly. This guy was so white as to be almost pink. Ray tapped the man on the shoulder, marveling at the contrast between his own dark skin and the man's paleness.

Well, Ray thought as he moved to wake up the man, *if I blow this job, I'm sure there's an exciting career in corporate security.*

***

Once he'd told the car where to go, Ray had it turn on a news channel. He preferred to listen to news in the car as opposed to reading it, so he had the car pull up the National Public News feed.

"This is Carl Cameron of NPN reporting as of four-fifty AM Eastern Standard Time. NASA reports this morning indicate that deep space control has lost contact with the interplanetary passenger liner ValuTrip *Cardinal,* in route to Earth from Mars. The vessel is now five hours overdue. Although interstellar ships frequently go much longer periods of time between reports, this long of an outage is unprecedented in the modern era. This is an ongoing story, and NPN will update it as events warrant."

The announcer paused for a breath, then continued. "A week ago today, commercial spaceflight quietly marked a major milestone: the fiftieth anniversary of the loss of the passenger liner *Fantasia.* That ship currently holds the distinction of the last passenger vessel lost in the Solar System. The 269 passengers and crew who died on her mark the largest single loss of life in interplanetary travel in one event this century. That event also started with a sudden and unexpected loss of communications. Here to discuss..."

The announcer brought on a pair of talking heads to speculate. Ray shut off the audio feed. He didn't want to listen to so-called experts babble on.

There was no other news of note on NPN, so Ray checked the weather. Unsurprisingly for May, it was expected to be hot and humid. His car pulled up to the Crowne Plaza's front entrance and was directed to a holding space just barely protected by the building's overhang. He stepped out of the car, travel cup of coffee in hand, and walked up to one of the bellmen. *Apparently, they got a new uniform. Wonder when the doormen went from red to blue? And when did they start hiring hunks like this?* "FBI," Ray said to the man, flashing a badge with his free hand. "Can I leave the car here for a minute? I need to pick up somebody."

"And I would know the answer to that why?" the bellman asked.

"Don't you work here?"

"No, and I've been on this planet less than a month." At that point, another uniformed man came up. His uniform was red. Ray recognized the man—definitely not a hottie—as one of the regular bellhops.

"Mister Volk," the bellhop said, standing next to the other man and allowing Ray to see all the points of difference between the uniforms. "What can I do for you?"

"I was wondering if I can leave the car here while I pick up a guest?"

"Sure, Mister Volk. Name of guest?"

"Mark Nagata."

The first man smiled wryly and offered his hand. "I'm Mark Nagata. Captain First Class Mark Nagata, Republic of Mars Navy."

Ray felt his face flush as he took the man's hand. *It's going to be impossible to get him into my bed if I keep messing up like this.* "Sorry about that. I guess I put my foot in it."

The Martian shrugged. "It happens. You are?"

Ray shook his head. "Ray Volk, FBI. Can I get a Mulligan on this meeting?"

Mark smiled, revealing a wall of white teeth. "Don't worry about it. At least you didn't ask me to park your car."

With the bellhop—the real bellhop—opening the door, they got into Ray's car, and it asked for the destination. He rattled off an address.

"What's Kay Cee Kay?" Mark asked, turning the A/C down.

"There are two Kansas Cities," Ray said automatically. Everybody from out-of-town asked. "One in Missouri—KC Mo—and one in Kansas—KC Kay."

"Ah. How long of a trip?"

"Twenty minutes or so." Ray waved outside the window. "Rush hour. Why does a planet with no oceans have a navy?"

Mark chuckled. "The ice under the sand is melting. We'll have an ocean in a century or so. In the meantime, the Martian Navy is the equivalent of your Space Force, with the added wrinkle of us being responsible for law enforcement and safety in space."

"Oh. So you're part of the Martian equivalent of the NTSB?"

"No, I'm actually here on a book tour before I go to your Air Force Academy as a guest instructor. I just happened to be in town when your safety board asked for a liaison."

Presumably because the ship left from Mars. *Good looking and an intellectual,* Ray thought appreciatively. "Captain First is a rank?"

"Equivalent of your bird Colonel. So, what do you know about this investigation?"

Ray gestured at the console in front of him. "Just what I heard on the news driving to pick you up. Spaceship Valu-something *Cardinal* disappeared off radar around midnight last night. Could have up to eight hundred people aboard."

"The vessel's name was ValuTrip *Cardinal*," Mark said. "US-flagged and registered. She declared four hundred twenty passengers and one hundred thirty-nine crew to Martian customs on getting underway." He moved the seat back. "She was five days out, and thus well outside anybody's radar range. And that, my friend, is pretty much all everybody knows."

Ray's car merged onto the interstate. "Do you think this will be a quick investigation?"

"Exactly the opposite," Mark replied.

"How so?"

"We haven't gotten a PSR from *Cardinal* in over eight hours."

"PSR?"

"Position and Situation Report."

"So, maybe they've got a big problem."

"All of those one hundred thirty-nine crewmembers are trained to contact Earth or Mars if they hit a problem. Since they haven't called, that suggests they are all incapacitated." Mark sighed. "The only thing that could incapacitate that many people is a massive loss of atmosphere."

Ray felt a wrench in his gut. "Don't these spaceships have backup systems?"

"Several," Mark said. "But some of those are only good for a couple of hours. We've exceeded or will soon exceed the life of some of those systems." He adjusted his seat. "I'm also really concerned about the time."

"The time?"

"The ship was on the same internal time as Kansas City," he said, gesturing. "Most American ships follow the time zone of their home office, for convenience's sake. If things go bad in the middle of the night, a lot of people would be asleep."

Ray had an uncomfortable vision of a ship full of people dead in their beds. "You think they're all dead? Crew and passengers?"

"At this point," Mark said heavily. "Probably."

"Won't the ship fly itself back to Earth?"

Mark chuckled humorously. "You've been watching too many bad videos. No, the ship is coasting right now, and will keep on coasting until she sails out of the solar system."

He's hating on *Spaceliner*, Ray thought. Although if that video was as accurate about space travel as *The Shen Files* was about police work, he was probably right. *The Shen Files* spent a lot more time worrying about who was hooking up with who than procedural accuracy.

"So, this will be a death investigation?"

"And a long one. We'll have to find a ship that can catch *Cardinal* and bring her back just to figure out what killed everybody."

"Which means you're not going to be in town very long?"

"Probably not."

Well, I guess I'll have to move fast or forever wonder what it was like to fuck a Martian. Even better, I won't be on this BS assignment very long and I can get back to real work.

Mark pulled out his handheld. "If you don't mind, I have a bunch of emails to catch up on."

"Sure," Ray said, pulling his ocular on and waiting for it to connect to his device. *After that downer, flirting will have to wait. Might as well get my inbox cleared out too.*

***

Ray's vehicle pulled up to a nondescript mid-rise office building—one of three surrounding a Marriott hotel—on the outskirts of KCK. Jayhawk Operations, the company that operated the ship, rented one floor of the building. The only indication of any importance attached to the building was a gaggle of reporters out front, watched by a handful of uniformed city cops and private security.

One of the rent-a-cops directed Ray's vehicle to a parking space in the front, next to an FBI white van which they used for airport runs. Ray and Mark climbed out and headed inside, escorted by the same security officer.

Other than the artwork on the walls—which consisted of spaceships and planets—it would have been hard to distinguish Jayhawk's offices from an insurance company. Ray and Mark ended up in an interior conference room, one wall of which was dominated by a giant picture of Saturn. A tall woman with red hair wearing an NTSB knit shirt was talking to a nervous man in a suit. She waved at Ray, who had his badge hanging from his neck.

"Get some coffee," she said, gesturing to a sideboard. She pitched her voice louder. "Then let's get started."

Ray counted seven men and women with NTSB logo-wear milling about the coffee service. He grabbed a fresh cup and took a seat at the granite-topped conference table as Nervous Suit left.

The redhead, Joanne Wagner, called the meeting to order and made introductions. When Mark introduced himself, Wagner asked, "Just out of curiosity, are you any relation to the Nagata that wrote 'From Gagarin to Pilgrim—Space Was Always Militarized?'"

"I wrote that, yes."

"Oh, cool," Wagner said, a smile creeping over her features. "I'll have to get a copy printed out so you can sign it."

"Great," the Martian said. "In fact, I was here on a book tour—self-funded, alas. I've got some hard copies at my hotel."

"I'll buy a copy," Wagner said.

So, the Martian wasn't just any old author, but apparently a good one. Ray thought. *Cool.*

"I assume everybody read their briefings," Wagner said. She looked at Ray. "Did you get one?"

"Sort of," he replied. "And Captain Nagata and I discussed it on the way in."

"So, you're up to speed."

Ray grimaced. "I'm not a spacer nor do I usually do crash investigations, but I'll muddle through."

***

A short time later, Ray, Wagner, and Mark ended up standing in an oversized cubicle. There was no nameplate, but a stuffed Teddy Bear was sitting on his worksurface. He looked too young to buy beer and had the chubbiness of somebody who sat behind a desk for too many hours. His cubicle had two banks of three monitors each. To Ray's eyes, the only readout that wasn't hieroglyphics was the time, although even that was complicated by having three different readouts in it.

"We got the quad-zero PSR at 0003 hours," Teddy said, addressing his remarks to the air just right of Wagner's head. "Everything normal, no indications of a problem. Then 01:03 came without a report, so I called. No reply, and nothing since."

We knew all of this before coming here, Ray thought.

"When did the BOLO go out?" Wagner asked. Ray assumed that was the same acronym for 'be on the lookout' as in police work.

Teddy looked at his pad of paper. "03:04."

"Anybody roger out on the BOLO?" Wagner asked.

"A container ship, the *Paul Carlson*. Had a CPA of ten million clicks but no joy."

"Not very close," Ray said, heading off the explanation of 'closest point of approach.' To his surprise, Ray remembered that ten million kilometers was something like forty times the distance from the Earth to the Moon.

"This is the readout from *Cardinal*?" Mark asked, gesturing to the right-most screen of the right-hand cluster.

"Yes, sir," Teddy said. "Once they were overdue, I switched focus to them."

Mark stretched out an elegant—and wedding-band-free—hand to a display on the screen. "Isn't this engine telemetry?"

"Yes, sir," Teddy said. He looked at the screen as if it had just materialized on his desk. "Hey, what's that?" Teddy reached for a keyboard and was stopped by Wagner putting a hand on his. "I swear that wasn't there five minutes ago."

"Maybe not," Wagner said. "Look at the update stamp."

"Could somebody clue in the fuzz?" Ray said.

"It's a main engine light-off," Mark said, "as of 04:18 and updated ten minutes ago." To Wagner: "Does a SpaceX Type 12E have an auto-engine-ignition feature?"

"No, it does not," Wagner replied.

"So, somebody's driving that thing?" Ray asked.

"This wouldn't be the first time a wreck generated spurious telemetry," Wagner said.

"Wreck?" Ray said, trying to keep up. "You think she broke up?"

"I don't think anything right now," Wagner replied. "We're just gathering data."

Mark

It would have been nice if the Federal Police had sent us somebody who'd at least been on a spaceship before, Mark thought, glancing at Ray Volk, the clueless Inspector they sent. *He apparently works out, though.* Not having any other duties, Mark had followed Joanne Wagner, and had been trailed by Volk, who also apparently had no particular assignment.

The trio returned to the conference room for Wagner to make a quick call to her bosses in Washington, detailing what little additional information they had and whom she'd assigned to do what. She ended the call by saying her team was still gathering information.

"I see that bureaucracy is the same on the Old World as on the New," Mark said.

"Consider it our gift to you," Wagner said with a wan smile. She leaned back in her chair. "This is the part I hate— waiting for people to get back to me." Another wan smile. "Although back when I was one of the people doing the gathering, I hated getting pinged by the boss every five minutes asking for an update."

"So, we sit and wait," Mark said.

"At least fifteen minutes, then I ping," she said wryly.

"Can somebody help me understand," Ray Volk asked, "who hired whom on this boat?"

Another Space 101 question for the cop. "Licensed crew work for Jayhawk and non-licensed for ValuTrip," Mark said.

"What does that mean?" Volk asked.

"Licensed crew actually operate the ship," Wagner said, keeping her clear irritation under check.

"They're the pilots?"

"Yes, except because it's a two-week trip each way you've got multiple 'pilots' and various support crew. Like electricians and life-support techs."

"And the non-licensed crew?"

"They are hired by ValuTrip," Mark said, "and work for the hotel department."

"So, they're cooks, maids—that sort of thing?"

"Yep."

"Who hired internal security?" Volk asked. "I assume the ship had some kind of Space Cops?"

"I assume so, yes," Mark replied. *Trust a cop to ask about the police.* "Martian practice is for them to be licensed astronauts and hired by the operating company."

"We usually do it the other way round," Wagner said. She grabbed a tablet device from the table and flipped through it. "Yep. ValuTrip hired the security. Not sure I see the relevance..."

"Okay, so there's two or maybe three reasons *Cardinal* is not talking to us," Volk said. "Hijacking, boarding or massive pressure loss."

Mark laughed out loud. "Are you kidding?" Wagner looked embarrassed and gave Mark a shrug as if to say she had no idea who sent this guy.

"What's so funny?" Volk asked.

"First place, the last successful pirate attack happened over a century ago, and even in the heyday of piracy, attacking passenger ships was very rarely done."

"Why?" Volk asked.

"Because you've got a shitload of passengers whom you need to control or kill," Wagner said. To Mark, she said, "I've heard there's still some activity in the Commonwealth."

Mark decided to cut her some slack on that. "A couple of rockers 'jacking a runabout in the ass end of the Asteroid

Belt is only piracy by courtesy." To Inspector Clueless, Mark said, "You heard the telemetry tech—nothing anywhere near *Cardinal.*" *Guy spends too much time in the gym and not enough in the library.*

"Then she was hijacked by people on the ship," Volk said.

"Maybe," Wagner said. "Why haven't they called us with demands?"

The Inspector chewed on that for a bit. "Okay, so massive pressure loss is still on the table, yes?"

"Pretty much," Mark replied. "By the way, the technical term is UPE. Uncontrolled Pressurization Event."

"So how would you create a UPE?"

"Create?"

"Yeah," Volk said. "Pretend I'm a nutjob who wants to die and is willing to take everybody with me. Or maybe I've got financial problems and the only way out is for my spouse to collect the insurance on an accidental death."

Wagner's handheld buzzed. She put a hand over her earpiece and listened. "Sorry...got to check on something." She got up, giving Mark a significant look.

"Okay," Mark said after she left the room. *Let's see if Inspector Clueless can be clued in.* "So, do the names *Fantasia* and *Blooming Lotus* mean anything to you?"

"No. Should they?"

"Yes," Mark said dryly. "They were a pair of ships lost around fifty years ago. *Blooming Lotus* was a Chinese-flagged ship and *Fantasia* Italian. Both suffered UPEs."

"Okay."

"From Earth's point of view, the situation started the same. Ships were talking to us, then they stopped. The causes of the UPE were different. *Lotus* suffered an electrical fire which caused a series of malfunctions while in *Fantasia's* case it was a MIAR."

"A mirror?"

Mark spelled out the acronym. "Madman In A Room. Although in *Fantasia's* case it was a madwoman—Gina Sacche."

"She locked herself in a room and opened the valves."

"Oversimplification, but basically, yes."

"And *Blooming Onion*?"

"*Lotus*. Electrical short which caused valves to open and prevented the crew from getting to where they needed to in order to manually override the system."

"I take it these were big deals," Volk said.

"Extremely," Mark replied. "Total loss on both ship and both ships ended up leaving the Solar System on random trajectories. Getting teams out to investigate was a major undertaking." Mark leaned in. "In any event, as a result of those accidents, there were a ton of changes made to ship design and operation to prevent UPEs, intentional or otherwise." Mark leaned back. "That's why we haven't had a UPE in a major ship since before I was born."

Volk pondered that for a bit. "I hate to ask based on a video, but..."

"Yeah, I saw that video too," Mark replied. "*The Cold Goodbye*. Had some nice eye candy on the cast and didn't mangle the tech too badly. The real ship that video was based on was a genuine JFILF."

"Jilf?"

"Junkyard Flying in Loose Formation."

"Which we don't think is an accurate description of the *Cardinal*," Volk said. It was a statement, not a question. Mark just let the statement hang there.

Finally, Volk said, "Well shit. This could be a really boring investigation." The inspector's handheld buzzed, relieving Mark from having to respond. The Inspector got up and went to a corner of the room and consulted his ocular. He returned after his call.

"Apparently," Volk said, "We have a checklist for crash investigations."

God, I hope so.

"Said checklist involves building a basic background report on everybody who's on the ship."

"You've got, if my math is right, five hundred fifty-nine people to look at," Mark said.

"Yep. Might as well get started." Volk sat down at the conference table and apparently started to review data on his ocular. After a bit, he said, "So, does ValuTrip book the passengers?"

"Of course," Mark said.

"How come all the passengers were single?" Volk asked.

That's a good question, Mark thought. "How so?"

"I mean, there's around four hundred passengers, and almost none of them are married. Here's another—how come the high-school kids are all one-to-a-cabin?"

Another good question. Not sure why it's relevant, but that does seem unusual. "That is a bit weird," Mark said.

"I guess I should go ask ValuTrip," Volk said. Before Mark could ask why, Volk added, "It looked to me like the Jayhawk people were running around like chickens with their heads cut off."

Mark's family had raised chickens for eggs and food. He'd seen actual chickens run around after their heads were cut off. A couple had even flown, albeit briefly. The Jayhawk people were busy but were both professional and purposeful—not something one could say of a headless chicken. "Yeah, Jayhawk's kind of busy at the moment."

Volk stood up. "You up for a walk?"

"Me? I'm just a liaison."

Volk waved at the empty conference room. "Not a lot of liaison-ing to do at the moment. I'm sure Wagner can find you if she needs something done."

Well, somebody's got to keep Inspector Clueless from stepping in it. "Yeah, lets."

***

Jayhawk Operations was on one side of and attached to the Marriott, and ValuTrip was in a similar office building on the other side. The lobby of the ValuTrip building was packed with reporters, watched over by another gaggle of uniformed police and private security. Volk's badge proved essential to get past the cops, and equally helpful in clearing the American-style security theater needed to get up to the ValuTrip offices, which took up the top two floors of the mid-rise building.

The main reception area was on eight and was decorated in generic corporate style. The receptionist had obviously gotten a call from the building's security officers and had a flunky waiting for them, who escorted the pair into the CEO's office.

The CEO introduced herself as Cami Niland. She was tall for a woman, and of that indeterminate age and race one could become if one had a lot of money. "You're with the NTSB?" she asked.

"No," Ray said. "At least not directly. I'm with the FBI and my colleague here is with the Martian Space Force."

"Martian Navy," Mark said, offering his hand.

"Ah," Cami replied. "Please have a seat," she continued, escorting the men to a grouping of high-end leather armchairs. "Why is the FBI here?" She held up her hand. "We're planning on being fully cooperative in any event."

"Truthfully I'm just trying to make best use of my time," Volk said. "While the NTSB is collecting technical data, I figured I could get started on what I need for my report."

"Please go on," Cami said.

"Well, we have a number of questions," Volk said. "Purely routine, at this point."

"Such as?"

"Well, for one, why were there forty high-school exchange students onboard?" Volk asked.

"That actually sounds light for this time of year," Cami replied. "We're primarily in the business of package tours— booking ten cabins and up. We have a whole sales department focusing on student and cultural exchange groups."

"So, everybody got their ticket via a tour?" Volk asked.

"Not everybody," Cami said. "We do get some single cabin bookings. Usually, about three to four weeks out from a sailing, we release any unbooked space to third-party aggregators. Most of our Martian business comes from Stateroom Select," she said, pointing at Mark.

"I'm an Interplanetary Lines man myself," Mark said.

"But most of the passengers would have booked through a tour group?" Volk asked.

"Upward of eighty percent, I should think," Cami said. "Our Director of Sales was on vacation—he's flying back from the Moon now—but we can get you the specifics."

"We'll need that," Volk said. "We'll also need to see the various department heads and review everybody's personnel records."

"I don't..." Cami paused. "I mean..."

"It's purely routine," Volk said with a smile. "I have to justify my being here somehow."

"We're glad to be of help," Cami said, standing up. "I obviously don't keep all of that in my office. Let me introduce you around to the people you need to see."

At least Volk knows how to be a cop.

***

The first office they came to was the Head of Security's, although she wasn't in. Cami left the two men and went to get her. Mark surveyed the office, noting the "I love me" wall. A picture of a spaceship in a presentation case caught his eye. "Let me take the lead on this, Inspector," Mark said.

"Special Agent," Volk corrected.

Apparently neither of us can keep our titles straight. I'll have to work on that.

Cami walked in, followed by another tall woman, olive-skinned with straight, gray hair.

"Morning, Colonel," Mark said, offering his hand. "I recognize a General-class destroyer, but darned if I can match hull numbers to names."

"USS *LeMay*," the woman replied, not taking his hand. "I'm a civilian now, Captain—Denise Ricardo. To what do I owe a visit from the Dread Red Menace?"

I would have to get a hardline nationalist, Mark thought, lowering his hand. "It's been a long time since we've been a menace," he said.

"We're here about the *Cardinal*," Volk offered clumsily.

"My grandmother was killed at Clavius," Denise said, ignoring him.

By the Martian Army was left unsaid. "I'm sorry. I lost a great-uncle in the war. He was on the *Vikrant*."

"Perhaps we could focus on the present," Volk said, more forcefully, a confused look on his face.

Mark assayed a smile. "I'm Mark Nagata, and my colleague here is Ray Volk of the Federal Police."

"Federal Bureau of Investigation, actually," Volk said.

Cami and Denise traded looks, and Cami took one of the guest chairs.

"What ships were you with?" Denise asked, settling behind her desk, ice in her voice. She glared at Cami, who replied with a shrug.

"My destroyer command was the RMS *Jim C. Hines*, and my major command was the RMS *City of Rivendale*."

"RMS?" Volk asked.

"Republic of Mars Ship," Denise said distractedly. "They let O-4s command ships on the Red Planet." She gestured at her wall. "*LeMay* was my only command. So, how'd you get assigned to this investigation?"

"Accidents, mostly," Mark said. "I happened to be in town," the truth, "and when I got out of boot I drew the short straw," a lie, "and got assigned to Crash and Smash. Mostly I made coffee, but the gig meant that when your ship went missing my name was on a short list."

Denise chuckled. "Apparently the Space Force is not the only bureaucracy in the world." She turned serious. "Any word?"

"I'm afraid not," Mark said. "The local crash-and-smash kicked us out." Mark gambled that she had the typical American's attitude to crash investigations. *I have to win a gamble one of these times.* "So, since I'm sure Agent Volk here will eventually have to fill out a report, we decided to come here and get a run on it."

"Well, I will do whatever I can," she said, looking pointedly at Volk.

"If you could start," Volk said, talking a bit slower than he usually did and lengthening his drawl, "by giving me the dollar tour of the security setup. I'm not an astronaut by trade."

"Neither am I," Denise said a bit sharply. "And why do you care about security?"

"Astronauts are enlisted personnel," Mark said. "Officers aren't." *I wonder if he knew that or was just poking Denise? Either way it's working.*

"So sorry," Volk said, sounding sincere. "I'm really at sea, or in space, here. To answer your question, I'm just going down my list, and your department was closest to Ms. Niland's office."

"No problem," Denise said. She looked at Mark. "Standard package, really. Three shift officers, a Chief and an assistant, and two cagers."

"Cagers?" Volk asked.

"Technically dispatchers," Denise said. "They sit in a locked room, monitor video and answer the phone."

"Armed or unarmed?" Volk asked.

"The five outside officers are armed with a pistol and there's an emergency pistol in the cage."

"Not a lot of security," Volk said.

"More police per capita than a typical US city," Denise replied.

Volk apparently did the mental math, then replied, "True. I assume that passengers are prevented from going to areas they shouldn't. How is that accomplished?"

"Locked doors, for the most part," Denise replied.

"Not physical keys?" Volk asked.

Denise shot Mark a "can you believe this guy" look. He replied, "Inspector, er, Agent Volk was telling me that their usual person for this detail was out." Mark was beginning to think Volk wasn't entirely as clueless as he was pretending to be. *Good.*

"Maternity leave," Volk replied. "Twins, who came early."

"They usually do," Cami said.

"So," Denise started, "all doors have electronic controls via access bands. Higher security levels require pin codes."

"Not fingerprints?" Mark asked.

"It's optional on SpaceX ships and we didn't buy that option," Denise said, shooting her boss a glance implying she did not agree with that decision. "But under ISFAR rules, certain critical locations need to be accessible no matter what the power situation is, so they have manual keylock overrides."

"Presumably as a result of *Fantasia* and *Lotus*."

Nicely played, especially since you hadn't heard either of those names fifteen minutes ago.

"Exactly," Denise said.

"And how are those keys controlled?"

"The keys are passed from person to person and are always in somebody's control. Several somebodies."

"But if they get lost?"

Denise shrugged. "The doors are alarmed and monitored. If they are opened by anybody, the cager gets an alarm."

"Sounds like an important job," Volk said. "Now, again for us groundlings, what was the ship's schedule like? I mean, I understand midnight here was midnight there, right?"

"Yes," Denise replied. "They had shifted to Earth time. Basically, everything except the core bar closes at midnight."

"Core bar?"

Denise ticked off items with her fingers. "Each ship has three bars. They have different themes and decors, but there's a piano bar, a dance bar, and the core bar. Also, a youth center, with a soft drink and snack stand and some activity space for the under-eighteen set."

"And this core bar? The one that stays open late?"

"Think hotel lobby bar. It's next to the Guest Services desk—the shipboard equivalent of the check-in counter."

"So after midnight, everybody who's drinking is at the core bar?" Mark offered.

"Correct. Also eating, because the core coffee shop's the only food place open, and the core mini mart is the only store open."

"And when do they close?" Volk asked.

"The bar at two in the morning—Federal law says we can't serve booze 24/7—and the other venues go to a self-serve mode."

Typical American weirdness about booze. Mark noted that Volk seemed equally nonplussed about that rule.

"We'll want a floorplan of the ship," Volk said.

"We sent one to the NTSB but I'll get you one," Denise said.

"And personnel records on the crew," Volk added.

"Of course," Denise replied. "Just for the record, I've known the Chief of Security on that ship for two decades—he was my Security Chief on the *LeMay*. He's solid."

"Good to know," Mark said.

The two men got up and left. In the hallway, Volk said under his breath, "Everybody's solid until they're not."

He may not know which end of a rocket goes up, but he does seem to know people.

Chapter 4

Victoria

After the takeover, Victoria' had set up her crew's base of operations in the piano bar. It made a good headquarters. Although on *Cardinal* the bar was open to everybody, the ship had been built with the idea that the bar would be reserved for first class passengers only. As a result, it could be easily closed off from the rest of the ship. Doing so was probably not necessary, but there was no point in taking unnecessary chances.

She walked into the bar from her new stateroom—formerly Hank's—refreshed after a quick shower. As she did, she adjusted the gun in her shoulder holster. *If I shoot somebody, they need to be killed, not stunned. This is not some historical video of flying eggshells—modern ships have self-sealing hulls.* She plopped down at the keyboard of the piano and started playing her usual warm-up song, the classic "Piano Man." She found music and routine soothing, and it had been a stressful night.

She rubbed her sore jaw, a parting gift from Hank. It was a shame the woman had proven so combative, but probably not surprising. Besides the fight with Hank, Zoren's failure had put another dent in last night's operation. He was a crewmember and, relevant to the operation, he had access to the cargo hold. His access badge and PIN being used to access the hold would not trigger any alarms. He wasn't fully briefed on the plan, rather they'd let him believe they were planning some kind of heist. She smiled at that. *We pulled off a heist, all right. Heist of a whole damn ship.*

However, Zoren's sudden burst of conscience or fear and thus not showing up had forced Victoria to improvise. She looked up from her piano to see one of her co-hijackers, Mike—aka "Commander Zero" and the public face of this operation—standing on the other side of the closed and locked glass doors, fishing through his pockets for his physical key. Mike was escorting Jack Otarski, her former boss as the ship's Director of Passenger Services.

"Let them in, please," she yelled over the music, something she had long practice in doing. The younger of Helen Grabowski's boys, a kid of twelve, set his stack of plates down and headed to the door. Before he got there, Mike found his key and came in. He and Jack stood next to her piano as she finished the song.

"I'm sure you didn't have your goon march me here to listen to a concert of music I've never heard before, Ms. Stevens," Jack said. He sniffed. "If that is your real name."

You sanctimonious prick! "That is my real name," *thanks to my late husband, who died much better than you will,* "and you've heard this song every day since I've been on this ship. I play it as a warm-up while you and Captain Octopus have your pre-dinner snort."

"He was a good man..."

"Who never met a woman he didn't try and feel up," Victoria finished.

"Is that why you shot him? Because he felt you up?"

Actually, I shot him because the SOB kept a gun in his cabin and was going to use it on me. Given that the last successful hijacking attempt had been in her grandfather's time, Captain Montoya's need for a gun was true paranoia. *Although he was an American, and those people have more guns than changes of underwear.* "No, Jack, I shot him because I wanted to make clear who the captain is now. That would be me, Jack, in case you're not clear on the subject."

"Aye aye, Captain," Jack replied with enough sarcasm that Mike reared back to hit him. Victoria waved him off.

"That one was free," she said, as Jack's face reflected the realization that he'd just escaped a rifle butt in the gut. "Next time, I'll let him hit you."

"My original question stands," Jack said, trying to keep his dignity.

"No, I did not call you here to listen to a concert. Your task is to keep our passengers and crew fed, watered, clean and calm for the next twenty days."

"We're only eight days out of Earth."

"No shit," Victoria said, leaning on her piano. "Tell me something else I don't know." She sat back.

"Why twenty days?"

"Again, not something you need to know. But since I'm feeling charitable, I figure that's about as long as I think it will take to negotiate the payment of the ransom."

"And what makes you think they'll pay?"

"Five hundred fifty-nine lives."

Jack made a sour face. "With Captain Montoya dead, who's talking to the company?"

Victoria stood up, and Jack reflexively flinched back. *Good.* "Is there some reason you're giving me the fucking third degree?"

"With Captain Montoya dead," Jack said, failing to keep his voice from quivering, "you could argue that I'm in command."

"You're barely in command of your bowels," Victoria said, flashing him a predatory smile. "But since you're all up in my business, and I'm feeling generous, I'll enlighten you."

"Thank you."

"At the moment, nobody is talking to Earth. We have, for all that they know, completely disappeared. We'll continue that silent act for another day or two, allowing them to work up a full sweat about a lost ship.

"Then," Victoria continued, "Staff Captain Davidoff will contact ValuTrip and start negotiations." *Well, not really, but it was a good story. Kept the hostages calm.*

"You're not going to be satisfied with just the insurance payoff, are you." Jack phrased that as a statement.

Oh hell no. These people were worth a lot more than the proforma insurance coverage. "We'll of course be asking for more." *And we'll get it, one way or another.*

"Where's Davidoff? I'd like to see her."

"She's safe, being held separately, and no you may not see her."

"May I ask why?"

"You can ask," Victoria said, resuming her seat. "I don't have to answer."

"There's a lot of work that needs to be done. Plantings, harvesting..."

"You have, in addition to the crew, all of the passengers."

"They're not going to like that."

Victoria smiled and pointed at Mike. "Ask him if he cares what they *like*."

Jack looked at Helen, who was inspecting her sons' work on the buffet line they were setting up in the lounge. "Am I to assume that I won't have the services of Grabowski?"

"Correct. Nor anything she's brought up to this kitchen." Victoria smiled. "We shall be as self-sufficient here as possible. Wouldn't want somebody to get any bright ideas." Victoria pitched her voice for Helen's benefit. "Do you have all the supplies you need?"

"Almost, ma'am," Helen replied. "We're waiting on a couple of cases of canned goods."

"Where we gonna put them?" one of her boys whined.

"Under the buffet tables," Helen replied. "Now get the silverware out."

"What's my count?" Jack asked.

"Fifteen less than it was yesterday," Victoria replied. *Plus the group from the cargo hold—like Mike here—that you don't need to know about, since it wasn't on your count anyway.*

"Jesus, that many?"

"Only a few of them are dead." *Four, actually. Montoya and the two ship's cops they'd killed, plus that Martian kid who'd gotten clobbered in the head.* She looked at Jack. *There will be a couple more, once I don't need them.* Victoria nodded at Helen, then looked at Otarski. "Most of them are on my team now. Also, we'll be feeding Davidoff out of our rations. Be grateful I didn't kill more people."

"Will there be anything else, Captain?"

"Not at this time, Jack. You will report directly to Mike, here. Please get his approval on your work and feeding schedules."

Jack turned and looked at Mike. "So, Commander Zero's not on your birth certificate?"

Well, shit, that was an unforced error.

"No," Mike said with a smile. "But you should probably just call me that. Let's move out."

As they did, Helen came up to the piano. "We're ready to serve, ma'am. I'm afraid it's just cold cuts."

"What, no lobster and cracked crab?" Victoria asked with a smile, getting up to head to the line.

"Soon," Helen replied. "We actually need to eat some of that up, so I have room in this freezer." Something in Victoria's glance prompted her to continue. "Our stuff is in a freezer on the cargo deck, and I've locked it with my key. It's tamper-proof. Besides, if we have to, we raid the hostages' food."

"Don't forget that the hostages are money," Victoria said. Actually, they were *all* the money, and 'inventory' would be a better term for them, but Helen didn't need to know that. *Once the people were all parceled out on Mercury, they would not be anybody's problem.* All she needed to know was how many people to be fed out of the small kitchen attached to the lounge.

"Most of the hostages could miss a couple of meals and nobody'd notice," she replied. "And did you really keep Davidoff alive?"

"For now, yes," Victoria said. "She may need to make an appearance. Jasper will take her meals to her."

Helen took that remark as a dismissal and stepped away. Victoria, reflexively, played an arpeggio on the piano. There were a number of ways things could go down on Mercury. Most of them required her, Grand Duke Victoria Hakken, to not be obviously involved in the hijacking. Thus

'Commander Zero' and thus the necessity for Otarski to have an unfortunate heart attack. *Do I have to do the same to Hank?* She played another arpeggio. *That would be a waste.*

***

"You look tired, Ted," Victoria said to the man sitting across from her.

He took a bite from his sandwich, chewed, and swallowed before answering. "I've been up since midnight, boss. I am tired."

You'd have more energy if you lost some of that spare tire around your waist. But since Ted Beale's big toe knew more about the actual operation of spaceships than she did, Victoria kept that thought to herself. "Well, you should be able to get some sleep now."

"For a while," Ted said. "With just three of us, we're going to be busy."

He meant three people qualified to stand watches on the bridge. Ted had wanted more bodies—probably so he could sit on his ass—but there were hard limits on how many people she could smuggle in. She'd hid most of the gunmen in what had supposedly been a refrigerated, thus powered, container. After five days, one of which was in zero gee as the container was being moved, the container had smelled like a sewer.

So, there were hard feelings between the "box people" and those—like she and Ted—who had been listed as crew or passengers out of Mars. To make matters worse, she'd had to pay Ted a double share for his ability to fly a ship. She hid a smile. Well, *promise* him a double share.

"Busy is good," Victoria said.

"Speaking of busy," Ted said, gesturing toward the main promenade, "when is somebody going to round up the bodies? The captain, well, he's gonna start to stink."

"I got the passengers on it."

"Good. Bunch of lazy-ass tourists."

Actually, most of them weren't lazy. A lot of them were members of various sports clubs. Young, healthy, physically fit people were worth more than the drug-heads and runaways who typically found themselves as slaves on Mercury. The older ones might even be able to ransom themselves to freedom.

"I assume we're on course?" Victoria asked.

"Yep. Eight days acceleration burn, four coast, eight days breaking burn."

"Other ships?"

"Nothing visible."

"Visible?"

Ted shrugged. "Radar's off." Victoria started to say something but Ted held his hand up. "I turned it off...for now."

"Because?"

"Because once we went 'missing' everybody with a radar-detector would be looking in our general direction. No radar means nothing for them to detect." He made a swooping gesture with the hand holding his sandwich, which narrowly escaped falling apart. "Once we're above the plane of the elliptic, there will be nobody looking for us."

"And why is that?"

"Because, except for a few asteroids, everything anybody wants to get to is on the plane." He took a bite of his sandwich. "Anyway, once we're well out of the way, then I can turn the radar back on—because anybody in radar range *will* be looking for us."

"When will that be?"

"Three, maybe four days from now."

Thrust came on again, causing Victoria's glass to slide toward the edge of the table. "And do we really need to keep turning the engines on and off?"

"Do you want to be found by the US Space Force?"

"No." She involuntarily shuddered. That would be nearly the worst case.

"So yes, we need to keep jacking the engines," Ted said.

"How does that help?"

"Sky scans," Ted said, talking around his sandwich. "Every space force has telescopes conducting automated scans of the Solar System looking for engine flares. When a wide-angle scan finds something, it tasks another, more powerful, scope to take a closer look. An automated look."

"So, you hope that when the second robot looks, it won't see anything."

"Exactly," Ted said. "Thus thrust on and off." He waved a hand, fortunately empty, in an expansive manner. "On warships, you can automate that throttling. On a commercial ship, it's a manual process by the watchstander. Makes the watches more involved."

Which gives you another reason to whine. "Okay. Keep doing what you're doing."

"I will," Ted said.

"Good. Keep me in the loop." Victoria's radio crackled.

"Jack says he's ready to feed our guests." Olga said through the radio.

"Fifteen minutes," Victoria replied into the radio.

"When are they going to start working on the depressurization valves?" Ted asked.

"Probably after I get the captives fed," Victoria said. "Everybody else is tired too."

"Just make sure they call the bridge when they start. Fucking with those valves will set off all kinds of alerts."

Tell me something else I don't know. "Will do."

Victoria got up and took her empty plate to where they'd set up a return area. It was critical that nobody figure out where the ship was going until they got there and got the passengers off. Then everybody could really cash in.

Chapter 5

Kansas City

Ray

Ray walked into the conference room at Jayhawk. There was a status display up, the letters and numbers hanging in air. One corner of the display was clearly understandable, showing time since last contact. The rest of the display was Greek to Ray, although the color-coding of green-yellow-red seemed clear enough. Ray noted two yellow items, both with numbers rapidly counting down. As he watched, the countdowns stopped, and the items went to red. There seemed to be a lot of red on the board.

"That can't be good," Ray said to no one in particular.

"It's not," Wagner said, sliding up next to him. "Two more emergency systems just went past their design operational life."

"One would hope they'd last a bit longer."

"In my business, hope gets people killed." She tapped his arm. "We had food brought in."

"I'm so hungry I could eat a horse," Ray replied, glancing at the sideboard. He walked over and grabbed some food. Judging by the napkins, the food was from the nearby Marriott.

"Investigating makes you hungry?" Wagner asked, grabbing an apple from the spread.

"No, missing breakfast makes me hungry," Ray replied.

"How's our Martian friend?" Wagner asked.

The Martian in question walked in at that moment, looking as cool as a cucumber. "Great," he said, walking over to the buffet where he perused the offerings and sat down empty-handed.

"What did you find out over at ValuTrip?" Wagner asked.

"Not much," Ray replied. "All the employees passed a background check, so finding anything of interest will be a slog." Which wasn't surprising. Ray had lost track of the number of people with clean background checks he'd sent to jail. It would have been surprising if they *didn't* do background checks, and even more surprising if something had shown up on those checks.

"The passenger group was a zoo," Mark Nagata said. "Everybody on Earth's calling in asking about their ship."

"I imagine," Wagner said.

"There was one thing that was a bit funny," Ray said. "ValuTrip's head of booking was on the Moon on vacation. They're coming back as fast as they can and have been in constant contact. Their subordinate, one Frank Malan, who's not on vacation, is not in."

"Work-from-home?" Wagner said.

"No, he's one of those office rats," Ray replied. "And even if he did work remote, well, he's not responding. You'd think the guy who actually handled the booking for the first ship to go missing in forever would be a bit more responsive."

"You'd think so." Wagner took a bite of her apple while looking around the room. "Where'd Nagata go?"

"Probably the restroom," Ray said.

"Good."

"Oh?"

"Yeah. We," she pointed at the room, "need to have a conversation in a few minutes. A conversation that we don't want to have in front of the Martian military."

"About what?"

"Well, to be honest, I'm not sure you're cleared for it, and I don't have time to find out."

"So, if the captain and I were to go take a road trip to Frank Malan's house in Overland Park, Kansas, you'd be obliged?" *And I'd get some alone time with Captain Hottie.*

"Yep."

"Then as soon as he gets back, we'll grab some food for the car and go."

"Thanks."

***

"So, tell me about this book," Ray said once they'd gotten into the car. *Having him talk about his book beat the hell out of asking him his sign as a pickup line.*

"Well, do you know who Gagarin and Pilgrim were?" Nagata asked.

"Gagarin? Wasn't she an early astronaut? Pilgrim—never heard of him."

"Gagarin was the first man in space. Janet Pilgrim was the first Commandant of the Martian Navy and helped win our War of Independence."

Ray shook his head ruefully. "Wow, not even close."

"Not too bad," Nagata said, clearly trying to make him not feel like an idiot. *Which, apparently, I am.*

"And given the title of the book," Ray said, "Gagarin was in the Imperial Space Force, or whatever it was in Russia."

"Gagarin was in the Soviet era—several decades after the collapse of Czars, and yes, he was Air Force."

"As you can tell," Ray said, lengthening his drawl, "space history was not my best subject in school."

"Actually, it wasn't mine either," Nagata said. "I got into history when I joined the Navy."

"So..."

"So, the book's part of an argument. During the last Congressional election on Mars, one of the issues was space policy." Nagata let out an exasperated sigh. "One major party adopted the position that we, modern-day Mars, were responsible for 'militarization' of space, and if we just stopped building so many 'flying palaces for admirals' things would be so much better."

"You don't agree, I take it."

"Well, we may have a few more admirals than we need, strictly speaking. Peacetime militaries get hidebound, and it's been a long time since there's been a war in space. But the broader gist...no, I don't."

"How'd that election go?"

"The clueless party," Nagata cracked a smile and covered his mouth with his hand, which was a cute gesture, "sorry, the Commerce Party, won. They immediately cancelled orders for two classes of frigates."

"Ouch. Although you'd think a party of businesspeople would be in favor of things which would generate more business."

"Yeah, I wondered that too. Then I read an article, which pointed out that the Commerce Party was dominated by small businesses, owner-operated, who mostly just wanted lower taxes. Cutting government spending appealed to them."

"You guys can't do deficit spending?" Ray asked, wondering how he was going to get this conversation out of politics and into more personal topics. He'd never yet gotten into somebody's pants by talking politics.

"We can and do. There are a lot of political parties on Mars, and the government is usually a coalition. Commerce formed this government on the fourth ballot and needed the Sound Money Movement to get over the top." Nagata clucked. "Those guys are really wackaloons, especially about deficits." He cleared his throat. "To be clear, these are my personal opinions and may not be shared by the Admiralty."

"Just two dudes out for a drive to find out why a third dude can't answer his damn phone," Ray said. "First time on Earth?"

"Yes."

"And I remember you said you were going to do a tour at our Air Force Academy?"

"Yeah. It's an exchange program—one of your officers teaches on Mars and we send one to Earth."

"Your spouse come with or are they back on Mars?"

"My exes—both of them—are back on Mars. You married?"

"Divorced. Only one ex. Couldn't handle my hours. You?"

"Ex Number One and I were too young to be married. Ex Number Two, well, that's more complicated." Nagata clucked his tongue. "A lot more complicated."

"How so?"

"I'm too sober to discuss it now," Mark said.

That doesn't sound good.

"Wouldn't you like to review the file on this Malan dude before we get there?" Mark asked, gesturing at his handheld resting in its bracket on the passenger side of the dash.

"I already looked through it," Ray said. "Not very useful."

"Oh?"

"I've done a shitload of white-collar crime investigations. The single most consistent thing I've found is that *everybody's* HR record looks as clean and shiny as a newborn baby's ass." *That came out a bit harsher than I wanted*

"I shall defer to the expert."

Yep. I was dismissive. Then Nagata's phone rang and the opportunity for conversation was lost.

Mark

Mark disconnected his call. "Sorry about that," he said to Volk. "Administrative stuff for the Academy."

"No problem." Volk had told the vehicle their destination and then ignored the road, alternating his focus between his sandwich and questions about Mark's book. Mark found it unnerving—he always paid attention when he was responsible for the vehicle. *But that's just my idiosyncrasy,* he thought. Both of his ex-spouses had done the same "set it and forget it" in a vehicle.

Volk crumpled up his napkin. "You know, another thing I was kind of curious about."

Which part of Space History 101 now? "What?"

"You and Denise—back at ValuTrip. What's was that all about?"

Mark sighed heavily. "I was warned Americans are either ignorant of history or have a distorted view of it."

"Educate me."

"You've heard of Clavius?"

"Yeah—it's one of the Lunar republics."

"Well, originally it was a US colony."

"Kind of figured," Volk said.

"The Battle of Clavius was President Garcia's attempt to keep an American presence on your moon."

"I do remember hearing about that in school," Volk said. "Long time ago."

"You didn't have a relative that served?"

"Maybe one of my grandparent's cousins. Nobody I knew of."

The war, at least for the Terrans, had been fought by volunteers. Mars had not had that luxury.

"I do know, however," Volk said, "we lost."

"Badly."

"Now, the follow-on to that, the succession of Texas and Alaska, that I'm more familiar with."

"How so?"

"My family's originally from Texas on my mom's side. They fled north, ending up here in Missouri."

"Ah." *For Volk, apparently, history is only important if it's personal.*

"And the invasion?" Volk asked.

"Mars had allied itself with America against China and India. Garcia's war broke that alliance, and we got invaded. If it weren't for anti-matter and force-field technology, I'd be speaking Chinese."

Volk yawned. "All this is ancient history. Don't know why Ricardo is holding a grudge."

The advantage of being ignorant of history is a reluctance to hold a historical grudge. "Nor do I, especially since the Republic of Clavius is practically American. Y'all have better relations with it than with Alaska."

Volk snorted. "Fucking Alaskans are all crooks. I guess they have to be—either that or starve."

That's harsh, Mark thought. *But then he is a cop and probably every Alaskan he's dealt with has been a crook.*

Volk squirmed in his seat. "And what was all that shit about 'crash and smash'?"

Mark chuckled. "Americans are notoriously hostile to their safety inspectors. Even, or maybe especially, the military."

"Oh. So, you drawing the short straw was not why you're on this gig?"

"Well, I actually requested Accident Investigation," Mark said. "I didn't know if I was going to make a career of the Navy, and AI was considered a good steppingstone to civilian jobs."

"Then why'd you stay in?"

"First they offered to pay my college and make me an officer, then they kept giving me interesting assignments, mostly in Second Fleet."

"Second Fleet?"

"Interstellar. Three of my four space tours were in different star systems."

"Cool," Volk said.

"It was," Mark replied. "This gig is actually the first non-cool assignment I've gotten."

"Teaching at the Air Force Academy isn't cool?"

"It counts as shore duty, but I'm not on Mars where the bulk of my family is, and it's not a major command which could line me up to be Admiral."

"So, this hurts your career?"

"It doesn't help." Mark stretched. The higher gravity was tweaking his back. "But I get to see the Old World and meet new people."

"Got plans to visit anyplace in your off time?"

"California," Mark said. "My family came from there. We've still got a couple of distant cousins who live in a place called Alameda. Been there?"

"Can't say I have." The car beeped, then announced they were one mile from the destination. Volk looked around. "How much does a booking agent make?" he asked.

Mark read him the salary figure. "Why do you ask?"

"Doesn't this look rather upscale for somebody making that kind of money?"

"I've been on Earth for two weeks. I have no idea what real estate values are like on this planet."

"Frank makes half of what I do, and I couldn't afford to live here."

That is curious. "Maybe he's got a wealthy spouse?"

"Maybe," Volk said as their car pulled to a stop at a security gate. Volk talked to the video pickup and whoever was at the other end granted him access.

"You Americans and your security theater," Mark said.

"You don't have gated communities on Mars?" Volk said.

"We do—we call them private pressure—and there'd be a hell of a lot more security to get in than that."

"Ah." They rode, then Volk grabbed the steering knob on the dashboard and took manual control of the car. "That house in the middle of the block is Malan's."

The house was—to Mark's eyes—enormous. There was a nondescript gray van of the type used for deliveries and repair people parked in the driveway in front of a closed garage door. Volk, driving somewhat jerkily, parked the car on the street in front of the house.

"Why are we parking on the street?" *Instead of in the driveway where the car wanted to go* went unsaid.

"Something's fishy," Volk replied. "See the window?"

Mark followed Volk's finger to a second-floor window which was open allowing curtains to billow out. *Pressure leak!* He shook his head. Earth didn't worry about pressure leaks.

"Does that look normal to you?" Volk asked. "Also, if he's having work done, you'd assume the workers would be coming in and out via the garage. But the door is closed."

"Good point." *The Inspector may not know a rocket from the tenth of June, but apparently, he's a decent cop.*

Volk unbuckled his seatbelt. "You stay here."

"Like hell," Mark said.

"If there's a problem, what are you going to do about it?"

Mark reached in his coat and pulled out his gun.

"What, you're going to shoot somebody with that antique?"

It was, in fact, Mark's grandfather's gun, but it was perfectly functional. "It works just fine. Besides, it's part of the uniform."

"There are laws here! You can't just carry a gun around!"

"In America? Y'all are more likely to carry a gun than to wear underwear!"

Volk glared. "You're a foreign national. Hell, foreign military even."

Mark shrugged. "Nobody at customs gave me any grief."

"There's a difference between having a gun and carrying one."

"So I've heard." Mark put his hand on the door latch. "We going in or are we going to sit here and sell tickets?"

"I'm going in. You're going to holster that museum piece and stay behind me. Got it?"

Mark holstered his gun. "You got nothing to worry about from me."

"Because that gun's never going to see daylight again."

"Not unless you're already dead, in which case you've definitely got nothing to worry about."

Volk sighed heavily. "I think you've been watching too many bad videos. This is not an episode of The Shen Files. Just remember you're an observer here, with no law enforcement authority."

Volk put the car in park and the door unlocked. Mark climbed out into the early May heat. *Supposedly this damn planet will get even hotter. Most of the ice at the poles has already melted*, he thought as sweat popped on his brow.

Mark fell in behind Volk. As they walked up the driveway, Mark unbuttoned his coat, the easier to get at his revolver. He'd really like to take his coat off—this damn planet was too hot for a wool, blue uniform jacket.

They walked past the closed garage door and up to a rather elaborate front door. To the entry sensor Volk said,

"FBI," and held up his ID so the camera could see it. They could faintly hear the entry system announce, "You have a visitor," inside the house.

"Door's not latched," Mark said.

"So I see," Volk replied, looking over his shoulder. "I still gotta announce."

As he did that, the door swung in rapidly, revealing a very large man with an equally large shotgun aimed at the two of them. Mark shouted, "Gun!" and pushed Volk forward and to the left. He used the momentum of that push to move himself right and down.

The shotgun went off like a bomb. Mark felt a wave of heat and pressure pass through where he and Volk had been standing. He landed on his right shoulder in the grass while pulling out his revolver with his left hand. He fired a shot wildly in the direction of the gunman, which caused the man to flinch.

Volk had rolled left and also came up with his gun, a modern slug pistol, which he fired on reflex. Shotgun Man, taking fire from two people, withdrew into the house. "Go around back!" Volk shouted at Mark.

So much for being a fucking observer. I hope The Inspector's alright, Mark thought, moving in a three-point crawl. As he did, he glanced over his shoulder to see Volk scrambling for his own cover. *If he's moving, I guess he's good for the moment.*

Mark got around the house to see it had a large brick patio area, walled off from a common lawn area with a low brick wall and accessed from the house by a pair of sliding glass doors. A figure in black came out of the open door. "Stop!" Mark yelled.

The figure turned and pointed a pistol at Mark, who dove around a brick pillar which was promptly hit by a slug from the other person's gun. "Shit!" Mark said. He swung around the pillar and fired a suppressive round in the general direction of the bad guy.

He heard a shotgun bark and several rounds from a pistol from inside the house. He peeked around the pillar to see the other figure dash out, firing wildly at Mark. Also firing too high. Mark squeezed off a round, saw the figure stutter step, and Mark fired again. The figure slowly dropped to the ground.

"Reload," Mark said aloud, fumbling with his speed-loader. He dumped the empties and unfired shells on the ground, and jammed a fresh six into his gun, then tossed the empty speed-loader to the ground. "One hostile down!" Mark shouted, hoping that Volk hadn't been hit.

"I'm coming out!" Volk shouted. An instant later he stepped out onto the deck. Mark stood up and walked toward him, noting as he did that Volk was talking to somebody on his headset. "Backup's on the way."

By the time they get here the bodies will be at room temperature. "Good."

"You can holster that," Volk said, pointing at his revolver.

Mark did so, noting that it seemed to be getting darker outside. He plopped down into an over-upholstered lawn chair before he went completely out.

***

"You know," Volk said, "I told you not to wave that gun around." The previously calm house was a buzz of activity as at least a dozen people milled about, a mixture of plainclothes and several different uniforms.

"Next time I won't."

"Also, for the record, thanks for not staying in the car."

"Well," Mark said, "next time, I *will* stay in the damn car." He looked up at the fierce sun. "Especially on hot days like today."

"It will get hotter," Volk said. "Nice shooting. Especially good for your first gunfight."

"Second, actually," Mark replied. "Popped a ventilator in the asteroids."

"A what?"

"Ventilator. De-air man. Guy who kills people for a living."

"We call those 'button men' or 'hitters.'"

"I guess ventilator is a Martian-ism," Mark replied. He gestured toward the house. "Frank Malan, booking man?"

"Presumably he's one of the two bodies wrapped up in plastic." Volk gestured at the house. "One body is on the kitchen floor, a second is in the trunk of the Malan's fully-charged car."

"Vent and vac, huh?" To Volk's quizzical look, Mark elaborated. "Vent you got. 'Vac' as in vacuum up."

"Remove the bodies."

"Exactly." Which in the asteroids frequently meant taking the body to the nearest airlock and sending them out of it without depressurizing the inner lock. On all but the biggest asteroids, the airflow thus generated would accelerate the body to the asteroid's escape velocity, sending the body off into space.

"Either this is one hell of a coincidence," Volk said, waving his hand to encompass the crime scene, "or something ain't right."

"Yeah. So now what?"

"Now I get to fill out one fuckload of paperwork." Volk pointed at a uniformed cop. "Unfortunately, you're going to have to go have a chat with their boss."

"Sounds like fun."

"Remember," Volk said, "better to be judged by twelve..."

"Than carried by six," Mark said, completing the saying. "Damn straight, sir." He stood up and to the cop said, "Where's my gun?"

"Evidence, sir," they replied.

"It's a family heirloom. I'm going to want it back."

"Not my call, sir. Now if you'll follow me."

Chapter 6

Kansas City

Ray

On arriving at the Overland Park Police HQ building, Ray found his boss, Special Agent in Charge Charlize Fetterer, was waiting for him in the lobby. She led him to an apparently unoccupied office just past the secure entry area. He had been dreading this.

"What part of 'don't fucking shoot anybody' did you not understand?" Fetterer asked as soon as the door was closed.

"He was shooting at me!"

"A fact which damn well better be backed up by forensics."

"It will be. Who was he?"

"Not carrying so much as a gum wrapper on him," Fetterer replied. "Fingerprints should be in any minute." She glared at Ray. "Stop shooting people!"

"I'll try."

"Don't try, do!"

"Okay," Ray said.

In a calmer voice, Fetterer said, "What do you have for me?"

"Well, Frank and Valerie Malan were both dead when I got there. Both had been wrapped up in plastic tarps and Frank was stuffed in the trunk of the family vehicle. Valerie was on the floor in the kitchen."

"How'd the perps get in?"

"Nothing obvious," Ray said. He pulled up his notes on his ocular. "Our perps got into the gated community posing as artisanal painters."

"As what?" Fetterer said, shooting him a quizzical look.

"Artisanal painters," Ray said with a shrug. "Apparently instead of just setting up a robot and letting it go, they paint your house by hand."

"And people pay money for this?"

"Those with more money than sense, yes."

"So, what did the painting company say?"

"These were not their crew. Somebody stole the company's van while our real painters were getting donuts."

"Tracker?"

"Disabled within three blocks of the heist. Tracker on the Malan's car was also disabled." *Clearly,* Ray thought, *the plan had been for the Malans to disappear and for the cops to spend the next week or so chasing their tails looking for them.*

Fetterer sighed. "These two were not gangers taking down the local RoboMart."

"No, they were proper vent-and-vac types." To Fetterer's questioning look, Ray explained the Martian slang terms and how he'd learned of them.

"So, you and our Martian are getting along nicely?" she asked, a sly smile on her face. "Good for you."

"He's very cute."

"That's what I saw from the pictures."

A beefy and pale uniformed cop came in. "The NTSB types want to talk to you."

Ray looked at his mobile. "Hasn't rung."

"They want a secure call," the cop replied. "In the FEMA room."

***

The room in question, buried in the basement of the building with a large "Federal Emergency Management Agency" sign outside, proved to be a virtual conference room. As Ray and Fetterer walked in, the other half of the room appeared to be the conference room at Jayhawk. Wagner was standing in the center of the room, consulting a handheld. "What you're about to hear is highly classified," she said without preamble.

"Is that conference room secure?" Ray asked.

Wagner smiled. "We bring our own anti-bugging stuff."

"Okay, so what do you have?"

"A highly-classified Space Force listening station picked up a significant amount of telemetry from ValuTrip *Cardinal*."

"What kind of telemetry?" Fetterer asked. "And why do we need a spy station to get it?"

"In reverse order," Wagner said, gesturing with a stylus, "somebody turned off the high-power transmitter that normally sent this data. They forgot the low-power transmitter."

"Even back in the 20th Century, humans could receive very low-power transmissions from spacecraft," Fetterer said. "Hell, the microwave in my kitchen puts out more power than some of those early spacecraft."

"True," Wagner replied, "but the transmissions were highly directional, and we were using big radio telescopes to receive them. Also, there weren't a lot of spacecraft sending out stuff."

"This is fascinating," Ray said, not that it really was, "but what did the telemetry tell us?"

"Engine light-offs," Wagner said. "Multiple. Plus attitude adjustments suggesting a change of course."

"Somebody's driving."

"Looks that way," Wagner said.

"Do we know where they are going?" Fetterer said. "Can our super-secret spooks track them?"

"Apparently not," Wagner said. "We got lucky they detected the signal in the first place. Now we're being told they can't even contact the 'installation'" —using air quotes for emphasis— "for another twelve hours."

"Huh?" Ray said.

"My guess is we've got some kind of automated tracking station on an uninhabited asteroid. When the asteroid's rotation allows the station to see us, we talk."

"And we would not like the Martians to know about the station," Ray said.

"Since they would consider it to be on their territory, no," Wagner said.

"Wonderful," Fetterer said.

Wagner held up a hand as, in the other room, one of her team came up to her. They conferred briefly, too quietly for the pickup to hear, then she said, "Clyde's got some ideas."

A gray-haired white dude, presumably Clyde, called up a 3-D image and tossed it up in the air. It looked like a schematic of the inner solar system. "*Cardinal's* last SPR had her here," Clyde said, using his hands to zoom the display in. "For our FBI friends, none of this is to scale."

The display dialed into a single dot, more-or-less midway between two yellow lines that Ray assumed were the orbits of Mars and Earth. A solid blue line trailing the dot Ray assumed was the past course of the ship, and a dashed blue line the intended course. "Stepping forward," Clyde said, again manipulating the display. The dot moved along the dashed blue line. "Here's the telemetry," Clyde said. The dot changed color, glowing bright red. "Normal engines light-off at 04:18, with an attitude change."

"We're positive that's good telemetry," Wagner said. "We got over a thousand discrete data packets. Can't possibly be anything but a normal light-off."

"We have LOS at around 07:18," Clyde said. "Which isn't a lot to go on."

"So where could *Cardinal* have gotten herself to?" Fetterer asked. "Assuming somebody knows how to drive and isn't just mashing buttons."

"I knew somebody would ask," Clyde said. He pressed a button on his display. The screen zoomed out, showing the solar system with a broad green band drawn through it. "Any place in the green band is accessible. The darker the green, the more likely, based on the new engine thrust vector."

"I see that Earth is still a possibility," Ray said. "Maybe somebody is trying to get home faster."

"Given reported fuel states," Clyde said, "the best they could do would be eighteen hours ahead of schedule."

"Would that be helpful?" Fetterer asked. "If they had an emergency and somebody wanted to get home sooner?"

"I'm hard-pressed to see how that would make any difference," Wagner said. "It's not like you can hold your breath for days."

"What if they don't?" Ray asked. "I mean, what if they don't know what they're doing?"

"Then they quickly make things much worse," Clyde said. "Like crossing Earth's orbit at speed but missing the planet by billions of kilometers because it's someplace else on its orbit."

"So, we better hope whoever's driving knows what they are doing," Ray said.

"Assuming that somebody is driving, and that they're not going to Earth," Fetterer began, "what objects are reachable?"

Clyde tossed up a list. None of the names were recognizable to Ray, and all of them had a number in front of them.

"A little help for the groundlings?" Fetterer asked.

"Asteroids," Wagner said.

"Which Mars governs," Ray said. "Right?"

"Yes, Mars governs the asteroids," Wagner said, a hint of disapproval in her voice. "They call it the Commonwealth of the Asteroids, but it's a Martian creature."

"Regardless of politics," Clyde said, "I ran the list. Only three of these rocks have anybody living on them, and none have more than a dozen people in total."

"Until we figure out who took our ship," Ray said, "we won't know where it's going."

"Probably not," Wagner agreed. "Although asteroids mean CIA. Not our CIA, but the Committee for Independent Asteroids. It's a Martian terrorist group."

"I'm sure that spaceship is worth a lot of money," Ray said.

Clyde chucked mirthlessly. "It's not like you could pull into a used-spaceship lot and sell it. If you're looking for ransom, why hasn't somebody called it in?"

"It's possible the hijacking went wrong," Wagner said. "They got control of the bridge, started to turn, and somehow there was a loss of pressure."

"But then who's driving?" Clyde said. "Has to be somebody."

Ray decided to assume that the auto-pilot had been ruled out.

"Which is where we come in," Ray said. "We need to pull background on everybody on that ship."

"Discreetly," Fetterer said.

"Why?" Ray asked.

"Because we don't know for sure what's happening," she replied. "I mean, if this was a straight ransom job, we'd have gotten a call by now. 'One trillion dollars or we blow the ship,' or maybe 'release this or that prisoner.' That kind of thing."

"Good point," Ray said, *if a bit Police Hostage-taker 101.* "Still, we have to ask. We can get Washington to parcel out the US-based people to their local FBI office for initial checking. What about the Martians?"

"I don't think forty high-schoolers could pull off a hijacking," Wagner replied.

"We need to ask," Fetterer said. "I'll talk to Washington."

"What about the non-Americans?" Wagner asked.

"We're only talking ten, if I recall correctly," Ray said. "An Alaskan, two Texans and the rest Canadians. I'm sure Washington can get that done as well."

"Why only North Americans?" Fetterer asked.

"Ship was part of a pre-clearance program," Clyde said. "You clear US Customs before you leave Mars."

Wagner had stepped aside and was conferring with another of her team. She came back online. "It gets worse."

"How?"

"The PSRs," she replied. Ray decided that meant something to the spacers. "O2 consumption is heavier than the soul-count would suggest."

"In English, please?" Fetterer asked.

"The amount of O2 being consumed was more than what the number of people onboard should be," Wagner said. She looked again at her handheld. "Suggesting that there were forty or so more people breathing than were listed on the manifest."

"Why wouldn't the crew notice that?" Ray asked.

Wagner shrugged. "It's not out of limit, and it's probably the same number as it was the last umpteen trips. Unless you actually do the math, you wouldn't. And the only reason we did the math is because the ship is missing."

Ray held up his hand and consulted his ocular. "Speaking of the manifest, *Cardinal* had a last-minute cancellation. Forty people from a square-dancing club didn't make the sailing."

"That's really odd," Wagner said. "They didn't take on some space-available people?"

"Not according to the manifest," Ray said, a hint of triumph in his voice. "Yet somebody or somebodies were sucking down the oxygen that should have been going to our square-dancers."

"So not only is the number in limits, but it's also what the crew were expecting based on the pre-flight brief." This from Wagner. "Convenient, that square-dancing club."

"Yeah," Fetterer said. "Schrödinger's people—there but not there. And they would have had to come onboard on Mars."

"Maybe we should ask our friendly Martian," Ray said. "Surely that's not classified."

"Good idea," Wagner said. She looked at her wristwatch. "We have a news conference in like five minutes. You two do your thing. We'll go out and play dumb."

Mark

The interrogation room of the police station at Overland Park, Kansas looked shockingly like the interrogation room of the base police office at Port Lowell, Mars—cheap and utilitarian. On Mars, the table was metal, here on Earth it was laminate over wood. Other than that, the two rooms were identical.

The sturdy metal door opened up and a terribly young woman, her brown hair framing a white oval face, walked in. "I'm with the Consulate," she said, handing over her card and flashing an ID proclaiming her name as Irene Yablonski

"Rumplemint," Mark said.

"Rumpelstiltskin, you mean," she replied.

"Yahoo."

"Bunting blue." Irene sat down, having proven her true identity. "Walls have ears."

Mark tapped firmly on the table and started to communicate in sign language. Since most causes of deafness were curable, the only people who learned it were spacers, for use in the event their suit radios crapped out. Even then, most spacers only learned a few words. Not so for the Navy. "*Need to call gov secure—urgent,*" he signed.

She nodded, fiddled with her handheld for a second and handed it over, signing, "*Go for it.*"

Mark looked at the screen, which looked like some adware-supported free texting service. "*How good?*" he signed.

"*Diplo,*" Irene spelled out.

Diplomatic. The Americans could break it if they really wanted to, but a pirate probably not. He nodded and typed a message for the Martian Naval Attaché at the US Embassy. They could get the message on to whom it needed to go.

Spaceship ValuTrip *Cardinal* probably pirated. Pirates had inside help.

He hit send, and when the acknowledgement came through, he handed the device to the diplomat. Her eyebrows rose fractionally as she read the sent message, but she was otherwise non-reactive.

The door opened again. The first person through was a tall black woman with close-cropped iron-gray hair and the ornate uniform of either a Texan general or an American chief of police. Based on context Mark assumed the latter and rose, noting she had a strong familial resemblance to Agent Volk. He was the second person through the door, followed by a white female, blonde, Marks' age, in good shape and conventionally beautiful.

"Captain," Volk said, gesturing at the blonde, "meet my boss, Special Agent in Charge Charlize Fetterer." He gestured at the uniformed officer. "And this is Chief Emily Volk." He smiled. "Your lucky day, Auntie Em here will fix you up."

Auntie? Really?

"Normally," the Chief of Police said, "we frown on foreign military shooting anybody in Kansas. In this case, I think I can make an exception."

"You're not charging Captain Nagata?" Irene asked.

"No. In fact," the Chief said, "we're not even telling people he was there. For now, the official story is that an FBI agent on unrelated personal business saw something suspicious."

"In that case," Irene said, "I guess I'm not needed."

She left Mark with the American police.

"Are you really his aunt?" Fetterer asked the Chief.

"Cousin, actually," the Chief replied. "But since I had to change his diaper, I got the title." She patted the woman on her shoulder in a friendly way. "Charlize, Ray never told you we were related?"

"No, he did not," Fetterer said, giving Ray a significant look.

Apparently the two women know each other. Volk managed to look embarrassed, although he had to have heard that line hundreds of times.

"Emily and I went through Quantico together," Charlize said with a smile. "She 'retired' and picked up this gig." Her smile faded as she offered Mark her hand. "I fear Agent Volk is a bad influence on you. We really don't like it when cops get in gunfights. It's not the 20th Century anymore."

"I'm not fond of them either," Mark replied.

"We need to talk," Ray Volk, said.

"There's a spare office you can use," the Chief replied.

***

"You really think forty people got smuggled on a ship past Martian Customs?" Mark said. He was standing in the office looking out the window. It was raining, something Mark hadn't seen until he was an adult and still found fascinating. He was also playing dumb, having already figured out what the Americans had regarding *Cardinal's* fate. Volk's boss, Fetterer, had walked away with the Chief, presumably on other business.

"Somebody's sucking down the air that the square-dancers were supposed to be using," Volk said.

Mark turned back from the window. "And how would you suspect that they got on board?"

"Stuffed inside a cargo container," Volk replied. "Happens on Earth all the time."

"Yeah, Earth has air," Mark replied. "Besides, do you know how big space cargo containers are?"

"No."

Mark gestured at the tiny office, barely big enough for a desk and a trio of chairs. "You could fit a container in this office. They're designed to be flown up from orbit on shuttles."

"And not pressurized?"

"No. In fact, for the standard container, if you tried to pressurize it the sides would rupture."

Volk sighed heavily. "Well, then who's breathing that air?"

It was a good question. *There's something you're not telling me.* "I don't know. I'll get Mars on it."

"Thanks."

"Are we clear to leave?"

"Yes."

"Then could you drop me off at the consulate? I need to make some calls and it would be easier there."

"Will do." Volk, who had been sitting on one of the guest chairs, got up. "Oh, on the way, tell me about the Martian CIA."

Gee, that's not half as subtle as you think it was. But we both have parts to play, so I'll play mine. "Stands for 'Committee for Independent Asteroids,'" Mark began.

***

The Martian Consulate in Kansas City was tiny—just half a floor in a downtown skyscraper. It did, however, have a secure room with encrypted communication gear. Mark was escorted in by Irene Yablonski.

"The Attaché has set you up to talk directly to Force Echo Actual," she said, pointing at a hard-sided briefcase. "Standard field setup—audio only."

Echo Actual was a Rear Admiral in the Martian Navy—stationed on a frigate somewhere in the vicinity of Earth—who commanded all Martian military units in the Earth area of operation. Mark couldn't for the life of him remember who had that job at the moment. "Thanks," Mark said. He put on the headset, keyed up the unit and toggled the press-to-talk button. "Kilo Charlie calling Foxtrot Echo, over."

"This is Echo actual, go, over."

The scrambler had significant distortion, making it hard to tell if he was talking to a man or a woman. Mark defaulted to sir, which was protocol if you couldn't tell. "Sir, US authorities seem to think ValuTrip *Cardinal* was hijacked. Over."

"Nagata, this is Teng, what makes them think that? Over."

Sally Teng. She'd been XO on his first ship when he was a newly-minted Ensign. "Copy, ma'am. Based on O2 consumption, they think approximately forty people were smuggled aboard. Also, I think one of their secret tracking stations may have seen something. Over."

"Copy," Teng replied. The US, the Chinese, hell, probably even the Russians who still suffered from delusions of grandeur, had salted uninhabited asteroids with 'secret' tracking stations. Sometimes when the Navy found a particularly obvious one, they dismantled it, but usually they just noted where it was and ignored it. "How confident are you on the tracking data? Over."

"Low confidence, ma'am. But the US investigator asked me about the CIA. Over."

Teng's snort was surprisingly clear over the link. The Committee for Independent Asteroids had always been a collection of cranks. What was left of them were mostly common criminals who shook down small operations for protection money. They were really just cheap thugs who were convenient plot devices in bad video dramas. "Understood. What do you propose? Over."

"We need to find *Cardinal* ASAP. Over."

"Agreed. I'll get Intel on it. Any other traffic? Over."

"Negative. Over."

"Echo out."

Mark broke the connection and stepped out of the room. Irene was waiting for him. "We need to get the Marshal's Service to investigate something."

"What?" she asked.

"How forty people got smuggled onto a ship without being detected by customs," Mark replied.

"Oh, that'll be an interesting story," she replied.

Chapter 7

ValuTrip Cardinal

Kelly

Kelly jerked awake out of a fitful sleep to yelling from the next cabin over. Half-awake, she found herself standing just behind Hank at the open door of their cabin to see a pair of guards walk down the passageway, guns ready. A few minutes later, one of them came back.

"Since you're here," he said, "come with me."

They went into the next cabin. In the tiny shower, a man—fat, old and balding—had hung himself from the exhaust fan. He'd used a ripped-off shirt sleeve which was wrapped around his neck. His tongue, blueish, was sticking out of his open mouth. The bathroom was so small that even Kelly could sit on the toilet and wash her hands in the sink. The guard, a short but bulky fellow, was standing on the toilet and cutting at the fabric with a knife.

What a waste, Kelly thought. *Surely this man had something to live for.* She stepped back into the tiny hallway between staterooms. "Spider," she said, noticing her friend. "What are you doing here?"

"His roommate," he replied.

"You two know each other?" Hank asked.

"Exchange students," Spider replied. In the cheap prisoner garb they'd been given, he looked even scrawnier and was turning green. "Alonzo Wilder the Third," he said, offering his hand to Hank. "Call me Spider." To Kelly, he said, "Go Vikings."

"Vikings are pussies," Kelly said, smiling despite her upset stomach. *Don't focus on the dead man.* "Tigers eat them for breakfast."

The dead man's body, suddenly free of the cloth, hit the floor of the shower with a wet thump.

"Body removal detail," the guard who'd gotten them said, gesturing at the three of them. "Another one. I'll be back with a body bag." He left, leaving them looking at the dead body, balled up on the floor of the tiny bathroom.

"Would somebody clue in the old lady?" Hank asked, trying to scratch under her cast. *Woman must have ice water in her veins*, Kelly thought.

"Spider here went to Franklin City South High School," Kelly said. "Home of the Vikings."

"You look pretty pale, Spider," Hank said, taking his hand.

"Having a really shitty day," he said, gesturing at the suicide. "Didn't even get his name."

"Oren," Hank said. "Oren Auric. Rich fuck had the cabin next to me in the first-class area. Wandering around with an hourly on his elbow."

"Hourly?" Kelly asked, fighting down bile in her throat. Ralph's bowels had cut loose, creating a powerful stink.

"Girl who charges for her presence by the hour," Hank said.

"Actually, I think she's a porn star," the guard with the knife said. "Worth a shitload more money than this sorry-assed old man."

"He said, 'another one,'" Hank said, pointing down the hallway. Well, actually, up the hallway which followed the curve of the ship.

"We lost a kid," the guard said. "Got clobbered this morning when he fought with a guard."

Oh shit. "Was his name Pete?" Kelly asked, her voice quivering.

"Fuck if I know," the guard replied.

"Enough with the bullshit," the other guard said as he returned. He had a black plastic bag in his hands, which he started to lay out on the hallway floor. The cabin was too small to lay it out inside. "Stinks in here. You three—hump the body out."

They did, with Kelly ending up holding the man by his hairy armpits. She surprised herself by keeping her sandwich down. Once in the hallway, the three put the man in the body bag with a minimum of fuss. It helped that Kelly's eyes were full of tears and she couldn't see very well. Not having to look at the man's bulging face helped a lot.

"You brought your own body bags?" Hank asked as they dragged the body out to the elevator lobby.

"No, ship had a supply," the other guard said. They reached the elevators. "Put him there. We'll get a cart later."

"Back to your cabins," the guard with the knife said.

"Can I not go back there?" Spider asked.

"We're not..."

"He can crash with us," Hank said. "Come on dude, cut the kid some slack."

The guard groaned. "Fine. For tonight."

***

The three of them retired to Kelly's cabin. "He's talking about Pete!" Kelly blurted out when the door was closed.

"Who?" Hank said.

"Oh shit!" Spider said, turning pale.

"Who, damn it?" Hank said.

Spider dashed to the toilet, followed by the sound of his retching. Kelly wanted to go there too, but kept her jaw clenched. "Exchange student. He was with us and got in a fight with a guard."

"They had non-lethals," Hank said.

"I guess the damn thing wasn't charged because it didn't work, so the guard hit him with it."

"Oh, damn. I'm sorry."

"Thanks."

There was silence for a bit, except for the sounds of water flowing in the toilet. Eventually Spider came out. By then, Kelly's nausea had changed over to gut-wrenching cramps. There were only two beds, and Kelly—as the one most able to fit in a tiny space—got the floor. Nobody seemed ready to sleep.

"I can't believe it," Spider said. "Just to kill yourself."

"I can," Hank replied from her bunk.

"Oh?" Kelly said.

"Dude was rich," Hank replied, "and more importantly didn't earn his money."

"What does that have to do with anything?" Kelly asked.

"It means he's a spoiled prick and this is the first time in his life shit has not gone his way," Hank said.

"I think he was one of the dudes who argued when we were in the theater," Spider said.

"Figures," Hank replied.

"Well, speaking personally," Spider said, "this shit is seriously scary to me."

"Yep," Hank said. "But have you thought about killing yourself?"

"No."

"My point exactly," Hank said.

"That's so fucking cold it's dry ice!" Kelly said.

"Look, kids," Hank said, "news flash. We're at war. Sometimes somebody has to die for the team." She sat up in bed and pointed to the other cabin. "But that—that accomplished nothing."

Kelly stared at her, slack-jawed. Finally, she said, "Okay, ma'am, exactly how many people have you had die for the team?"

That got a flash of embarrassment from Hank. "None," she finally replied. "Never been in combat."

"Neither had Oren, neither has Spider, and neither have I. So just maybe, ma'am, you can spare us the cheesy speeches you cribbed from the old war videos." Kelly waved her hand dismissively. "Just a thought."

Hank was practically glowing with anger. Eventually Spider spoke up in a very quiet voice. "Maybe we ought to get some sleep?"

For Kelly, sleep was a long time coming.

***

Both video screens in Kelly Rack's cabin popped on. One of the guards, unmasked, appeared on the screen. "Breakfast," he said, loudly. Apparently, the video screen volume could be adjusted remotely. "Listen carefully to the following procedure. Those who don't follow it to the letter not only won't eat but will be dealt with forcefully."

"Get the shit kicked out of them, he means," Hank said. Spider grunted from his much-more comfortable top bunk.

Sleeping on the floor would suck on Mars—on this gravity it's super-sucky. Kelly nodded, not that her roommates were watching her. All eyes were on the video monitor. They watched the instructions, which were repeated twice.

Everybody in Kelly's group of cabins—200 through 262—were ordered out into the hallway and formed one line facing spinward. In their case, that meant they turned right. Then the goon opened the pressure door that cut the hallway in half and her group walked into the spinward half of the cabin block and got in line behind that group. Kelly ended up last in line, and the mid-corridor pressure door automatically closed behind her.

Once everybody was in the corridor, the door in front of them—which led to the small lobby with the stairs going up to the promenade deck—was opened. A pair of armed guards were there, and they directed the line of people along. The line filed up the stairs to another set of guards, and down the promenade, which had single guards stationed at intervals.

About halfway to the main dining room, a woman in front of Kelly stopped and faced a guard. She spat into his face and slapped him. He punched her full in the face, knocking her down. "That one was free," he said. "Next one gets you in the hole."

"Move on!" the other guard shouted to the prisoners behind her. They did, stepping around the bleeding woman as if she was contagious.

"I want to talk to her," Hank said over her shoulder. When the two women came even with the third, Kelly found herself helping the injured woman up. *Resistance or not, it's the right thing to do.* Spider held their place in line.

"What's your name?" Hank asked, offering a sleeve to help with her bloody nose.

"Maria," the woman replied.

"Let's walk, Maria," Hank said.

Inside the dining room, a serving line had been set up. The prisoners were marched through the line, and food was placed on their plates by people on the other side of the line. They were wearing the same prison-style uniform as Kelly. She recognized one of the servers as her table's waiter. The whole thing was surreal—they were being treated like and looked like people in a prison movie yet they were eating off good China in a fancy space.

"Notice how they're controlling portions?" Hank asked.

"No," Kelly replied. She was holding a plate for Maria and herself, while Hank had her plate which she was holding gingerly in the hand with the cast on it. Hank was using her good hand to help Maria.

The trio sat down at a table which had been set with water glasses and utensils. A metal detector had been ostentatiously set up at the exit to the room. It had been removed from the ship's access area, and the exposed wiring at the base showed that it had been spliced into a power supply. Completing the prison atmosphere, not only were there guards on the main floor, but a pair of guards with rifles were on the balcony overlooking the main area.

"Why'd you hit that guard?" Hank asked.

"Fucker handed me over to them," Maria replied. "He's a ship dick."

"A what?" Kelly asked.

"Cop. Security. Supposed to protect us from goons, not be one," Maria said.

"Which explains how they were able to take over," Hank said. "Inside job. That's two crewmembers so far."

"Who's the other one?" Kelly asked.

"Victoria Stevens."

"Vickie?" Maria said. "She was my roommate!"

"Well now she's in my cabin," Hank said dryly. To Maria, she asked, "Do you know if any of the Security team is on our side?"

"They shot the ones that were," Maria said.

"You sure?" Hank pressed.

"Yeah." Maria glared at her. "I'm in housekeeping. I was vacuuming the game room when the shit hit. Dominic—the night dick—was making his rounds and a couple of goons shot him. I saw it. I followed protocol. Larry—the guy I hit—found me in my hiding spot. Said he was trying to get a distress call out and needed my access card to get to Damage Control. Instead, he marched me right into the same holding area with the rest of the crew."

"So how many people were in ship security?" Hank said.

Maria counted off on her fingers. "Five," she finally said.

"Two executed in the theater, the night guy dead—wanna bet the missing cop is on their side?" Hank asked.

Not really, Kelly thought. She looked at Hank, who appeared to be as pleased as if she'd been promoted to Fleet Admiral. *If they had two fucking ship's cops on this, we are very extremely fucked.* Kelly was glad to note that nobody else in their group seemed impressed with the Earthling's detective work.

"So," Hank said. She looked around. "Kelly, do you see that bald guy with the black glasses?"

"The one two tables over?" Kelly asked.

"Yes. I think he's with maintenance. He had to come fix my HVAC when I checked in."

"Okay?"

"I want you to talk to him on the way out of here."

"About?"

"Well, to start with, communications." She gestured at her completely dead access wristband. "We need to get these back up."

"And do what with them?" Kelly asked.

"Organize our internal communications," Hank said. "With us being stuck in our cabins, communications are difficult."

What exactly are we going to communicate? We're fucked? "We who?" Kelly said. "I don't recall signing up."

"I'll do it," Spider said.

Kid was acting like a lost puppy dog, Kelly thought. Although turning off the access bands was a neat trick. The wristbands controlled everything. Want to change programming on the video monitor? Use your access band. Charge booze to your account? Use the band. Want to call somebody on the ship—especially important since regular mobile devices didn't work—use your band. Lock your cabin door? Use the band. With the bands dead, they were practically back in the Stone Age.

Kelly realized Hank was still talking. The woman did have an air of command about her. "The other thing is," Hank said, "is food. Why are they rationing it?"

"Are they?" Kelly asked.

"They could just as easily put out four or five buffet lines as two served lines," Hank said. "And did you note that they were very conscious of how much food they put on your plate?"

She hadn't cared, but the two large men in front of them had asked for and been denied extra scoops of everything, even the oatmeal. "Okay, so they're rationing food."

"Why?" Hank asked.

Because they're mean fucks? Half of the shit Kelly had seen in Basic was done just to jack with people. "Any idea on how to find out?" Kelly asked.

"They put the crew in with the passengers," Maria said.

"Your job, Maria," Hank said, "is to find a cook and ask. Can you do that for me?"

"Of course."

***

"He got put in 262," Spider said referring to the maintenance guy they had seen at breakfast. They were back in her cabin. A work schedule had been issued on the video screens, and the details would be forming soon. Kelly and Hank were on laundry detail, while Spider got assigned to a 'general cleaning' detail.

"His name's Stanley Wo-joe-something," Spider said. "Goes by Stan W.—there's a Stan C. who's a cook."

"Useful," Hank said, scratching under her cast. "He got any tools?"

"Didn't ask," Spider replied.

"They surely took his tools from him after they were done with him," Kelly replied, her arms crossed.

"Well, we'll have to find him some," she said.

Are we supposed to shit them?

"Where is he?"

"The other side of the secondary pressure door." Spider said.

"What's a secondary pressure door and where's it at?"

Spider stared at Hank as if she'd asked what a napkin was.

"You are an Earthling, aren't you?" Kelly said. *And I'm supposed to follow you on some fucking passenger resistance? You don't know your ass from the 60th of Taurus!*

"Yes, I am, you smart-ass Greener," Hank replied, using the derogatory term for Martian. "So, throw me a fricking bone here and explain yourself."

"Primary doors are those designed to be opened and closed on a regular basis. Like the doors from the passageway to the stairway lobbies, which are closed every night. Secondary doors, like the one in the middle of the hallway, are only closed in emergencies."

"Except they've closed that door," Hank said.

"Yes. Keeps us more separated."

"Great," Hank said. "Spider, find out from Stan where that anti-spinward door goes."

Hopefully nowhere useful, Kelly thought. *Then she can abandon this resistance game and not get her head blown off.*

Kelly shuddered. *Between Pete and the ship's cops, there are more than enough heroic dead people on this ship.*

Chapter 8

Kansas City

Ray

"We got names on the hitters," Ray said as Nagata rubbed his neck. They were in the NTSB conference room at Jayhawk.

"I keep forgetting how heavy my head is in one gee," Nagata said as he stopped rubbing his neck.

"I know a great masseuse," Ray said.

"I may take you up on that," Nagata said. "You were saying about the ventilators?"

"Yeah," Ray said. "They're professional muscle out of St. Louis." One of the NTSB people was circulating, asking about dinner orders. Ray waved them off.

"Who were presumably going to make the Malans disappear," Nagata said.

"If we'd gotten there half an hour later, they'd have been gone." Ray finished his thought in silence. *And if they were gone, it would be a couple more days until we convinced the right people that we had a hijacking.*

"Frank handled booking," Nagata said. "What about his wife?"

"Collateral damage, we think."

"So, since I never got inside, did anybody find anything in the house?"

"If you mean like a big book with 'here's the plan' on it, no."

"That would have been too easy."

The NTSB aide handed a paper menu to Nagata. He looked at it and made a face.

"Nothing appealing?" Ray asked.

"Not really." Nagata looked around the room. "Also, I find this place light on atmosphere."

"You like steaks?"

"Yes."

"Good," Ray said, standing up. "I know a place." *Time to make my move.*

***

"What's good here?" Nagata asked.

"Pretty much everything, Mark," Ray replied, looking at the man over his wine list. *Not that I need it—I've got it memorized.* Ray was a regular, and thus able to score a quiet table overlooking the river. More importantly, the video newsfeed in the bar—wall-to-wall coverage on the *Cardinal*—wasn't visible from their table. "I can call you Mark?"

"Of course," he replied. "Mark, Captain, Nagata—just don't call me late to dinner."

"I won't and you're not." Ray looked around the dining room. "We're actually a bit early. So, you a beer or a wine guy?"

"First I need a whiskey," Mark replied. The waiter arrived, and Mark ordered a local bourbon and water. This confused both Ray and the waiter, but they eventually got it straightened out.

"A 'local' bourbon around here is Kentucky?" Mark asked.

"I think there's a couple of distilleries in Missouri," Ray said, "but anything you'd want to drink is from Kentucky. You ordering steak?"

"Is it good here?" Mark asked.

Bless you, son, Ray thought. "Best in town."

"Then yes." Mark put down his menu. "You order—medium rare is my only requirement."

Ray did, and got a bottle of wine as well. "So why a wheelgun?"

"My revolver?" Mark asked, patting his coat where it should have been. Auntie Emily had confiscated it for evidence. "They don't jam in zero-gee. Even your Space Force carries them."

"I read an article on *Popular Mechanics* about the coming revolution in personal lasers," Ray said.

"Yeah, I read that too," Mark replied. "And the one they ran five years ago. And the one five years before that."

"Not a laser fan, huh?"

"Just the opposite. My first two jobs in the Navy were weapons. Care and feeding of lasers." Mark took a sip of his bourbon. "It's physics—lasers generate a lot of waste heat. Something small enough to carry and powerful enough to drop a man will just melt itself."

How come every time I end up trying to be romantic we end up talking about the least-romantic topics possible? "So, you're a weapons expert?"

"Aren't you?"

"No. I use a gun but that's about it." Ray leaned back in his seat. "I've always been a bit surprised we're using a technology that's stuck in the 20th Century."

"It's the fork problem," Mark said, holding up his salad fork.

"Go on," Ray said. Mark apparently liked to pontificate. Fortunately, he seemed knowledgeable.

"Imagine that you've got some wonderful new bit of tech that will replace the fork. Here's your problem—the fork is simple to use, highly reliable, and cheap enough that if it breaks," he mimed throwing the fork over his shoulder, "you pitch it and get another." He set the fork down. "Nothing has cleared that bar, except for special cases like non-lethal crowd control."

"Ah." The wine arrived.

Mark took a sip, nodded approvingly, then looked at the label. "I see 'local' wine means California."

"You seem surprised."

"On Mars, most food is produced within five hundred clicks of where you eat it," Mark said.

"I heard there are some wineries in the area, but nothing you'd want to drink," Ray said. "You seem awful calm. About the missing ship, I mean."

"Resigned, more like it," Mark replied. "Spaceships move fast, but the distances are so far that things take days to happen. You just learn to deal with it or resign early due to ulcers."

After that, Ray decided to not talk about the case. Fortunately, Mark proved very curious about police work and the Kansas City area, both subjects that Ray was able to cover in depth.

After dinner, Ray drained the last of the bottle into Mark's glass. "So, what's on your evening plans?" Ray asked.

Mark gave him a funny look. Not good. "Are you trying to seduce me?"

Ray flashed his best bashful smile. "Afraid so."

Mark had a startled expression on his face. He tried to hide it with his napkin, but it wasn't working. "I'm sorry," Mark said. "It's not you, really."

"Oh?" Ray said, confused. Things had been going so well.

"I'm sorry," Mark said with an embarrassed look on his face, "but I'm straight. *Really* straight." He blushed. "I mean, I did my homework, if you know what I mean."

"And?"

"And I kissed a guy, said, 'yuck' to myself, gave him a goodnight hug and left. I'm sorry to have led you on."

"You didn't," Ray said. *So much for my gaydar. Clearly the man knows what he likes and doesn't like.*

"Also, I told a little white lie earlier."

"Oh?"

"Ex Number Two isn't quite officially ex yet."

"But she's on Mars?" Ray waved his hand. "I assume she's a she, I mean."

"Most definitely," Mark said with a grimace. "And to say we don't get along any more is an understatement. Which is why the divorce isn't final yet. She's contesting it."

"She wants to stay married?"

"No, she just wants to piss me off." Mark took a breath. "Well, that's my take on the matter. I'm sure she's having a conversation with her friends about what a shit I am."

"I'm sorry."

Mark waved his hand. "No need to be—not your problem." He took a sip of his wine. "Sorry—I really should be flattered. Not often a grandfather gets hit on."

"You don't look old enough to be a grandfather," Ray said truthfully.

"Lower gravity and less UV exposure," Mark replied. "I actually look a bit older than my peers—most of the extra-solar worlds are more Earthlike."

"Ah," Ray said. Damn—all the good ones were straight. "I suppose you'd like me to take you back to the hotel."

"If you've got a hot date," Mark replied. "Otherwise, I'd probably just sit in my room and stare at the wall."

"How are you handling it?"

"The shooting?"

"Yes."

Mark looked surprised. "Oh, no," he said. "I didn't mean I was going to mope or that dropping that thug bothered me. I just meant that I have no plans for tonight."

"Well, in that case," Ray replied. He held up the empty bottle in the direction of the waiter and pointed at it. "You know, I should probably talk to Charlize—Special Agent Fetterer. See if you can talk to our department counselor."

"About the shooting?" Mark asked.

"Yeah," Ray replied. "We've got a good guy. I'm seeing him tomorrow." *Again.*

"Thanks, but I'll skip," Mark replied.

The new bottle arrived, stalling conversation for a bit. After the glasses were refilled, Ray continued. "What do y'all do for after-shooting support?"

"Last time?" Mark asked. He grew serious. "I was an ensign, straight out of college, when I ventilated my first person. She was a pro, sent by the mob to solve a problem on 243 Ida."

"Which is?"

"An asteroid. Fairly big one, but not many people. I was assigned to a destroyer, the *Richard Chwedyk*. Twelve officers and one hundred fifty total crew. The captain and

the XO—the 'Old Ladies' were in their thirties Earth-years—
and the eldest person on the ship was the Chief of the Ship.
He was younger than I am now."

Mark took a sip of his wine, nodding appreciatively at his
glass. He continued, "After the shooting, the Chief of the
Ship took me into his office and asked me if I was in a hurry
to die. I said no, and then he asked if I had a problem killing
professional assassins. I said no again, and he said good, then
reached into his desk drawer and pulled out a bottle of
bourbon and two juice glasses. We had a couple of good
snorts and called it a night."

So much for grief counseling. "Wow."

***

"Tell me again how this worked?" Ray said, draining the
last of the second bottle into his glass.

"The senior female enlisted would hand you a note,"
Mark said, "asking if you wanted to attend a fuck party."

"And if you said yes?"

"You showed up in the Chief's mess in your briefs and
shower shoes. They tied your hands behind your back, put
a bag over your head and the girls would come in. They'd
paw over you for a bit, decide who was doing who, and
you'd fuck. If you were a good fuck, they'd send you out of
the mess and keep your underwear. If not, you'd be handed
your underwear when you left."

"What did they do with the underwear?"

"Actually, they'd wash it and return it," Mark said.

"But you never knew who you fucked?"

"Well, you weren't supposed to know," Mark replied.
"But with a ship of one hundred seventy people, you had a
good idea."

"I was never in the military," Ray said. "I had no idea they
did shit like that."

"I don't think the Americans do that," Mark replied with
a smirk. "Y'all have a reputation for not liking sex much."

"While we think Martians are second only to the French when it comes to sex," Ray said. "But don't discount the US of A. There are some places I could show you that would change your mind on that,"

"You done?" Mark asked.

"Sure, but I need to hit the men's room."

"Meet you in the bar," Mark said, getting up stiffly.

When Ray returned from the men's room, Mark was staring at the newsfeed.

"Problem?" Ray asked.

"Maybe," Mark replied, gesturing at the feed. "They found out about the engine light-off."

"We knew that would come out sooner or later," Ray said. He'd have preferred later.

Chapter 9

ValuTrip Cardinal

Kelly

Kelly glanced at the wall-mounted time readout. *Zero-three-fucking-fifteen.* She heard the sound again. It was coming from the tiny cubbyhole that served as the closet for the cabin. There was a dim light coming from within. She got up and wandered over, finding a blanket had been rigged, blocking the light from the sleeping area. "What the...?" Kelly said.

"This had better be really good," Hank growled, her voice rolling into Kelly's ear from behind. Everything in the cabin was no more than three steps from everywhere else and they'd determined last night that Hank was a light sleeper.

"Aren't you a bit big to be tunnel-ratting?" Kelly asked. She gestured at the access panel Spider had removed, revealing a dark void.

"I had a late growth spurt," he replied.

Kelly gestured at the void. "Spider here just found a tunnel."

"Tunnel-ratting is the time-honored Martian sport of exploring tunnels, air-ducts and related areas," Spider said. "When I was smaller, I was the best rat in town." He leaned into the tunnel. "I still think I could fit in here."

"So I see," Hank said. "Where does it go?" She tapped Kelly's shoulder. "I told you that we could resist."

"Ma'am, all 'we've' done is find a utility tunnel," Kelly said. "A tunnel which I'm sure is on ship's drawings, so it's not like we could even hide out in it."

"Always with the negativity," Hank said, grinning broadly.

"Huh?" Spider asked.

"Very old video," Hank said.

"So, who's going in?" Spider asked.

"You're the rat," Kelly said.

"It's really tight," Spider said.

"Who's smallest?" Hank said with a smile.

Fuck me sideways, Kelly thought.

***

"It's asshole dark in here," Kelly said. The tunnel was barely a meter wide at its widest and lined with pipes, cables and related shit. At three spots so far, Kelly had had to turn sideways to squeeze by something. It was also dark—pitch dark. She'd moved about four meters down the tunnel, going slowly and working by feel.

"Gotta be a light switch somewhere," Spider said. "There always is."

Which was off. How the fuck did I draw this detail? Well, actually, I'm shorter than Spider and thinner than Hank, plus younger. Kelly again cursed her genetics and kept inching along in the dark tunnel. She came to a sudden stop.

"Found a door," she said, trying to keep her voice down. There were people on the other side of a thin metal wall.

"Light switch is probably right next to it," Hank said in a stage whisper.

I would have never thought of that, Earthling. She carefully felt around the door, looking for the handle. You would think the light switch would be right inside where the door opened. She felt around—finally!

"Let there be light!" Kelly said, throwing the switch.

The tunnel wasn't what you'd call brightly lit—the occasional LED wall-warts—but damned if that wasn't a million times better than black. She looked around, and realized the place was dusty and grimy. "Janitors don't get back here very often," she said.

"Good," Hank replied. She stuck her head inside and looked spinward. Like any long corridor on the ship, both ends of the corridor gradually sloped upward, and it always looked like you were at the bottom of a circle. *Because I am. We're in a tin can that's spun to simulate gravity.*

"Spider, check out that bulkhead," Hank ordered, pointing spinward while leaning into the space Spider moved from, responding to Hank's air of command. *Big chicken—now that the fucking lights are on, he's suddenly small enough to fit.* "Solid," he reported when he got there. "No bolts or nothing."

Makes sense. The corridor functioned as a way to route plumbing and power to the cabins. Those utilities probably came down the central elevator and staircase lobbies, separated from the cabins by the primary pressure doors. Half the cabins on each side of the lobby got supplied from the lobby.

Somebody in one of the cabins flushed a toilet and Spider jumped half-a-meter, emitting a squeak as he did so.

"Keep it down, damn it!" Hank hissed.

"Sorry."

"We gotta find out what's on the other side of that door," Hank said.

"Some kind of maintenance closet," Spider said. "Think about it—you've walked through that lobby every day and it's not as deep as a cabin."

Spoken like a true tunnel rat, Kelly thought. The door swung out, unlike the cabin's pocket doors. There was an access band reader—apparently dead—next to the door. She tried the knob. "It's locked."

"Good thing it's not alarmed," Hank said dryly.

Maybe a bad thing. Getting busted might put an end to this commando shit. "So now what, boss?"

Hank sighed heavily. "Well, come on back, but leave the light on."

***

"What I don't understand," Hank said at breakfast, "is why that door was locked when the rest of the doors on that level aren't?"

"Expected behavior in the event of a power outage," Maria said. After yesterday's fight with the guard, the rest of the passengers were treating her as if she was radioactive. Which was a shame—even with the big bruise on her cheek, she was quite a good-looking woman. *Christ Jesus—two weeks away from Leah and I'm checking out girls.*

"I thought you weren't a licensed astronaut," Spider said, talking around a slice of apple. This morning's fruit offerings were half of an apple. "Being a maid and all."

Sexist much? Or would it be classist?

"Well, first off, young man," Maria replied with more than a touch of heat, "even us humble maids had to take a ship safety course. Second, I'm taking astronaut classes. When we get to Earth, I'm going to sit for my first exam."

Nicely done.

Hank rubbed her good hand on Maria's shoulder while staring daggers at Spider. "Maria, would you like some of my fruit?"

Wow, Hank moves fast.

"Sorry—that was mean of me," Spider said. *Well, at least he can learn.* "So, we were talking about expected behavior."

"Space is unforgiving, as everybody at this table should know," Maria said, glancing at Hank's cast. "Therefore, we always need to think about what happens in the event something goes wrong. In the event of a power outage, some things—like doors to passenger cabins—you want to fail open."

"So people can get out," Kelly said.

"Or crew can get in if we need to find somebody or fix something," Maria said. "Other things, like doors to maintenance areas, you want to fail closed."

"But what if you need to get in there?" Spider asked.

"There's a manual backup." Maria smiled at Spider. "You're not the first tunnel rat this ship has seen." The smile faded. "Two or three trips ago, a couple of kids your age went ratting and scaring people in their cabins. It was a big hoopla."

"What happened to them?" Hank said.

"They got put in the brig," Maria said. "And their parents were pissed. Captain almost put them in a cell too."

"We're assuming these were turned off by cutting the power," Hank said, pointing at her dead access band. Kelly— who was not used to wearing watches or bracelets—had taken hers off.

"See the guard with the green hair?" Maria said, gesturing with her chin.

The guards wore black cloth hoods with holes for seeing and breathing. One of the guards, a giant of a man, was standing by the door. Some of his long green hair was peeking out from under the hood.

"Name's Bruno," Maria continued. "He's one of the ship's electricians."

"How damn many crewmembers were in on this damn thing?" Hank asked with exasperation.

"Apparently enough," Kelly said, earning an acidic look from Hank.

Victoria

Victoria yawned heavily and poured herself a cup of coffee. The metal carafe felt light and proved to have only enough for half a cup. "Need more coffee," she yelled in the direction of the kitchen. In the meantime, she took a sip of the lukewarm liquid. *At least it has caffeine.*

"Here you go," Helen said, walking out with another carafe. Victoria offered her mug to Helen who filled it up. "You look..."

"Tired," Victoria said. "I got used to keeping nightclub hours." She took a sip of the coffee. *Much better.*

"So," Helen said, "any word from Earth?"

"Haven't called them," Victoria said, truthfully. Helen gave her a surprised look. *Shit. She's on the D team.* "Figure give them another day to stew, then talk."

"You're the boss," Helen said. Another one of the crew came in and Helen went over with her coffee pot. Victoria grabbed her usual bagel and went to the bar.

Victoria's crew was divided into several groups. One group, whom Bruno had christened the A team, knew what the real plan was, which was go to Mercury and sell off the hostages to the highest bidders. Those bidders could then either ransom them off or put them to work. There had been an I-as-in-idiot team, composed of people who thought they were engaged in some nickel-dime robbery. Those poor sods were down with the rest of the hostages.

D Team—for "in the dark"—thought the plan was as described to the hostages, namely ransom back the entire ship to ValuTrip. *D also stands for dumb.* Ransoming back an entire ship, at least anywhere Earth or Mars had a naval presence, and living long enough to count the money—let alone enjoy it—was impossible. Although, if they got to Mercury, which was not troubled by those organizations, the whole-ship option was a viable backup.

Kelly

"It's fish or cut bait time," Hank said.

"Huh?" Kelly asked. They were sitting in their cabin waiting for the lights out order after dinner. Spider was in their tiny bathroom taking one of his over-long showers.

"You need to decide if you're in the Passenger Resistance Group or not."

"I thought I already decided I wasn't in," Kelly replied. Kelly recognized the game Hank was playing—it had been covered in a psychology class. Act like you're in charge and tell people what to do. By the time they figure out they don't have to obey you, they're already doing it. *Ain't gonna work on me.*

"Then we're going to have to move you out."

"It's my cabin, and the hell you say." How Hank was going to move anybody anywhere was left unclear.

Although, she moves me out and maybe I'm not sleeping on the floor.

Hank held up her hands. "Okay. Let me try another way."

"I'm listening."

"Assume you're right, and they are going to ransom the whole ship. That means they need to keep us alive, right?"

Kelly nodded her agreement.

"Then what's the risk?" Hank said. "They catch you, what's the worse that will happen?"

"I get a beatdown," Kelly said. "Which as we saw with Pete"—her voice caught at that—"could be lethal even if they don't mean it to be."

"And if I'm right?" Hank asked. "That they intend something more nefarious?"

"I don't understand why you assume 'nefarious' anyway," Kelly said.

"So, I've never been in combat. However, a few years back, a group of people hijacked a small cruise ship. The why's not important. What is important was that they tried to hand off the ship and got curb-stomped."

"By whom and how?"

"The PLAN—Chinese Navy. The hijackers either got dead or captured, and the cruise people got their money back. Handing over live, adult kidnap victims is the hardest crime to pull off. Especially if the kidnap victim is still alive."

"So?"

"So," Hank said pleadingly, "even if they are trying to hand back the whole ship, the odds are high we don't live to see it."

She's got a point there.

"Somebody needs to go up to the maintenance terminal. It's you or Spider."

The maintenance terminal. Today's Holy Grail of the 'Passenger Resistance Group,' which still existed mostly in Hank's mind. The goons were doing a damn fine job of keeping passengers in small groups segregated from each other, which made organizing anything extra hard.

Cardinal, as an intraSolar-System ship, did not have an FTL drive. It also did not have an FTL communication system. If you wanted to talk to somebody not on the ship, you sent an old-school email, which got sent over a radio at lightspeed. Every passenger had been given an account on the ship's network specifically to send and receive such messages.

Supposedly there was an unmonitored path from the cabins to an unwatched and open terminal from which they should be able to send messages to Earth and Mars. There was enough uncertainty to make Schrödinger's cat look like a sure bet.

"Spider's a better tunnel rat."

"He's too scared right now," Hank said. "First time the ship creaks he'll come running back."

"Not my problem."

"I'd go myself," Hank said, "but..." she held up her wrist cast.

"Have Maria go tomorrow."

"That means we spin our wheels for another day."

And you don't want to risk your girlfriend. "Again, not my problem." Hank didn't reply. The silence dragged on.

The door to their bathroom opened and a shirtless Spider, his hair damp and spiky, walked out. *Boy is kind of cute.* Kelly flushed and looked away. *Been away from Leah for less than two weeks and that's the second boy I've checked out. She'd kill me if she knew. And since when have scrawny-ass people—boys or girls—been my type? That's why she'd hooked up with Leah—girl had curves.*

And the first boy I checked out is dead. "Be that as it may," Kelly said to Hank, "I'm a hard no."

"That's disappointing," Hank said. "But you haven't heard my final offer."

The in-cabin video monitors popped on. "Lights out in five minutes," it announced. The screens showed a countdown clock.

Ignoring it, Kelly asked, "And what final offer would that be?"

"I'll get you a bed."

"How?"

"I'll tell the guards they can move me into Spider's old room." Hank looked at her pleadingly. "I only need this one thing."

Kelly looked at the floor. "Shitiest deal in the Solar System."

"Is that a yes?"

"It's a yes."

***

Kelly woke up to Hank's watch beeping. "Shit," Hank said in a low voice. "I was just having a margarita in my dream."

"Great," Kelly replied in similar volume. Her interrupted dream had been more erotic in nature. The room was dark except for a little light that shined in from the passageway through a vent in the door. Kelly sat up and noticed that Spider was still sound asleep. She pointed at Spider's bunk, not knowing if Hank could see her or not. "Man could sleep through an explosion."

"Good trait to have, I guess." She heard Hank's bed creak and assumed she was sitting up as well. "I used to be able to do that, then I got the *Shah*."

"The ship you commanded?"

"Yeah."

"So, what changed?"

Hank chuckled. "Night orders."

"Huh?"

"Captain's night orders. Very old tradition in the US Navy. When the captain—me—went to sleep we'd leave written night orders for the watch. They gave the team orders to wake me up for any of a half-dozen reasons." Another wry chuckle. "Underway, I don't think I got a single uninterrupted night's sleep."

I swear the American Navy designed their ranks specifically to confuse people. She's a Commander but also Captain of a ship? "That why you retired?"

"That and my divorce."

"She not like the hours?"

"He, and the hours didn't bother him. Gave him more time to stick his dick into women other than me." Kelly heard more rustling. "Hang on, gotta pee."

"I'm hanging," Kelly said, scooting toward the cabin door to allow enough room for Hank to get out.

On Hank's return—even the loud flushing didn't seem to bother Spider—she said, "Time to wake up Spider."

"I'm up," he said, still lying down.

"Ready to pick a lock?" Hank asked.

"As ready as I'll ever be."

***

Here goes nothing, Kelly thought as she stepped into the cabin utility corridor. At least now she had light—although to her dark-adapted eyes it was a bit too bright. Spider was ahead of her, squeezing around some pipes. He'd jury-rigged a lockpick out of a piece of plastic.

Maria had spent all day trying to gather information and reported it to them at dinner. She said the door wasn't alarmed nor was there a video camera on the other side. Also, according to what laughingly passing for intel, the door led to a "fan room." There was a ladder leading up into another fan room directly above. She could, in theory, follow the ladders all the way up to the fifth deck, where all the life support was.

"The cabins are on First Deck," Maria had said at dinner. "Which is the lowest. What passengers call the Promenade Deck directly above, that is second deck. Crew and first class are on third deck, aka Sports Deck."

"Which is where the pool is," Kelly had replied.

"Yes. Above that is fourth deck, mostly storage and grow houses, and then fifth deck, life support and more equipment."

"Where are the generators?" Hank had asked.

"Way back by the engines—astern of the fuel tanks. Crew never goes there—they fix stuff by robots. Before you ask, because of radiation, mostly, and parts are open to vacuum."

Now, Kelly stopped just behind Spider, who was fiddling with the knob and muttering to himself. Finally, he said, "Got it."

"Well, let's do it," Kelly replied. *Supposedly the door wasn't alarmed. I guess we'll find out.* Spider opened the door and stepped through, followed by Kelly.

The lights were on, which was good. Also good was that the space was noisy. It wasn't a large area—maybe five meters by three—and full of air-handling equipment, which was roaring.

"Okay," Spider said. He leaned in and kissed her on the cheek.

"What was that for?"

"Luck," he said, then stepped back into the maintenance corridor and closed the door behind him. Kelly checked to make sure she wasn't locked out. "So far, so good."

There was another airtight door to her right, which had to lead into the public elevator lobby. That was locked on the outside—to prevent nosy people from coming in—and had a camera covering it. Directly opposite it was the ladder going up, ending in a small round airtight hatch. She started climbing.

The climb up was monotonous and tiring. Each of the little round hatches she opened—besides being heavy—was a potential trap if somebody was in the room. The fan rooms on the various levels may have been slightly different, but the only way Kelly kept them straight was by the compartment numbers painted on the walls.

The fifth deck, on the other hand, was radically different. It was a huge space, running the width of the centrifuge and far enough along the sides to show some curvature of the floor. It had four giant air-handling units and some pipes that looked big enough for Kelly to fit inside. Per Stan W., there was a workshop with a terminal that would have access to external comms in this space. *He said it was anti-spinward.*

She walked in that direction and found the terminal just on the other side of a large electrical distribution panel. The area looked heart-wrenchingly similar to her dad's garage—a workbench, a free-standing tool chest, some open metal shelving with various boxes and jugs on it, and in one corner a stand-up table with a terminal. She smiled—even the pin-up calendar holo looked like Dad's.

The terminal was an industrial model, designed to be used by people with greasy hands, but it had power, unlike the ones in their cabin. *Can't hack a brick,* she thought, recalling what a fellow passenger had said about the dead terminals in their cabins. She started to yawn, then snapped her mouth shut. *Fuck—I need an access band to log into the terminal!*

It took her a minute to remember that she'd put her band in her pocket. She took it out and tapped the reader. The little red light which showed it was working did not change to green. She tried Maria's band and had the same result. Even Stan W.'s band—which as Chief of Maintenance should have worked—did not. *Well shit. All this for nothing. Time to go.*

***

Kelly opened the hatch leading into the Second Deck Fan Room. *One more floor and I'm done.* As she climbed down the ladder, the door going into the public space clicked. *Shit!* She turned and looked to see the door clearly ajar. She glanced around franticly and scrambled behind one of the air-handling units.

As she did so, the door opened fully, and a man stepped in. Fortunately, the door swung in, blocking the man's view of her. He said something, apparently talking to somebody in the hallway, then closed the door. She squeezed deeper into the cubbyhole—for once glad to be tiny. *Although if the guy comes looking for me, I'm fucked.*

He did not, and after a couple of minutes she carefully peeked out from her hiding spot. The guy, wearing a ship's maintenance uniform with a pistol on his belt, had removed an access panel on the other side of the room. He then walked over to the ship's phone and dialed a number.

Phones aren't working, she thought. At least they weren't in the passenger cabins. They were, however, apparently working here, because he had a brief conversation with somebody then hung up. The man then resumed his work, by cutting some wires inside the access panel.

Whatever he was doing, it took about fifteen minutes. At the end, her muscles were screaming in pain from her awkward hiding spot.

He got almost out the door before he swore under his breath and picked up the phone. He dialed a number, said "Shit, damn access code," and hung up to redial. Kelly watched this time, noting that he dialed something, waited, and dialed another number before talking. This second conversation was even faster than the first, and he left.

Kelly counted, slowly, to one hundred, then unwound herself from her hiding space, stifling a groan. She walked over and inspected the work. The man had taken an extension cord, cut one end off, and spliced the cut end into some wires on the open access panel. The other end, still with a plug attached, was plugged into a white box which then went into a standard power outlet.

Stan W. needed to see this. It certainly didn't look like standard maintenance.

Chapter 10

ValuTrip Cardinal

Kelly

Kelly woke up to Spider shaking her. "Breakfast!" he said. "The guards are waiting for us."

"Shit," Kelly said, rolling out of the bunk. On her return, Hank had given up her bed, choosing to sleep sitting up on the floor. She'd said it was the least she could do.

"So much for a shower." Her uniform was a bit dusty from crawling around in the maintenance areas, but not too bad, and more wrinkled than anything. *It'll pass.*

She stepped outside to find all of her fellow prisoners lined up to head out and a pair of cranky-looking guards barreling down the line toward her. "What's your malfunction?" one of them barked at her.

"I overslept," Kelly said, keeping her own crankiness out of her voice. *No need to draw a beat-down.*

"I ought to..." the guard said, a scowl on her face, then she looked at Kelly's red face. She also glanced at Hank, who was standing by the door and hadn't been in the cabin when Kelly was woken up.

A smirk came over the guard's face. "Ah, young love," she said. The guard tapped Kelly's chest with her stick, then pointed with her chin at Spider. "Good thing your boyfriend's quick."

Kelly's face flushed. "He's—" she cut herself off, avoiding saying 'he's not my boyfriend.' *If I wasn't screwing, then I'll have to explain what I was doing.* The logic didn't help her red face. "I'm sorry. He's sorry. Won't happen again."

"Good," the guard said. She raised her voice. "Move out!"

The knowing looks from her fellow prisoners were even more embarrassing than that from the guard. *Damn you, Hank! If you just told people what was going on.* But she didn't—Hank was worried about "collaborators" so only a few people were being told.

Spider wasn't helping—a cat-that-ate-the-bird grin was plastered on his face. "Are you amused?" Kelly hissed over her oatmeal.

"A little," Spider said. "Relax."

Easier said than done, Kelly thought.

***

During the day, the guards told Hank to move back into Spider's old cabin. Maria, the housekeeper, was also moving in with Hank. Conveniently, the toilet in Maria's cabin had stopped working and the guards were not interested in having it fixed.

They were waiting to go to dinner, and it was the first time she'd been alone with Spider since breakfast—as inmates all had work details in the morning. They were lying on top of the covers of their bunks. He was taller, so he'd gotten the top bunk and Kelly was below him.

"Do you want to die a virgin?" Spider asked.

"Oh for fuck's sake, you're not going to use *that* line on me? What *is* it with boys anyway? Do you explode if you don't have sex?"

"Well..."

"Don't answer that!"

And it's not a line," Spider said, his voice breaking. "It's a question."

"What makes you think I am a virgin?"

"I have a very finely-tuned virgin-detection radar, and it's locked on you."

"My girlfriend would disagree with you."

"She got a name?"

"Leah. Leah Cartman." *And very talented fingers and tongue.* "You're not my type."

"You're only into girls? What about Pete?"

Who's dead, you jackass. "And like I told him I have a girlfriend back on Mars."

"So, you don't like boys."

Kelly rolled out of bed and stood up, her face next to Spider's. "I like boys too. Just not now."

"Just not me, more like it."

Kelly felt her eyes water. "Just not anybody, damn it! What part of 'I got a girlfriend back home' do guys not get?"

"Remember Zola?"

"Yeah. It was only a couple of days ago." *Felt like an eon.*

"You told her that your girl back on Mars was dumping you."

"I was drunk."

"In vino veritas."

"Go to hell."

Spider smiled, recognizing that he'd gotten her goat. "So, you and Pete. You go all the way?"

Kelly punched him. "Fuck! Is that all guys think of?"

"Ouch! And no, we think of sports and food too!"

Kelly chuckled. "Well, think of food for a while." She laid back down on her bunk. "And take a nap."

"I will," Spider said, "But just to be clear, am I your type? Do I have a chance?"

A week ago I'd have said you have no chance at all. "I'm not into virginal guys who look like beanstalks."

"Ouch! And I'm not a virgin!" His voice wavered on that last in a completely unconvincing way.

Yeah, that was kind of harsh. On the other hand, Spider had been chuckling at her expense all damn day. She decided to stick to her guns. "We're going to have another late night tonight. I'm going to get a nap."

"Another patrol for Captain America? Now with the ability to log on?"

"I think they call three-stripe navy types 'commander,'" Kelly said.

"Commander America then," Spider said, a note of exasperation in his voice. "And way to seize the capillary of the argument."

"You mean jugular."

"No, I mean capillary, as in the least important part of my statement." Spider sighed heavily. "She's gonna lead us into a charge at the pirates' guns."

I didn't hear any of this last night when you were picking a lock. "If you think that, why are you helping?"

Another long silence. "I'm scared," he finally said. "Of her, of the pirates, of the whole fucking mess."

That took some guts. "I'm scared too."

They were quiet for a bit. Finally, Spider said, "You didn't answer the question."

"We're not going to die," Kelly said, trying to sound like she meant it. *Although whatever was going to happen to them might be worse than dying.*

"Everybody keeps saying that," Spider said.

"If they wanted us dead, we'd be dead."

"Well, there's what they want and there's what Captain...sorry Commander...America wants."

"It's time to wander over to see the boss lady," Kelly said. She got out of her bunk and stood up to look at Spider. "I wasn't quite ready to play bangola with Pete and I'm not ready to bangola with just anybody."

"I'm not just anybody," Spider said, a grin rippling over his face as he rolled out of his bed.

"You're growing on me."

This was 'social time' so the pair could just walk down the main hallway as opposed to using the utility tunnel. They walked over to Hank's cabin, aka the Suicide Special. Kelly could still see the dead man hanging in it every time she closed her eyes.

"Well, howdy there," Spider said as he walked in the door. "Are we interrupting anything?"

Kelly glanced around Spider to see that Maria's shirt was off and Hank had a hand on her bare breast. "Well, obviously," Kelly said, not bothering to hide her smirk. "We'll just..."

"Close the door," Hank said as Maria pulled her shirt on. "We lost track of time

"Closed," Spider said. "What can we do for you?"

"We have a solution for the terminal problem," Hank said.

"Oh?" Kelly replied. "What would that be?"

"You'll need to hotwire it," Maria said.

"How?" Kelly asked.

"First by springing Stan W.," Maria said. "He's the maintenance guy."

"Yeah, I know," Kelly replied. "I tried his band last night."

"Yes, but get him and some tools in front of the terminal, and he can bypass it."

"Would you like me to also get you a pink pony?" Kelly asked.

"Don't be a wiseass," Hank said. "Here's the plan." She looked significantly at Spider. "It will involve both of you and you're going now."

"Now?" Spider asked, his voice breaking.

"Since there were people in the fan rooms at oh-dark-thirty," Hank said, a smirk on her face, "we're hoping that there won't be people in there now."

"Two questions," Kelly said, feeling heat on her face. "One, why do you think that? Two, wasn't this a one-and-done deal for me?"

"One, while we're up and about, they need more guards. Once we're tucked in for the night, people who would be guarding us are free to do other things. Two, you didn't finish the mission, which was to contact Earth."

Earth. The Holy Grail. "Not my recollection of the deal."

"I'm not going," Spider said.

"You won't be alone," Hank said. "Kelly will go with you."

"The fuck I will," Kelly growled.

***

What the ever-living fuck is wrong with me? An hour ago, I said I wasn't going! It had taken a mere five minutes for Hank to cajole Spider into going. Spider had then done his best puppy-dog imitation, which resulted in Kelly saying she'd go as well. She sighed. *Here I am.*

"Ready?" Spider asked. He'd gotten the access panel to the maintenance tunnel off.

Would it matter if I said no? Kelly nodded. "Do it."

Spider stepped through the opening he'd created and Kelly followed. Now she was squeezing through the narrow and dirty tunnel. Spider had done something to the door— the knob still wouldn't turn but the door could be pushed or pulled open.

"So, this is what the fan room looks like," he said.

"A beautiful space, no?" Kelly replied.

The maintenance tunnel they were in was in the aft part of the ship. Stan the Maintenance Man's new cabin was on the forward part of the ship. Getting there required crossing a corridor on every level. They didn't know which—if any or all—of those corridors had a camera.

That's where Kelly came in. Her job was to go up to level three where the ship's laundry was, then walk out and get picked up by a guard. She had been assigned a work detail in the laundry, and so she'd say she got left behind. Hopefully, while that was happening and distracting the guards, Spider could slip over, find the other tunnel and some tools, go down, find Stan the Maintenance Man, get him up to one, hotwire a terminal, send a message, then get back without getting caught. *This is truly a shitty idea.*

***

"Hey, you! Stop right there!"

Kelly stopped and reflexively put her hands up. She slowly turned to find herself facing a mountain of a man in gray coveralls. A bit of green hair peeked out from under his mask.

"I'm lost," she said, trying to sound as weak and fearful as possible. Given that she was so scared that she was barely in control of her bladder it did not require much acting skill.

"No shit, little girl," the guard said. "Where were you?"

"Laundry," she replied. "I was folding sheets, then suddenly realized I was alone." *If he buys this, I'll eat my shirt.*

The guard walked up to her and put his hand on her head. "You on laundry detail?"

"Yes, sir," she said. He started stroking her hair with his giant hand. She felt a wave of revulsion and nausea. She ducked her face down, avoiding looking at him.

"How old are you?"

"Nine and a half." Kelly could hear her voice quiver.

"What's that in real years?"

"Seventeen."

"Seventeen?" the man chuckled. He walked behind her and then began running his hand down her back. "Girl, woman, your age, should have a man and a baby or two. You got a baby?"

"No sir." *You creep.* She felt her skin crawl wherever his hand touched.

"Well," he said, whispering in her ear, "I might be able to fix that for you."

What exactly do you say to that?

"You should pay more attention to what's going on," he said, his voice husky.

"Yes sir," she replied.

His hand moved from her back to her arm, running slowly down to her hand. He then walked around her. When they were facing, he touched her chin and forced her head up to look at him. "Let's get you back to where you belong."

She nodded, not trusting herself to open her mouth.

***

The giant, who's name she finally remembered was Bruno, walked her down to the passenger deck, his ham-like arm on her shoulder. There was a guard stationed in the elevator lobby, scratching vigorously under their stab-proof vest. "What's this?" they asked, pointing at Kelly.

"Special project," Bruno said. "I may need her for additional work." Kelly shuddered involuntarily at that remark.

He walked her to her cabin, opened the door for her, waved her in, then closed the door behind him. Hank and Maria were waiting for her in her cabin.

"I see you made a friend," Hank said.

Kelly threw jab at Hank's face, catching the woman flush on the mouth. She fell back, getting tangled up with Maria. They both ended up on the bed. "Get the fuck out of here, both of you," Kelly growled.

Hank made to take a swing at Kelly, who moved to defend herself, but Maria grabbed Hank's arm. "Not a good idea," Maria said.

Hank struggled with Maria for a second, then stopped. "You're right, Maria," Hank said. She looked at Kelly. "I was out of line and I'm sorry."

"You better be!" Kelly barked back.

Hank opened her mouth to say something but apparently thought better of it. "So, Private Rack, let's be clear. He likes you. You may have to use that."

"Fuck him, right?"

"No," Hank said, drawing out the word. "Fuck with him, which is different."

"How so?"

"We'll talk later, after you get a chance to calm down," Hank said.

"After you both calm down," Maria said firmly. "She's just a kid for Christ's sake." Hank ripped her arm free of Maria's grasp. "We're out of here."

Maria hustled Hank out of the cabin. Kelly glared at the door for a minute, then broke down in tears.

Sometime later, Kelly heard the access panel slide back. Spider came in, a pleased smile on his face. "We did it," he said. "Messages sent!" He looked very pleased with himself. Then his face fell as he looked at Kelly. "What happened?"

"I think one of the guards wants to make me his special pet," she replied.

Spider wrapped her in a hug. "I'm sorry," he said.

Kelly started to cry.

Chapter 11

Kansas City

Mark

Mark was unpleasantly reminded of Earth's gravity—his back twinged as he stepped out of the ground car onto the FBI's parking lot. He'd not slept well, because of thunderstorms, and thanks to gravity his back was kinked. He tried and failed to stretch the kink out. *At least the storms blew in some cooler weather,* he thought.

Mark looked up at the FBI building. Despite being surrounded by the steel, brick and glass of downtown Kansas City's skyscrapers, the low-slung white stone building stood apart. The building was ringed by a small park planted solely in grass, which led up to a chain-link fence surrounding the compound. It looked like a fort. Or a prison.

He stepped through the metal and glass automatic doors—which appeared to have been cannibalized from a grocery store—and walked into the musty-smelling lobby, carpeted in a busy industrial pattern. The A/C was on, its wet slap unneeded today.

The elderly gentleman receptionist gave Mark a gimlet eye. Several of the FBI types were upset at Mark's having shot somebody, even if that somebody was a bad guy. *At least I don't have to go through comic-opera security theater,* Mark thought. They'd taken his gun for ballistics testing, although it was due back today. *Let's hope today isn't another wasted day.*

Yesterday, the day after Ray Volk had made a pass at him, hadn't been productive. *It's your own damn fault for being Mister Secrets.*

Nothing Mark had said the other night had been a lie. It just hadn't been the full truth. Mark was asexual. *And it only took me twenty-four Mears to realize it.* He rubbed his neck again. *When on Earth, do as Earthlings do.* He did the math in his head. *That's forty-four Standard years, sports fans.*

Yeah, he'd participated in a grope session on the destroyer, but he'd been a one-and-done kind of guy. The reason that both his marriages had failed was that he just wasn't that into sex. The first time he'd not accepted it, the second—or current, given that his lawyer had sent yet another lengthy missive last night—he'd finally figured himself out. Now he was dealing with the fallout.

At least Ray had made progress on the investigation. It turned out that Mrs. Malan, Arlena, had worked as head of HR for a local bank. She was also heavily invested in the same, and when the bank went bust she lost her job and savings. She was supposedly doing some free-lance work, but judging from their bank records it wasn't very lucrative.

As a result, the Malans were broke and facing foreclosure until about six months ago. Then, a few small infusions of capital arrived, tiding them over. Presumably, the Malans thought the ventilator squad was delivering the big payout. *Which they were*, Mark thought with a smile. Just not the kind of 'payout' the Malans were expecting.

As Mark finished signing in, the receptionist said, "There's a visitor waiting for you. Says he has information on ValuTrip *Cardinal*."

"Great, thanks," Mark said. There were a surprising number of crazy people in the world, and public events brought them out of the woodwork. He wondered which conspiracy theory this person had for him. He stepped through the inner metal security door to the industrial hallway.

Just inside, there was a man in a white uniform sitting on a green fabric and metal guest chair. The man stood, and Mark realized it was an American naval uniform.

I'm going to assume four stripes means the same thing in their Navy as it does in ours. "Good morning, Captain," Mark said. "Can I help you?"

"Maybe," the other man, trim and tan, said. "I'm looking for somebody in charge of the ValuTrip *Cardinal* investigation. Somebody is pretending to be a friend of mine and sending me fake messages from the ship."

"Well, Captain—"

"Wheeler," the man interjected. "Captain Tom Wheeler, USN."

"I'm Captain First Class Mark Nagata, Martian Navy," Mark said, offering his hand. "I'm assisting your FBI on the investigation. Let's step inside." *I can at least keep the riffraff out of Volk's hair. Well, I should probably talk to Ray too.* Wheeler handed Mark his ID, which at a glance looked legit. Mark quickly had it run, and discovered it and the bearer were both legitimate.

Mark stashed the American captain in a small conference room, barely big enough for four seats, huddled around a small laminate table, and got them some coffee. "Tell me about this message," Mark said, taking a sip from his cup.

Tom handed over a neatly-folded printout.

"Old-school, huh?" Mark asked.

"Sometimes a piece of paper is more secure," Wheeler replied.

Mark unfolded the sheet.

To: Wheeler.Thomas.M@Navy.mil.gov
From: HSolis@ValuTrip.Cardinal.P-link.space

Subj: Hey, Flounder!

Hey, Flounder, it's me, Hankie-Pankie. You've probably heard that the ValuTrip *Cardinal* has gone missing, or maybe told that she blew up.

Not so. We've been hijacked. The passengers are confined to second-class cabins with most of the crew. Armed men are controlling access. I don't know who's driving the boat, but the cooks have been told to make the food last for three weeks.

Please contact any mil- or LEO-people you know. It needs to be somebody you trust—if the hijackers find out we're sending out messages we're really FUBAR.

We'll check for replies tonight at 2300 ship time.

Hankie
WGNB

Mark's eyes widened as he read the message. "What makes you think this is a fake?"

"It has to be, right?" Tom said. "You can't just hijack a passenger ship."

Well, yes you can. "So, how many people call you 'Flounder'?"

"Not many," Tom allowed. "It's a nickname from when we were in college."

"And 'WGNB'?"

"World's Greatest Naval Battalion," Tom said. "Our ROTC unit at U of I."

Mark set down his coffee with exaggerated care. *Well, hijacking is our working hypothesis. But he doesn't need to know that.* "At the moment we have to keep an open mind." He gestured at the printout. "What I need to know is whether this is somebody jerking your tether or what?"

"Chain. Jerking my chain."

"Whatever. So, I ask again, how many people would know to call you 'Flounder' and her 'Hankie-Pankie'?"

Tom's face went through several changes of expression, finally settling on acceptance. "Maybe thirty. None of whom would pull bullshit like this."

"The code-boffins are going to want to see this electronically," Mark said. "Can you do that?"

Tom held out a handheld. "Yes."

"Make yourself comfortable," Mark said, standing up and accepting the handheld. "I need to round a boffin up."

Ray

"We need to talk," Nagata said. Ray had run into him in a hallway at FBI's headquarters in Kansas City.

"Yeah, I heard a Colonel came in with info. What did he have to say?" Ray asked.

"Well, that too," Nagata said, "but also about our personal relationship."

Ray waved that off. "Dude, not a problem. I asked, you said, 'no,' we're good." *Not the first time my gaydar needed calibrating.*

"Thanks, but still..."

"I know a great lunch place. So, the Colonel?"

Nagata smiled at him. "Not military and not a spacer, are you?"

"I went to Orbital Disney once," Ray said. "Stayed at the Holiday Inn Express the night before. Took a pass on the Army."

"It shows," Nagata said. "He's Navy, so he's a captain."

"Same as you."

"Yep."

"So, what did he say?" Ray said, wondering what was eating Nagata.

"A Navy buddy contacted him from a ship address," Nagata said. "Said they got hijacked."

"We believe him?"

Nagata shrugged. "Seems legit to me. Computer geeks are checking the message routing."

"Well, I'm not surprised. Not after the vent-and-vac on the Malans." Ray watched as Nagata leaned back against the wall. "Back bothering you?"

"Yeah. Gravity sucks."

"I hear you," Ray said. "I loved the zero-gee playroom at the Disney. Right until I puked."

Nagata nodded. "Stayed in too long, right?"

"I guess?"

"Space sickness usually hits after the four-hour mark," Nagata said. "Ask me how I know."

"How?"

"For me, it's like a clock—right after the four-hour mark I start turning green."

"Wow. You'd figure somebody who got spacesick wouldn't make a career in space. It would really be nice to know where the hell our hijackers are going."

"Clyde's got a theory," Nagata said.

"Clyde?"

"One of the NTSB guys. There's a 75% ISFAR-compliant flight path to Mercury."

"In English please?"

"ISFAR is International Space Flight Safety Regime," Nagata said. "If you ever wanted to print it out, it would be a stack of papers a meter high. For the purposes of this discussion, commercial flight plans must be 100% ISFAR compliant. A 75% compliant flight is not 'legal'"—he used air quotes—"but private ships and miliary do them all the time." He sighed. "This particular 75% flight isn't that risky."

"Oh?"

"*Cardinal* has four main engines. They can only lose one of the four during this trip."

"I assume that's not very likely?"

"Not unless somebody's shooting at them."

***

Yet another conference, Mark thought, glancing at his watch. His stomach gurgled, reminding him that it was past lunchtime. The virtual wall at the other end of the table faded away, replaced by four figures and a blank segment of screen. It was a surprisingly high-level conference, at least in Mark's eyes. He ran down the group from left to right.

At far left, Major General Carol Lopez, US Space Force, sitting in front of a blue drape. Next was a stocky man, General Portman, US Army. Mark noted that there was no command associated with him, which probably meant he was special forces. The next screen held a hatchet-faced man identified as FBI Director French. Rounding out the cast was Rear Admiral Sally Teng of the Martian Navy's Force E. Mark nodded at Teng, who returned the nod.

"Let's get started," French said.

A new screen appeared. The chyron underneath identified the person in it as Robin Liu, Chief of Staff, pronouns they/them. "I'm just here as an observer," Liu said. "Please continue."

"Admiral Teng?" French said.

She leaned into her screen. "The Martian Army, specifically a Major in it, got a message last night from somebody claiming to be his niece and a passenger on the hijacked *Cardinal*."

"The Royal Canadian Mounted Police got a similar message," French said, "via a retired Mounty who has a grandson, a crewmember, on the ship."

"And FBI headquarters here received one as well, from a Navy captain who is a former classmate of one of the passengers," Mark said.

"Once is accident, twice coincidence, three times is enemy action," General Portman said in his surprisingly high-pitched voice. "We've got a live one."

"And we have no idea where she's going," Teng said.

"We have a theory," Mark said.

"Which is?" French asked.

"Mercury," Mark said.

"Well, that makes perfect sense to me," Teng replied. To the group, she said, "The Syndication of Mercury is not known for their respect of law and order."

"But would they just let a hijacked ship fly in and not stop it?" French said.

"Depending on who's getting paid off, maybe," Lopez said. "And under the Treaty of Copernicus, they are strictly neutral."

"So, neither military has a significant presence there?" This from Liu, who was clearly not just an observer. Mark wondered what they were chief of staff of.

"Correct," Lopez said. "I don't even know if we, the US, have diplomatic relations with the Syndication." She held up one hand to indicate a pause and another one to her ear. "We don't," she said. "Mars does."

"But how certain are we that she's going to Mercury?" Liu asked.

"Right now, it's a theory," Mark said. "We need to get a good fix on *Cardinal*."

There was an uncomfortable pause. General Lopez finally filled it. "We might be able to help. We've gotten intermittent hits from one of our classified tracking assets."

"And?" Portman said.

"And it doesn't make a lot of sense that this particular asset is getting a hit," Lopez said reluctantly.

This is like pulling teeth. "How so, ma'am?" Mark asked.

"It's in-system from Earth," Teng said. She held up her hand. "Just a guess."

"A correct guess," Lopez replied.

"Could somebody help me out?" French asked.

"There's only one inhabited spot closer to the Sun than Earth," Lopez said. "Mercury."

"In other words, the one place in the system where there's no law and order," French said.

"Pretty much," Teng said. "Even Venus has more legal presence."

"Really?" Portman said.

"Quad Power Observation Group," Teng said. "Four Earth nations maintain a small task force in orbit there." She waved her hand dismissively. "Not more than two or three ships, but enough to handle a hijacked passenger liner."

"Which is apparently more Earth forces than on Mercury," Liu asked. "What happens if they get to Mercury?"

"There's several million people on the planet," Teng said. "If they get the hostages off of the ship, finding them could be nearly impossible."

"So, we've got a ship that's maybe been hijacked and maybe going to Mercury," Liu said, "and if they get there and the Synod—"

"Syndicate," Lopez corrected.

"Syndicate can't or won't stop them from offloading the passengers, they're screwed. What do I tell the President?"

"Not to lecture my superiors, but we need to get somebody to sit on this egg immediately," Mark said.

"Pardon?" Liu asked.

"Navy jargon for put a ship on her tail and make sure nothing comes on or goes off," Teng said. "So where do we think she is?"

"The US Space Force can handle this," Liu said.

"Maybe, maybe not," Lopez said sheepishly. "It depends on if we have a ship in the right place."

"When will we know for sure?" Liu said. Lopez had a pained look on his face. "Surely you can tell me that?"

"Six hours," Lopez said. "We'll have a better location in six hours."

"Good. Call me as soon as you know. In the meantime, what are the President's options?"

"Piracy 101," Lopez said. "Quiet, Hard, or Talkative. We either sneak a counter-piracy team onboard—quiet—or send them in guns-blazing with the pirates alerted—hard— or negotiate—talk—with the pirates."

"Negotiate means that at least the pirates get a walk," French said.

"If not payment," Lopez added.

"I really hate paying crooks," Liu said. "Risks of hard and soft?"

"It's not at all clear we can even do soft," Lopez said. "Sneaking up on a ship in space is very difficult."

"General Portman?" Liu asked.

"General Lopez is correct, ma'am," he replied. "Also, my team would not be familiar with the ship."

"The problem with any option is that the pirates can threaten to kill the hostages," Teng said.

"How hard would that be, operationally?" French asked.

Teng shrugged her shoulders. "Depressurizing the ship is the quickest way. Overriding the safeties is merely a matter of time, if you have physical access to them."

"I should point out that we will have to get the passengers off," Mark said. "*Cardinal* will be out of food and nearly out of consumables for her water recycling system."

Liu took a deep breath. "General Lopez. What time constraints am I under with regards to a rescue? Assuming she's going to Mercury."

"Which is just an assumption at the moment," Portman interjected.

"If she's going to the asteroids or outer system," Teng said, "we'll be waiting for them. Ships are already moving."

"So," Lopez continued, "assuming Mercury, we need to leave in three or four days, depending on the speed of the ships. I have a Wing scheduled for a routine week in the training area which leaves in three days. Besides being my most ready force, sending them means less questions to answer from the media."

"But you need time to prep them, yes?" Liu asked. Lopez nodded affirmatively. Liu took another deep breath. "Here's your orders, General. Get a force ready—whatever you need. I do not want to pay pirates, but if it's that or a slaughter, we'll pay. Find and procure a suitable ship for the passengers to evacuate to." They waved at the camera. "Write that up and I'll get POTUS to approve. Anything else you need from me right now?"

"What about the pirates?" French asked.

"What about them?" Liu said. "Generals. If you end up with live pirates under your control, I'm sure the Attorney General can deal with them. If not, God *will*. Clear enough?"

The generals and admiral nodded. "If I may, ma'am?" Mark said. "I believe that *Cardinal*'s sister ship, *Bluejay*, is ready for space trials. She may be available."

"That would be great," Portman said. "My team could practice on her on the way."

"Get her," Liu said. "Charter or seize, I don't care which. Anything else for now?"

"Actually, yes," Ray Volk said. Mark turned around to see him just out of camera range. Mark waved him in and introduced him.

"The messages sent to the US and Canada were put on the Net in Wasilla, Alaska," Ray said. "Where we can't operate."

"Shit," Director French replied. "Those loons..."

"How ironic," Liu said with a smirk. "My next meeting is with their ambassador."

"Do you think they will help?" French asked.

"They will if I tell him that his country helps or I bomb them into the Stone Age," Liu replied. "We just sent a third aircraft carrier to the Gulf of Alaska."

Mark wondered what this months' diplomatic tiff was about, but knew in general terms that the relationship between the two countries was contentious. "We really, and I mean really," Mark said, "need to get control of the communications to *Cardinal*. This operation could leak out at any time."

"Then I guess Agent Volk is going to Alaska," Liu said. "Director French—I'll conference you into the meeting with the ambassador. Anything else?"

There was not. Mark broke the conference connection.

"I can't believe a Republican is going to green-light the biggest military operation in a decade," Volk said.

"Not a whole lot of other options," Mark said. "Agent Volk. I think you need to see a woman about a ship."

"Sounds fun," Volk said.

"And we need to get a message to *Cardinal*." Mark stood up. "I'll work on that with Captain Wheeler."

To: HSolis@ValuTrip.Cardinal.P-link.space
From: Wheeler.Thomas.M@Navy.mil.gov
Subj: Keep the Faith—Hanoi Hilton

Hankie-Pankie:

Got your message. Keep the faith and find out as much information as you can. We're listening and need you to be eyes and ears onboard.
Flounder
Now Jayhawk Battalion, NROTC

Ray

Between the lengthy meetings and Ray's need to pack for his Alaskan adventure, lunch had turned into an early dinner. Clemente's, Kansas City's finest Italian restaurant, was practically empty.

"So, you had something you wanted to get off of your chest?" Ray said, wondering why Nagata seemed so agitated.

"You know what asexual means, right?" Nagata asked.

"Yeah. Ace. Not into sex, or not very much," Ray said. It clicked. "You're ace?"

"I am."

"Okay." Ray ripped off a chunk of bread.

"Okay?"

"Yeah, Mark, really." Ray shrugged. "I mean, I'm not bothered. Really." Ray looked at Mark. "But you are."

"It took me two failed marriages to figure this out about myself," Mark said painfully.

"That's rough," Ray said. "I feel for you. I do."

"What about your sexuality?"

"Oh, man, I was lucky," Ray said. "Really lucky. I don't remember a time where I didn't know I was gay." Ray leaned forward. "I know a lot of people who don't know themselves or took a lot of time to find out. It happens and it sucks. But bottom line, my feelings were not and are not hurt."

"I'm glad to hear that," Mark said. He still sounded a bit pained to Ray's ears.

"I really meant that," Ray offered. "Figuring out who you are is tough. Friend of mine in high school either couldn't figure it out or didn't like the answer."

"How'd that end?"

Kid tried to blow his head off with a shotgun and didn't quite get the job done. "Not well at all," Ray said.

"Well, this is awkward," Mark said.

"Not to me," Ray replied. "Seriously. We can just be friends, or if that's doesn't work for you, coworkers."

Mark smirked.

"What's so funny?"

"You." Mark gestured with his chin. "You're checking out the waiter's ass."

"And he has a fine ass," Ray said, surprised at his bashfulness. "I'm afraid I'm going to do that a lot."

"Okay by me," Mark said, "as long as you're okay with me getting a chuckle out of it."

"I'm always glad to be a source of amusement," Ray said. "So, what do you do in your free time?"

"Golf, for one thing."

"Any good at it?"

"A one handicap."

"Wow," Ray said. "We should get you on the course with my boss Charlize. We make her tee off from the men's tees and she still kicks everybody's ass."

"Sounds like a plan," Mark said.

Well, at least we patched up this relationship, Ray thought as the salads arrived.

Chapter 12

Anchorage, Alaskan Free Republic

Ray

Ray Volk stepped out onto the airport concourse, glad he'd packed a jacket. It was raining outside and looked damn chilly. There was a woman, tall and red-headed, wearing cowboy boots and jeans, standing in the middle of the concourse holding a sign with his name on it.

"I'm Ray Volk," he said.

"Andrea Huggens," she replied. "Mister French told us you're coming. I've got a car outside."

"Let me claim my bag first."

She smiled. "Certainly."

The car proved to be a black stretch sedan, about ten years old and practically screaming 'government.' Ray climbed into the back seat and found a wrinkled old man in a bad suit sitting on a rearward-facing jump seat. The car started rolling.

"Kratman, National Police," he said. He pointed at Huggens. "Her boss's boss."

"Director," Ray said. "I'm..."

"No time for small talk, Volk," Kratman said. "Here's the deal. President Palin called me this morning. Your President called her last night. Gave her some speech about 'with us or against us' and suggested we either get to the bottom of your terrorist problem or start ducking bombs."

"I'm sorry—" Ray started.

"No, you're not," Kratman interjected. "But at any rate, understand this: My priority is defending this country from all enemies, and right now whoever's running around 'jacking civilian spaceships classifies as an enemy. So, you need anything, call. If we *can* do it, we *will*." He pointed at Huggins. "This is national security Red. Got it?"

"Yes sir," she replied.

"We're dropping you off at the Hyatt," Kratman said. "Rent a car there. Make sure you carry your pistol, but if possible don't use it."

"Yes, sir."

***

Ray was glad for the jacket. "It always this cold?" he asked.

Huggins smiled. "This is actually pretty warm for May."

Ray shivered. At least there wasn't snow on the ground, which he half-expected. A gust of wind blew a cluster of cold wet drops in under the canopy of the Hyatt. *That ain't snow but it's damn close,* Ray thought as a few drops found their way down his collar. The rental car agent handed Ray the keys to their mid-sized sedan and Ray climbed in, grateful for the warmth.

"Where are we going?" Huggins asked.

"You got the report from the FBI coders, yes?" Ray asked. "Where would you think?"

"Wasilla," Huggins replied. "Which is just up Free Road 1. Any idea where in Wasilla?"

"That's where I was hoping you'd come in," Ray said, giving the car their destination. "Apparently the messages we got were dumped on the network from a residential aggregator." The car asked for a location in Wasilla and Ray told it 'downtown.' The vehicle acknowledged the directive and quietly started rolling.

"Well, that's a problem," Huggins said. "Legally, we have no authority to make an aggregator provide customer information."

"I assume we can get a warrant," Ray said.

"Sure," Huggins replied. "If you want your bad guy to get a formal notice from the court and forty-eight hours to respond to it."

Ray cursed under his breath. Bullshit 'rules' like that had made the Alaskan Free Republic a haven for white-collar crime. "So, I guess I should just get back on the plane?"

Huggins frowned. "Special Agent, I don't think you were paying attention to my director."

"Enlighten me."

"We're not going to get a warrant. National Security Red means I'm to ignore all those niceties and get what we need."

Maybe we should threaten to bomb nations back into the Stone Age more often. "Then, which aggregator are we going to illegally visit first?"

"Your coders were able to narrow it down to one aggregator." Huggins reached over to the central console and started to enter an address. "Threeper Services."

Ray converted his involuntary gasp to a cough. Threeper Services—founded by some of the characters who'd made Alaska independent and named after the idea that only three percent of Americans ever fought at any one time in the American Revolution—was the premier data services provider for every slimeball in Alaska. The FBI had been trying to get inside of Threeper's operation for years, and had always been stymied by Alaskan law. "We're just going to walk into Threeper's and ask?"

"Pretty much," Huggins replied. "And no, this is not an open-ended fishing expedition for the FBI. We're just pulling data pertaining to this case."

***

Wasilla proved to be a long and narrow town sandwiched between a pair of lakes. The main road into town was four lanes, but slowed by a number of stoplights. The car turned off the main road just west of what apparently passed for downtown Wasilla, and headed north for a couple of blocks, then pulled into a parking lot for a five-unit strip mall.

The end unit was a bar, Frito's, and three of the other four units were various franchise retail outlets. Threeper

Computer and Network Services occupied a middle unit, sandwiched between a franchise deli and a haircut place. "We just gonna walk in and ask?" Ray asked.

"No, I'm going to walk in and ask. You're going to stand behind me and keep your mouth shut and your gun in your holster," Huggins replied. Ray noticed that she undid two buttons on her blouse. "Got it?"

"Yep."

The pair stepped out of the car. Ray followed Huggins into the storefront. Just inside the door was a small and very plain waiting area with the kind of cheap furniture one got on sale at a business supply store. There were a few metal wire-rack shelves lining one wall, offering a spare selection of computer accessories. Judging by the sun-faded packaging, they rarely sold anything.

Huggins marched up to the counter, manned by a pale and chubby kid who clearly spent too much time behind a keyboard. "Picking up or delivering?" the kid asked.

"Neither," Huggins replied. She leaned over the counter, giving him a decent look down her blouse. "Need some information."

The kid smiled wanly. "Tourism bureau is downtown."

"Customer information," Huggins said. "One of your retail net customers."

The kid frowned. "We can't release that without a subpoena," he said.

"Even as a favor?" Huggins asked.

A large black man walked out of the back area to the counter. He scowled at Huggins. "Clean out your ears, lady. No court order, no info."

"Hi, Mike," Huggins said. "Nice to see you too."

The man softened slightly. "Andy, you know the drill. Turn your pretty ass around and head back down to The Anchor."

Huggins made a hurt face. "You're no fun, Mike." She turned and walked out the door, leaving Ray to follow her.

"That went well," Ray said when they were outside. "Now what."

"You hungry?" Huggins asked.

"Not especially," Ray replied.

"That's a shame," Huggins said. "Bushwhack Bob's has great salmon."

"Didn't come here for the food," Ray said, not bothering to hide his irritation.

"Actually, neither did I," she said, "and the salmon is the only item on Bob's menu that I can stomach. But you'd be surprised who stops by Bob's."

***

Bushwhack Bob's Bar and Grill—hard on the shore of a lake—was a rundown-looking shack. The inside of the bar wasn't much better, and poorly lit. There was one man behind the bar. The three waitresses wore short shorts, push-up bras and too much makeup. Huggins got a table in the back, looking out of one of the few windows onto the lake.

Their waitress handed them a pair of grease-stained menus and two plastic glasses of water. The menu was heavy on burgers, chicken wings and other fried foods. "Two grilled salmons," Huggins ordered, "and two Moosehead bottles."

"What makes you think I don't want a burger?" Ray said.

"You want food poisoning?" she retorted. "Bob, whose real name is Justin, pays off the local food inspector. The fish at least is fresh and local. God knows where the beef comes from." She shuddered. "Assuming it is beef and not horsemeat."

Mike, the guy from Threeper's, arrived at the same time as their beer. Huggins ordered a beer for Mike.

"You like this table," Mike said.

"Good view of the rest of the bar," Huggins replied.

"Especially after four," Mike said, winking at Ray.

"They go topless at happy hour," Huggins said. The waitress returned with Mike's beer, which he promptly took a large gulp from.

"What do you need?" Mike asked.

"One of your customers," Huggins said. "Like I told your counterman."

"Which like he told you means court orders."

"I don't need a court order to revoke your parole," Huggins said.

Mike took another long drag on his beer. "If it gets out, our customers—"

"That's Threeper's problem, not yours," Huggins said. "Yours is staying out of jail."

Mike sighed. "Do I at least get to know why you need this?"

"No," Huggins said.

"Who?" Mike asked.

Huggins slid over a piece of paper. He glanced at it. "Call you in an hour." He drained his beer and headed out. Ray noted that he stopped at the counter to pick up a takeout order.

"You know, Andrea," Ray intoned.

"No," Huggins replied. "I am not going to ask for a data-dump of every one of Threeper's customers. He'll get caught, and if they don't kill him one of the burnt customers will." She took a sip of her beer. "Besides, if it weren't for crooks this country would freeze over and blow away."

"I thought you had minerals up here?" Ray said.

"It's cheaper to mine an asteroid than to dig in winter," Huggins said, "and now that the oil is gone, all we've got is some trees and fish."

"You could always come back to the US of A," Ray said with a smile.

"If it were up to me, I'd do it in a minute," Huggins replied. "But there's enough old farts and 'freedom lovers' to mean we won't."

After eating, they took their second beers out to a small deck in back overlooking the lake. Huggins' phone chirped. "Got the address," she said. "About thirty minutes away. Need to use the john?"

"That would be nice," Ray said. "Meet you at the car?"

She nodded.

Chapter 13

Victoria

Apparently even pirates have paperwork, Victoria thought, looking at the stack before her. "Do I really need to sign off on each meal?" she said.

Jack Otarski, standing before her, replied carefully, "You said you were the captain now. This is what he would have seen."

She looked up from her table. She'd be much more comfortable at the piano, but it was hard to do paperwork at it, so she'd commandeered a booth behind the piano. Several piles of paper littered it.

"In hardcopy?" she asked, gesturing at the stacks. "I didn't know we even had a printer on this ship."

"We have three," Otarski said dryly. "Which is good, since you locked me out of the system, ma'am. In order to get what I need, I have to have one of your guards print out reports, which I then modify and provide to you." Otarski shuffled his feet. "I'm open to other suggestions."

Victoria looked at him. "Let's start with the question you haven't answered. Why am I signing off on every meal?"

Otarski leaned over and pointed at one of the reports. "You're signing off on the consumption estimates, ma'am." He pointed at a chart. "This shows how much food we served, how much is left, and how much we expect to get out of the grow-houses over the next few days. For the record, we can't feed everybody out of the grow houses. This is just extending the margins."

Victoria looked at the chart, variously hand annotated. "Why is this column negative?" She referred to a fourth column, written in by hand.

"The original report was based on our going to Earth," Otarski said. "Which was a fourteen-day trip. I am recalculating based on a twenty-one-day trip. That figure is number of days food left at the end of the projected trip."

"So negative two means we'll run out of food two days before we get there?"

"Yes, ma'am," Otarski replied.

"I thought we had a margin sufficient to make it?"

Otarski shrugged. "We might. If you compare that with yesterday's number, we're actually improving. Yesterday we were at negative three days."

"What's driving the improvement?"

"Grow house production. We put in some fast-growing seeds, and they are sprouting as anticipated. Also, we're conserving leftovers better. Tomorrow's lunch is stew, which will mostly be recycled leftovers." He smiled wanly. "Lastly, less menu options means less waste."

"How so?"

"Remember when you were a kid? Mom or dad told you 'eat what I put on your plate or go hungry.' Well, everybody's a kid again."

Nobody ever told me that. As far as she could ever remember, food was brought to her on a plate by a servant and she ate whatever she wanted. "So, all of this pile of paperwork is telling me that you'll keep our passengers happy and fed until we get to our destination?"

Another shrug from Otarski. "It will be close. Calculating things by hand means some slop."

He's apparently smart enough not to complain about lacking computer access again. Victoria let loose a sigh. "Fine, fine, you win, Jack." She looked at his guard. "Get him computer access. Tell our geek to keep it limited but get him some."

"Thank you, Captain," Otarski said.

"Anything else?"

"Water recycling," he replied.

"What about it?"

"You're not letting my people into the recycling plant," he said.

"No shit," Victoria replied. "We're drinking that water too."

"There are filters to be changed and consumables to be replenished," he said. "Are you keeping up on that?"

Good question, Victoria thought. "Your concern is noted. Anything else?"

"Cooling. I've noticed that the radiators aren't dumping quite as much heat as we'd expect."

They were just inside Earth's orbit, so he must have an eagle eye on whatever gages he's using. "Also noted. Anything else?"

"No, ma'am."

Victoria waved him away. Once he was out of the lounge, she picked up a wireless ship's phone, which she had because shutting down the wrist access bands also killed any other wireless communication. She dialed the access code and then called the bridge. "Is Beale up there?" she asked.

Whoever answered said "yes" and put Beale on the line. She filled him in on Otarski's question about water.

"No, ma'am," Beale said, "I'm not doing anything with water recycling except looking at the alerts. That's Hotel's job."

Fuck you too, Beale, Victoria thought. *How the fuck am I supposed to know about water recycling?* "Do we have anybody who knows how to keep the units running?"

"I sure don't know," Beale said. "I just drive the boat. I'll ask around."

"Don't bother," Victoria replied. "I'll get Otarski to put somebody on it. Our maintenance guy will just have to watch their people." She sighed, then asked about radiators.

"That I do know about," Beale said, "and I figured a native Mercurian would too. We'll need to go EVA and rig sunshades soon."

"What's involved with that?" she asked.

"Five or six people out on shifts for two or three days," Beale said. "It's hot work and since we're still under thrust, dangerous. A tenth of a gee isn't much but if you fall off the ship, we'll just keep on going."

"Can you do it without involving the prisoners?"

"Yes, but I'll need a couple of the more space-handy guards."

"Guards are spread too thin now."

She could hear the irritation in Beale's voice. "You wanna be cool, we rig shades. No shades, we sweat."

True. On the other hand, it was a temporary thing. They were going to Mercury, where keeping anything cool was a chore. Dumping waste heat in a vacuum was hard, but with the extra solar heat it was even worse. "Will we overheat anything critical if we don't rig shades?"

"Probably not. It will just be warm."

I grew up on Mercury. Never saw snow until I showed up on Earth. "Then I guess we'll sweat."

"You're the boss."

You're damn right. She hung up and then called Otarski's guard. "Tell Otarski we need to get somebody on water recycling."

Victoria turned her attention from the mass of paper to her ship-provided handheld. It used the same secondary wireless as the phones so at least had connectivity, although at a glacial speed. The secondary network had been built for reliability in the event of an emergency, not convenience. She'd programmed in some keyword searches, monitoring the news feeds for any updates on the "disappearance" of ValuTrip *Cardinal*. There were a large number of updates, most of them speculative rehashes of the same old non-new news. She smiled, although she would have been smiling more broadly if the news wasn't talking about their engine light-off. Still, it told the NTSB nothing useful.

Her smile faded when she came across a news item announcing that the NTSB had chartered the *Cardinal's* sister-ship, the ValuTrip *Bluejay*, and were taking her to space to "test various theories about the accident."

What 'theories' are the NTSB testing? She checked the timestamp: noon today US time—yet only a handful of the feeds had updated their stories with that news, even though it was late evening in the US. She felt a shiver. *Something's not right*. She sent an email to her US operative, asking them to investigate. It was all she could do.

Kelly

"That sucked," Kelly said as she was putting her clean clothes—a few items of prisonwear—in a drawer in the cabin. More like staring at them. And feeling sorry for herself. *All those nice new clothes Mom bought for me—gone.* She glanced at the thermostat for the cabin. It was at its lowest setting and the room still felt a bit warm. *Maybe I'm just stressed.*

"Yeah," Spider replied. "It did suck."

At lunchtime, they'd all been marched into the theater instead of the dining room. Four prisoners, were on stage, tied to some metal scaffolding. Commander Zero had made a speech, announcing that they had been 'stealing rations.' In one poor sap's case, it had been an apple. Their shirts were ripped off and another of the guards whipped them on their bare backs with a belt. The show had ended with everybody being told that they would not get any lunch today and would instead have to go back to work.

If they whipped him for an apple, what the hell would they do if they knew I was talking to Earth? Although the fact that they were talking to somebody without the fucking goons knowing about it was nice.

This was especially on Kelly's mind because—during the afternoon work detail—she and Spider had provided the replies they got from Earth to Hank and Stan the Maintenance Man. She wondered again what a "POTUS" was and why references to a hotel in a place called Hanoi got Hank all watery-eyed.

"What did your reply say?" Spider asked.

"Remember the dragon," Kelly replied. "Bradbury's coming."

"Oh," Spider said.

It was a reference to a battle during the Martian Revolution, when forty militia troops held off eight hundred Indian Army regulars for three days until the Bradbury City Regiment arrived to relieve them. Kelly assumed it was supposed to cheer her up, but she couldn't help but remember that twenty of the defenders had died in the battle.

"So, what do you think Earth's gonna tell us?" Spider said.

Kelly pushed the drawer closed and turned to look at Spider, who was sitting on the room's only chair. "We're screwed, that's what they're going to tell us."

Spider stood up. "You're not being very optimistic."

"Fuck optimism," Kelly said. Her eyes started to water, and she wiped them angrily with her sleeve. "And fuck Henrietta Solis and the motorbike she rode in on!"

Spider, looking awkward, took a step toward her—as close as he could get in the tiny cabin without being on top of her. "Look—"

"No, you look," Kelly cut him off. "I'm sick of this shit!" Her eyes went from watery to full tears, and she felt her face flush. *Goddamn I'm not going to cry.*

Spider reached out and put one hand on her shoulder. Kelly lost what little control she had and started bawling as Spider wrapped her up in a hug. "Big girls don't cry," Kelly sniffled into his shoulder.

"Shame, because big boys do," Spider replied. Kelly looked up and realized he was crying too.

ValuTrip Bluejay

Mark

Our cover's about to be blown, Mark Nagata thought. He scratched himself—there hadn't been time for him to wash the NTSB shirt he'd been given, and the damn thing itched. "Say again?" Mark asked, playing for time.

"I said, what exactly kind of ship are we supposed to meet up with?" The Third Mate, a chesty young woman with curly blonde hair, fixed a gimlet eye on him. Her very obvious 'sex kitten' looks were very similar to Mark's second wife, a woman he'd married hoping to 'fix' his low sex drive. It hadn't worked, and he found himself irritated at the Third Mate. *It's not her, it's you, Sport.*

"A deepspace tug," Mark replied. "In case our testing develops problems."

"Well, that so-called 'deepspace tug' on our bow sure looks a hell of a lot like a *Kowalski*-class Martian destroyer."

Considering that it was the RMS *Marian R. Kowalski*, lead ship of the class, the kid's eye was pretty good. "The tug may have been based off of a military hull," Mark offered lamely.

"Kinda like those White Sox, huh?" she asked.

They had told everybody that Mark was from Chicago because that accent was closest to his, but unfortunately the Third Mate was a baseball fan. The arrival on the bridge of Captain Brass saved him from having to comment. He was followed by Denise Ricardo, former head of ValuTrip security, now wearing a Space Force uniform.

Finally, I can stop the bullshit. "All will be revealed shortly," Mark said.

"It still fits," Ricardo said to him in a low voice, gesturing at her working military uniform.

Considering how baggy US military uniforms were, Mark figured she could add at least twenty kilos before it was too tight. Captain Brass keyed up the ship's public address system, sending audio and video throughout the vessel.

"This is your captain," he said. "I have an important announcement. You have been told that we are going to space to help the NTSB test theories as to what happened to our sister ship *Cardinal*. Well, we are going to help *Cardinal*. It turns out she has been hijacked, and we're part of a task force to rescue her. I'm now going to give you Colonel Ricardo, who many of you know is Chief of Security for ValuTrip. Colonel."

Ricardo moved in front of the camera, graceful under the ship's modest acceleration. "I'm Denise Ricardo," she said. "On the direct orders of the President, I have been recalled to active duty. Those of you with a military background will be getting notification soon that you too have been recalled."

"You will also note," she continued, "that a number of people came aboard, ostensibly with the National Transportation Safety Board or various contractors. Almost none of them are actually with the NTSB. They are all either Space Force or US Army Delta Force personnel and are tasked with retaking *Cardinal*. They will be studying this ship with that goal in mind, and this ship will be receiving passengers and crew when we retake *Cardinal*. Please extend all cooperation to the Delta Force team. I will be commanding this ship, with Captain Brass reporting to me. We have one other person to introduce."

Mark stepped up to the camera. "My name is Mark Nagata, and I am a Captain First Class in the Martian Navy." He then briefed the crew on the plan, not mentioning that most of the details were yet to be written.

Mark took a breath. "As senior officer, it has fallen to me to give everybody the bad news. Effective immediately, all communications on and off this ship will be subject to military censorship. Right now, the pirates on *Cardinal* think they have gotten away clean. That is the only tactical advantage we have, and the lives of five hundred passengers and crew hinge on keeping our mission a secret. So, all messages will be reviewed before transmission. There will be additional information as necessary."

Mark handed back the mic and walked over to the watch officer's station. He picked up the bridge-to-bridge radio handset. "Mike Romeo Kilo, this is Victor Bravo, the bird has sung. Over."

"Victor Bravo, this is Mike Romeo Kilo, roger that. Interrogative station? Over."

"Kilo, this is Bravo. Station Lima Ten Lima. Over."

"Roger. Out."

"What does 'lima ten lima' mean?" the bridge officer asked.

"No closer than ten clicks in front of us," Mark answered. He reached into his backpack and pulled out a binder. "International Tactical Signal Book 1-Charlie," he said, handing it to the befuddled officer. "It's your bible now. Learn it and love it."

"A binder?" the officer asked.

"Never have to reboot it," Mark said, "and can't be hacked." He turned to Brass and Ricardo. "I'd like to assemble all officers and chiefs not on watch somewhere so they can meet up with the Delta people."

"We can use the first-class lounge," Brass said. "What about the reporters?"

Mark swore under his breath. Bringing reporters aboard had not been his idea. "I'll deal with them later."

"Assemble them in the auditorium for now," Ricardo said. "One of us can brief them." Mark nodded his assent.

"What's the agenda for the officers meeting?" Brass asked.

"Training, scheduling, getting this ship ready to take on refugees," Mark said.

"May I ask where we're going?" Brass said.

"Mercury," Mark replied. "Got the tracking data an hour ago."

"Christ," Brass replied. "They've got a big head start on us."

"Three days," Nagata replied. "We're going to be burning a lot of reaction mass to catch up. Hope you're up to speed on underway replenishment."

"Never done it before in my life," Brass said, turning slightly pale.

"I have," Ricardo said. "It's not as hard as it looks."

"If you say so," Brass said. "How good is that tracking data?"

"One of our heavy frigates, RMS *Cydonia*, got a targeting visual on her," Mark said. "She's been diverted to sit on

Cardinal." Mark left unsaid that the US covert tracking station that had found *Cardinal* had been set up to monitor the transit of Martian warships like the *Cydonia* as they transited in and out of the Solar System.

"I guess we're gonna sweat," Brass said.

"Probably," Mark replied. "Oh, and communications. The USSF likes to talk on scramblers as opposed to tactical code, so we'll need to get those installed."

"And see if we can get better communications with the hostages," Ricardo said. "Once a day updates from PassengerLink are slow."

"Why don't they use the captain's radio?" Brass said.

"What 'captain's radio'?" asked Mark, Ricardo and the Third Mate more-or-less at once.

"Captain Montoya and I keep a radio in our cabin," Brass said. To Mark's puzzled look, Brass added, "Carlos Montoya's the captain over on *Cardinal*. He's a personal friend—stood up at both of my weddings."

Mark smiled. "Apparently nobody knows to look for it."

Brass looked embarrassed. "That's actually the general idea. It's supposed to be secret."

"Not anymore," Mark said.

The radio crackled. *Kowalski* reported she was in station and announced in code she had updates on the other ships. Mark waved the other two officers to go below and turned his attention to the radio.

After dealing with the *Kowalski's* news, the Third Mate said to him, "Now you get to be a fleet captain, right?"

"Technically," Mark said. "How do you know?"

"I'm a big fan of 'Station Thirteen,'" she replied. "A fleet captain in the Martian Navy is any captain who commands multiple units but does not command an individual ship."

Mark stifled a groan. Station Thirteen was a kid's show, centered on a fictional Martian Navy rescue station in the asteroids. The character who played Captain Mendel was getting promoted to fleet captain once a season and applying her rank tabs was always treated as a big deal.

The Third Mate was right, and at some technical level fleet captains were equivalent to US Space Force brigadier generals. At a practical level, since fleet captain was a temporary rank and paygrade, most such officers didn't make a big deal about it.

"Well, I'm not Emilia Mendel," Mark replied, "and besides I don't have tabs in my pocket, so they'll be no ceremony. In any event, once we hook up with the *Oklahoma* battlegroup I'm back to just captain."

"That's a shame," the Third Mate said with what could be taken as a flirtatious smile. *Your charms are wasted on me.*

***

Mark had changed into his service dress khaki uniform. It was as dressed up as he was going to get on a ship. He paused at a mirror, straightened his tie, then stepped through the door to the stage of the auditorium. The stage was cluttered, littered with boxes and props for the various shows the ship was planning to put on once it went back into service. Mark navigated around them to a stylish glass-and-metal podium. A small gaggle of maybe twenty reporters and their hangers-on were clustered at the foot of the stage, glaring at a uniformed crew member. The mood in the room was ugly.

"What the hell's going on?" one of the reporters, a bald man of indeterminate origin, barked out.

"That's what I am about to tell you," Mark said, arriving at the podium. "As you probably heard, my name is Captain Mark Nagata, Martian Navy, and I am commanding what we're calling Task Group 304. This task group, consisting of three Martian destroyers, a US supply ship, and this vessel, are due to rendezvous with the US Space Force's 30th Space Wing. That unit's flagship is the USS *Oklahoma*. Upon rendezvous, we will proceed to Mercury, where we will attempt to retake the *Cardinal* from the so-far unknown group of pirates holding her."

"When can we report this?" the bald reporter asked. "The public has a right to know."

"The five hundred passengers and crew on *Cardinal* have a right to live," Mark replied. "And right now, the only tactical advantage we have is that the pirates think they got away clean. So, we're not allowing any communications off for the next twenty-four hours. After that, all, and I mean all, communications will be approved by me. We do have two NTSB reps aboard, who will assist you in generating useful content."

"You mean lies?" Baldy asked.

Mark shrugged. "Anything broadcast needs to meet my approval. You can send content that meets my specs or nothing. I don't care."

"So, we're sending bullshit for a week?" Baldy asked. "While all these troops get a pleasure cruise?"

"We won't be in a position to intercept *Cardinal* for nearly twelve days. During that time, we'll be rehearsing and testing our plan to rescue the hostages." *A plan that hasn't been written yet.* "The troops will be busy practicing that plan."

"What is the plan?" Baldy asked. Mark wondered who'd made him king of the reporters.

"All will be revealed," Mark said. "And you'll have a front-row seat."

"But still the public..." Baldy said.

"Five hundred of your countrymen, civilians all, were hijacked and are running hell-for-leather to Mercury, a planet with a great demand for slaves. We're going to try and stop that."

Baldy looked modestly abashed. "And who authorized this?"

"Your President, personally, in consultation with my Chancellor." Mark took a deep breath. "I want to be clear here. The planets wait for no man. To have any opportunity at all to be in a position to intervene, we had to leave when we did."

The room's mood had gone from ugly to serious. "So, this is a crap-shoot," Baldy said.

"Yep, and we gotta roll a hard six," Mark replied.

There was a long silence. "What can we do to help?" Baldy asked.

"For now, hang tight. Then help us keep up the fiction that we're in Earth orbit working with the NTSB." Mark smiled. "And you will get front-row seats to whatever happens with *Cardinal*."

Wasilla, Free Alaskan Republic

Ray

The address Huggins had gotten from her contact proved to be well out of town. "Paging Jeff Foxworthy," Ray said as they rattled down yet another dirt and gravel road.

"Who?" Huggins asked.

"Early 21st Century comedian," Ray said. "Still surprisingly funny."

"Brainiac, huh?"

Ray grimaced. "You take one blow-off course on 'history of humor,' and everybody thinks you're an egghead."

"Sorry," Huggins said.

They rolled on in silence for a bit. The heavily wooded terrain was scarred with small irregular valleys. "Lots of erosion," Ray said.

"Not erosion," Huggins said. "Permafrost melt from global warming."

Just then the car came to a stop in front of a sagging and rusted metal gate. Huggins laid on the car's horn.

"So much for surprise," Ray said.

"Around here, surprised people shoot first and ask questions later." She pointed at the gate. "Get the gate, please."

Ray got out, undid the chain, then opened the gate. Huggins drove the car through manually, and waited while Ray closed the gate and climbed back in. They rolled down the rutted gravel road slowly, Huggins periodically hitting the horn.

The road ended at a small lake or large pond. A rambling wooden house that had seen better days was in front of them, flanked by a pair of faded barns. There was an old man standing on the porch of the house, his hands in the pockets of his coveralls.

The two agents got out. "Afternoon," Huggins said.

"You two lost?" the old man asked.

"Not if you're Ted Beale," Huggins said.

"I am," the man replied. "Do I have business with you?"

"I'm afraid so," Huggins replied. She flashed a badge. "Andrea Huggins, ABI." She did not introduce Ray, and as he'd been advised not to advertise who he was, he said nothing.

"I'm a Member of Congress," Beale said.

"So I've heard," Huggins replied. "Which was why I hoped you'd see fit to cooperate."

"Cooperate with what?" Beale said.

"We're investigating a spaceship disappearance," she said, walking up the grassy path to the porch. Ray followed a few steps behind.

"Don't know nothing about spaceships," Beale said.

"Not what I've heard," Huggins said.

"Then you've heard wrong," Beale said.

By this point, Huggins was within arm's reach of the man. "Our American friends are very upset about this."

"They'll get over it," Beale said.

"Before or after the *Nebraska* battlegroup bombs Anchorage?" Huggins asked.

"Americans bluster a lot," Beale said, moving to block Huggins from walking up the steps. "Either get a warrant or get gone."

"I was hoping we could do this easy," Huggins said. She stepped up onto the first step. Beale tried to stop her with a hand and Huggins jerked out a collapsible baton. She hit Beale with it twice almost faster than Ray could see it. He drew his gun as Beale, falling to his knees, struggled with something in his pocket.

"That better be a handkerchief you're going for!" Ray shouted, pointing his pistol at the man.

Beale flashed Ray a look of desperation. "It ain't."

"Easy," Ray said, gesturing with his gun. "Slow and easy."

Beale slowly produced a small revolver, which he sent clattering down the porch. "Your boss—"

"Will either give me a medal or send me to America," Huggins said. "Where's the radio?"

"Red barn," Beale said.

***

The barn had been red at one time, but only a few splotches of paint remained. Inside the wooden structure with its odd—and radio-transparent—fiberglass roof was a five-meter radio dish antenna and a workbench full of computer and electronic gear.

"Don't ask me what all this does," Beale had said. "I just fuel the generator and push buttons when they tell me to."

Huggins had called her boss, and Kratman flew in with half-a-dozen agents. A pair of the agents had taken Beale into his house to clean him up, and a computer agent had tackled the electronics. Ray and Huggins were watching the tech work.

"So much for being a Member of Congress," Ray said, cocking a thumb back toward the house.

Huggins laughed. "In college, I was a Member of Congress. We've got one Congressperson for every thousand people, and my dorm complex was a district."

Further conversation was diverted by the arrival of Kratman from the main house. "Do we believe him?" Kratman asked, referring to Beale's story of being just a caretaker.

"I have no idea," Ray said. "And at the moment, I don't care. We need to keep this system up."

"Keep it up? Why?" Huggins asked.

"If it goes down, the hijackers might get jumpy," Kratman said.

"Besides which, we lose what communications we have with the hostages," Ray said. "And I lose any link to the groundside team."

The computer expert, a short man, walked up to the group. "I'm in," he said.

"Does anybody know you're in?" Kratman asked.

The expert shrugged. "As far as I can tell, no."

"How well can we track messages in and out?" Ray asked.

The expert smiled. "I own that. Nothing goes without my approval."

"Good," Kratman said. "Call the feebs in Kay-Cee. Cut them in on everything. If they're not happy, I'm not happy."

"Yes sir," the man said.

"What about Beale?" Huggins said.

"His heart look good to you?" Kratman asked. "It didn't to me. In fact, he's having a heart attack. Good thing his 'girlfriend'"—he pointed significantly at Huggins—"came up to see him or he'd be dead now. We'll air-evac him to the military hospital while his girlfriend stays here and keeps an eye on things."

"I like you, boss, I really do," Huggins said, "but do you think I'd go for him?"

"Well..." Kratman said.

"Call me his niece," Huggins replied. "And can I go home to get some underwear?"

"We'll send you up some," Kratman said. "As for you, Agent Volk..."

"As soon as KC is happy, I'm gone," Ray said. "Thanks."

"Darn," Huggins said, "here I was hoping you'd stay the night. We could keep each other warm."

Now I know how Mark felt. "Sorry, dear, you're not my type."

"Don't like girls with guns?"

"Don't like girls."

She snapped her fingers. "Damn."

**

It was well after five when Ray got back into Anchorage. He checked into the fortress-like American Consulate and was escorted into a room deep in the bowels of the building. A staffer fiddled with some communications gear that looked like it was designed to be thrown out of a moving train and finally said, "We have a secure link."

"Mark," Ray said, talking to the video image of Mark Nagata. "How's it going?"

"Can I shoot reporters in America?" he asked plaintively.

"Well, not unless you want to go to jail," Ray said with a smile.

"Damn. Because they are a pain in the ass."

"Sorry to hear that."

"So, what do you have for me?"

Ray briefed him on the situation with the barn. When he finished, Mark said, "Okay. For now, we need to keep everything running as it was before."

"Which means the hijackers have comms," Ray said.

"Yeah, but we're using the same system to talk to the hostages." Mark paused for a second, then asked, "What did you say the old man's name was?"

"Beale. Ted Beale."

"We've got a Ted Beale as passenger on the *Cardinal*," Mark said.

"I thought that name sounded familiar," Ray said, feeling a twinge of irritation at himself. *I'm supposed to be the cop here.* "It's not an uncommon name but let me do some digging."

"Please do," Mark said.

"Can I do anything else for you?"

Mark chuckled. "Unless you can magically make reporters disappear, no." His smile faded. "As we get farther away from Earth, these conversations are going to be more one-sided."

"So I've heard."

"Well, stay safe."

Ray nodded. "You're the one gallivanting off into space. I'm here on Terra Firma."

Chapter 14

ValuTrip Cardinal

Kelly

"Does this room feel hot?" Kelly asked.

"I'm fine," Hank replied, talking around a yawn. "The first couple of days on this ship I was freezing my tits off."

That's a shame—they're nice tits for an old woman. Kelly blushed and tried to hide it with her hand. She realized the conversation had moved on.

"They want us to do what?" Hank asked, yawning again.

Old people need sleep, Kelly thought. They were trying to be quiet—it was after lights out and per the guards everybody was supposed to be in their own cabins. "Apparently Captain Montoya kept a radio in his cabin. They want us to get it."

"Captain Octopus was full of surprises," Maria, the former housekeeper, said.

"Who?" Cody asked, rubbing his hand over his bullet-shaped bald head. Kelly could never remember his last name, so he was just "Cody the Cop." He was in the next group of cabins over and had appointed himself in charge of that area's resistance.

"Captain Montoya," Maria said. "He was very good at feeling women up. Hands everywhere."

"I'm surprised he didn't get fired," Hank said.

"He was very good at not getting caught," Maria replied.

"All this is very interesting," Kelly said. *Not that it is but why argue,* she thought, while trying and failing to hide her irritation. "But why do they want us to get a radio and how do we get it?" *And remind me again why the hell I'm having this conversation instead of keeping my damn head down?*

"Why is simple," Hank said, gesturing vaguely in the air. "There's a ship chasing after us, and they want to get more information about what's going on here."

"We've been hijacked," Maria said. "What more do they need to know?"

"I did some time on SWAT," Cody said. "In a hostage situation, more information is always better."

Don't know what a swat is but you don't have to be a supercop to know more intel is better.

"Why is not important," Hank said. "They ask, we do. Question is how?"

"Otarski," Maria said after an uncomfortably long pause.

"Who?" Kelly asked.

"Steve Otarski," Maria said. "Director of Hotel Operations. The pirates are letting him go into crew quarters to use a computer."

"How generous of them," Cody said sarcastically.

"Probably tracking water and air recycling," Kelly said. Since the takeover, crew and passengers had been divided into a number of work details. *Probably in part to keep us distracted.*

"And how would you know, little girl?" Cody asked.

"Martian, remember?" Kelly said, bristling at the jib. "Air isn't free on Mars."

Cody turned and looked at Hank. "I've been meaning to talk to you about that. We're relying an awful lot on kids like her."

"I'm nine-and-a-half, mister," Kelly said, feeling heat in her face. *Am I going to have this conversation with every damn Earthling I meet?*

"What's that in *real* years?" Cody asked.

"Seventeen," Maria said.

"And you know this how?" Cody asked.

"I also bartend," Maria said. "I have to calculate the legal drinking age."

"Whatever," Cody said. "She's a kid."

"She's gotten military training," Hank said. "Which is more than ninety percent of the people on this boat can say. Including you, SWAT-man." Hank yawned again. "Besides, resistance groups historically relied a lot on kids. Read your history of the 20th and 21st centuries."

"What kind of 'military training' did she get?" Cody asked.

"Basic training in the Franklyn State Militia," Kelly said. "I also completed scout-sniper school."

"Which would be helpful if you had a sniper rifle," Cody said.

"We covered unarmed combat. That's the 'scout' part of training."

"All the Martian 'kids' have militia training," Hank said, a sigh in her voice. "American kids go to summer camp to learn how to row canoes. Martian kids go to boot camp and learn how to shoot people. And I had seventeen-year-olds on my ship."

Not every Martian kid went to boot, Kelly thought. Her cousin Ryan, for example—he hadn't gone, at least not yet. But most did.

"Look," Kelly said, "I didn't come on this trip to be GI Jane. But we all got handed a shit sandwich. So, how to we get hold of Mister O?"

Hank and Cody glanced at the dead phone hardwired to the cabin wall. Kelly remembered the first time she'd seen a hardwired phone—it had been when she'd gone with her parents to Disney Mars North and they'd stayed at the hotel. It made sense—people would want to talk to the occupants of the room, not to a specific person.

"We need to get those phones up," Hank said.

No shit, Commander America.

"I've seen the hijackers use phones," Cody said.

"Wireless units," Hank said. "Which they probably brought with."

"No," Maria insisted, "wired units." She pointed at the unit on the wall. "I was in the freezer today. Phone rang, guard answered it. Then he made a call out."

"So, some phones work but others don't," Cody said. "Probably by location."

"No," Kelly said. "The phone in the fan room on this deck worked."

"So?" Cody asked.

"So," Kelly replied. "It can't be by location."

"Fuck this," Hank said. She picked up the handset, which was not wired into anything. "I got a dial tone."

"Try to dial," Cody said.

She did. "Nothing," she said, holding the phone out.

"Not nothing," Maria said. There was a voice saying, 'your call cannot be completed as dialed.' "Something."

"Access code," Cody said.

"So?" Hank said.

"So, we try all of them."

"That could be millions of numbers," Kelly said.

"Not really," Cody replied. "I happen to be familiar with phone systems from my SWAT days. Ninety-nine percent of access codes are three digits or less." He waved his hands. "After all, you have to dial it every time you make a call."

***

It was tedious as fuck, but they tried every key combination they could think off. Much later than even Kelly wanted, by brute force, they found the code. If you dialed 2-5-3, you got a triple beep. After the triple beep, you could dial normally.

"It's too late to call," Hank said. She pointed at the time display on the cabin's video monitor. "We'll try tomorrow."

***

"We got him," Cody said to Kelly as she was finishing dinner.

"Who?"

"Otarski," he replied. "We're making our play now. Roll with it."

Kelly walked her tray up to the return station and dumped the bones from her baked-chicken dinner into the foul-smelling organic trash receptacle. Before the hijacking, the wheeled container had been kept in a back room and a crewmember loaded it. The woman behind her wondered aloud why it made such a difference. "Composting," Kelly said over her shoulder.

"She'll do," a man in a prison uniform with a clipboard said.

"You sure?" the guard next to him asked. Kelly involuntarily shuddered. The guard was a giant of a man with green hair—the same guy who had caught her when she had faked being left behind in laundry.

"Positive, Bruno," the prisoner, pale, balding and gray, said.

"Who's Bruno?" the guard asked.

"Oh for fuck's sake," the prisoner said. "How many two-meter-tall giants with green hair are running around on this ship?"

The guard thought for a minute. "You're right," he said, removing his full-face mask and using it to wipe sweat off his pale face. He sighed deeply. "Much better."

For a second, Kelly felt sympathy for him. *Even creeps get hot, and apparently nobody's taking care of the A/C on this ship.*

"You're Kelly Rack, right?" the prisoner asked.

"Yes," Kelly replied.

"She's a Martian, took ecology electives in high school," the prisoner said. "If I can't have O'Brian, she'll do."

"I told you about crew," Bruno replied distractedly. He was holding the tail of his stab-proof vest out away from his waist and trying to fan some air up through it.

"And I understand that," the prisoner said. "But I need somebody who understands enough about basic life support to collect the data."

Bruno turned and looked at Kelly. "What's an acceptable level of atmospheric CO_2?"

"For non-agricultural usage, under six hundred parts per million. Four hundred fifty is Earth-standard, and most people shoot for four hundred."

Bruno consulted a piece of paper then asked, "For agricultural use?"

"The book answer is one thousand parts per million. I've seen growhouses up to fifteen hundred. Depends on the type of plants and stage of growth."

"Why not higher than fifteen hundred?" the prisoner asked.

"I'm told it generally doesn't help the plants and people start to get tired and irritable at that level."

"Okay," Bruno said. He smiled, which made Kelly feel very nervous. "I guess she's not an idiot." He tapped the other prisoner lightly with his baton. "Otarski here says he needs a rover to check CO2 levels. Still not sure why."

"Ever hear of the wreck of the *River of Stars*?" Otarski, asked.

"No," Bruno said.

"I have," Kelly said. *Vaguely*, she mentally added.

"And?" Bruno asked.

"They weren't watching CO2 levels," Kelly said. "They died." *And that's the sum total of my knowledge, so don't ask me any more questions.*

"That's why we had O'Brian out," Otarski said.

Bruno tapped Kelly lightly with his baton. "When did all of this go down?"

"Damned if I know," Kelly said truthfully. "But my cousin Lewis damn near died from CO2 poisoning a couple of years back. His parents got him just in time."

Bruno sighed, a bit theatrically. "Fine. I'm convinced." He pressed a bit harder with his baton. "You fuck up, Little Miss Muppet, and I'll fuck *you* up. We clear?"

"Very, sir." She looked at Otarski. "When do I start?"

"Now."

The three of them went to a little cubbyhole off the kitchen, obviously intended to be an office for the cooks. Otarski provided Kelly a map for the ship, and Bruno handed her a small metal thing on a string like a necklace. He put it on for her. "Since those outfits don't have pockets."

They did but this is not the time to point that out. She grabbed the metal thing. "What's this?" Kelly asked.

"A key," Otarski answered.

"For what?" Kelly asked.

"We've turned off the access bands," Bruno said. He ran a hand thru her hair. "This will open some of the doors you need to do your job." He took his hand back. "I want this back," he said. To Otarski, he said, "Get her up to speed." He cocked a thumb. "I'm going to the john."

I swear, if he touches me, I'm going to fuck him up and if I survive I'm going to fuck Hank up. When he was gone, Kelly carefully said, "Did you actually have a guy manually checking CO_2 detectors?"

"Yes," Otarski said. "But it was mostly for training—you really understand a system if you go over it hand-over-hand. Your cousin Lewis really have a CO_2 emergency?"

"Yes, actually, but it was a malfunctioning spacesuit, not a fixed hab." She pointed at the map. "Any CO_2 sensor near the captain's cabin?"

"No," Otarski said. "But there's one in the crew office, here." Otarski pointed at the chart. "In the office, there's also a machine the hijackers brought aboard to copy physical keys. Make a copy of that, give the original to Bruno, and go fetch the radio tonight."

"Got it," Kelly said, wondering how one copied a physical key.

Chapter 15

ValuTrip Cardinal

Victoria

Victoria finished her last song and smiled. *It's good to be the boss. I can indulge my hobby and run the show.*

The piano in the former first-class lounge was, of course, electronic, and in the right mode could replicate a symphony. Otarski, that ignorant jackass, had insisted she only play 'cool and calming' songs in the piano mode. She grimaced at the thought of her former boss. Well, soon enough he'd be trying to breathe vacuum.

"What was that song, boss?" Ted Beale asked, standing to her right. She waved him to a chair at the built-in bar around the piano.

"'Where The Streets Have No Name,'" Victoria replied.

"Never heard of it," he said. "It's nice, though."

"You wouldn't have heard of it," she replied. "That is, unless you took a degree in music history. My Master's thesis was on 20th century popular music. Very popular in its day." She favored him with a look. "I don't think you came over here to talk music history."

"No, ma'am. I think we have a problem."

"I'm all ears."

"Supposedly, my dad had a heart attack."

"I'm sorry," she said, wondering what that had to do with her.

"Supposedly," Ted said. "But his heart was perfectly fine a year ago. At any rate, he's no longer manning our ground relay station in Alaska."

That was a problem. "Who is?"

"His niece. Except he doesn't have a niece."

Shit. "We know who this niece really is?"

"No."

"Can we have somebody get hold of your dad? I mean, he could actually be sick."

"Dad's supposedly at Elmendorf-Freedom Hospital."

"Which means?"

"That's the military hospital in Alaska," Ted said. "Which isn't entirely unusual—a lot of civilians end up there."

"But on the other hand," Victoria said. "If he was taken there, he could easily be sitting in the Free Republic's brig, which I assume is on the base."

"That's what's got me worried," Ted said.

Me too. "How certain are you?"

"The local sheriff and I go way back. She emailed me."

"The sheriff know about us?"

"No. And if she did, she wouldn't be blabbing—most of her income is from bribes to ignore criminals."

Alaska was such a wonderful place. "Have you told anybody else?"

"No."

"Good. Don't. This email—going to a ship account?"

"No. I've got it encrypting and auto-forwarding."

"So, if somebody's listening to our comms, they don't know that we know we're being monitored."

Ted shrugged. "I would guess so."

"Let's hope so. For now, keep everything normal."

Ted stomped off to do whatever he did when he wasn't on watch.

There is a way to test if the Americans are monitoring our communications. I'll send them a message they won't be able to resist responding to.

***

"That ought to do it," she said to her terminal in what had been Hank Solis' cabin but was now hers. She'd sent two messages—one to the people who'd ventilated the Malans for her, telling them good work and offering them another job, and another to the person at Martian Customs and Immigration who'd gotten her people and weapons on the ship. If the cops were eavesdropping, they'd move on one, the other or both of them. Her other resources would see it and contact her.

Kelly

Kelly found it more than a little spooky wandering around the ship. She'd been in the public areas on the promenade deck, so they were familiar, but now empty of people. Somebody had turned many of the lights off, or, not turned them on, so they were full of shadows. She walked by one of the bars. Glasses were stacked on one corner, apparently still waiting to be put away.

Stan the Maintenance Man had said the goons had shut off the access bands by the simple expedient of killing both primary and secondary sources of power to the main controllers. Bruno, Giant of the Green Hair, was one of the ship's electricians and obviously knew how to do that. Whoever designed the system assumed that loss of power equaled major emergency and so not only had normally closed security doors defaulted to locked but several fire and pressure doors had also automatically closed. The hijackers had then manually locked a number of those doors.

"Which is just peachy," Kelly said. Her rounds had taken her to the main lobby. There was a door just to one side of the customer service counter. In normal times, the band reader next to the handle would show a red light. It did not, of course. Kelly fished out her metal key. She'd seen keys used in historical videos, but never actually used one herself. It took her several tries to figure out which way to insert the key, and then she had to guess which way to turn it. "Finally," she said when she got it open. She wiped sweat off her brow.

The door opened to a narrow corridor. Unlike the fashionable carpet and wallpaper, the corridor was very industrial—painted metal walls and metal floor. The corridor was also dark, illuminated only by what light sneaked in past her from the lobby. She took a deep breath and stepped in. Overhead lights came on, presumably triggered by a motion sensor. She headed down the corridor.

The office had a service counter opening into a passageway. A metal security gate closed off the counter and was locked down, allowing light from the passageway to spill into the office through the open grating. Inside were several tiny built-in workstations—their surfaces barely a meter square—the occasional bric-a-brac sitting there waiting for its owner to return. At the desk closest to her, somebody had taped a picture on the side of the workstation, which was cycling through several faces, presumably family members. To the side of the counter, there was a personnel door, metal as opposed to the usual fiberglass. It had been forced open with a crowbar, and now wouldn't close.

She stepped inside, but unlike the hallway, no lights came on. Just inside the door there was a metal cabinet bolted to the wall. The door had also been pried open, damaging the electronic lock in the process. There were a dozen small metal hooks inside the cabinet which looked like they would have been ideal for holding the metal key she had. Taped to the inside of the cabinet was a piece of paper— faded and tattered at one corner—listing which numbered hook corresponded to which security zone.

"What are you looking for?" Bruno asked.

Kelly jumped back. "Sorry, didn't hear you."

"I know," Bruno said with a smile. The smile faded. "What are you looking for?"

"Light switch. So, I can find the sensor."

"By the other door."

Kelly followed his eyes. There was a second door into the room on the other side of the counter. She walked over there, noticing as she did the very old-looking and out-of-place mechanical device sitting on the counter. There was a grinding wheel on one end of the thing. Must be the key copier.

She found the light switch and turned it on. "Much better. So, if I were a sensor, where would I be?"

He grunted, then pointed into the room. "Probably in the back."

"Thanks," Kelly replied. She found a wall-mounted unit with an integral lighted display. She took her reading, logged it on her clipboard (on paper!) and went to the front of the office. "So, what happened here?"

"What do you mean?" Bruno asked.

"Door busted, the cabinet behind the door busted."

"We needed stuff, so we took it. Since you're here, come with me," he said.

She followed him down the corridor, a sense of dread and revulsion washing over her. They went farther down the utilitarian corridor until they arrived at another metal door which had been busted open. A sign on the door declared it to be 'duty-free.'

"What's duty-free?" Kelly asked.

"Passengers were able to buy stuff on Mars and ship it back to Earth without paying import taxes," Bruno said. He opened the door and held it open for her. "Go on in."

"Why?" Kelly asked, her tongue thick.

"Shopping expedition," he said with a smile.

She stepped inside, followed by Bruno. The room was lined with shelves stacked with individual packages in clear plastic. Some were sealed, others had been cut open. A few empty plastic bags were littered on the floor. "It's been a bit picked through," Bruno said sadly. "But a lot of good stuff is still here. You like wine? Whiskey? Pick what you want."

"I, I don't..."

He put his giant hand on her shoulder. She resisted the urge to jerk away. "You sure?"

"Yes, sir."

He patted her shoulder, surprisingly gently. "Well, maybe tomorrow night. Finish your rounds and stop by cabin 4-104. You can give me the key back." He leaned over and whispered into her ear. "We can be good friends, you and me. Where we're going, you're going to want a friend."

"We're going to Earth!" Kelly blurted out.

He chuckled, the sound coming from deep in his throat. "That's what you've been told."

"Where are we going?" she asked, turning to face him.

He touched her nose. "Someplace warm. You'll see. And trust me, you'll really want a friend." He smiled. "Now, go finish your job and bring the key back to 4-104. Got it?"

Kelly nodded, not sure she could trust herself to speak.

***

"You two should probably keep your voices down," Maria said as she was lying in the bed. Judging by the fact that she had her sheet up around her neck and Hank's shirt was wrinkled, the two of them had not been sleeping.

"Okay," Hank said to Maria. To Kelly, she said, "If he offers you another shot at the booze locker, take him up on it."

"What part of 'he wants to get me pregnant' are you not getting?" Kelly asked.

"I'm getting all of it. I'm just saying that you can use that." Hank smirked. "Men have two heads and only enough blood to use one of them at a time."

"I would have thought that fat lip I gave you would have made it clear that I don't want to have sex with him."

"*I* don't want you to have sex with him," she said with a note of exasperation. "I want you to fuck him over. We all are going to have to do things we don't want to do."

So far, 'we all' doesn't seem to include you, Commander America.

"What I'm curious about," Maria said, squirming in bed and revealing that she was not wearing a shirt, "is where *are* we going?"

"He didn't say," Kelly said.

"Well," Hank replied, "we need to get him in a talkative mood, and fucking ask him."

"I. Do. Not. Want. To. Be. Fucked. By. Him."

"Maria!" Hank said.

"Damn it, woman," Maria said with some heat, "I am not your translator!" She glared at Hank. "Although apparently I am." To Kelly, she said, "You're going to make a visit to sickbay and talk to a friend of mine."

"I took a long-term birth control pill before I left."

"Good. They're going to give you something for Bruno."

"To kill him?"

"I hope not," Maria said. "But they will explain it better than I will."

Hank frowned. "Now that that's settled, we still need those damn keys, so get hopping." She glanced down at Maria and smiled, then back up at Kelly. "Anything else?"

Kelly didn't trust herself to speak so she got up and exited through the maintenance tunnel.

Chapter 16

The 30th Space Wing (aka Oklahoma Task Force), en-route to Mercury

Mark

Mark looked at the American brigadier and took a deep breath. *If I were in her shoes, I'd be every bit as frustrated too.* They were standing in her flag plot, which was just a corner of the ship's Combat Information Center—or CIC—looking at one of the tactical displays.

On the one hand, she commanded a decent task force. The USSF's 30th Space Wing consisted of two heavy ships the Americans called battleships, the *Oklahoma* and *Kentucky*, two light American ships designated cruisers, *Boston* and *Atlanta*, and three American destroyers. Nagata had the Martian heavy frigate *Cydonia*—equal to the American battleships—trailing *Cardinal,* and three Martian destroyers detached from First Fleet's Force E. It was a sizeable force, although not quite enough to defeat the entire Mercurian fleet.

On the other hand, it might just be a collection of ships glaring impotently at the Cardinal.

"Non-compliant boardings of ships underway are the hardest things we do," Mark said.

"Captain, please don't patronize me," she replied.

"I'm sorry, ma'am," Mark replied. "That wasn't my intention."

Brigadier General Nicola Morehouse favored Mark with a glare. Her face, angular, light-brown and topped with short gray curls, slowly softened. "We've been at this for a while," she finally said. "Tempers will flare up."

It didn't help that the *Oklahoma*, her flagship, was having air conditioning problems. The flag plot was normally cool, even with the half-a-dozen people standing around a small 3-D tactical display. But only half the ship's A/C units working, now everywhere was warm and flag plot was downright hot. They were heading sunward, and temperatures would only rise.

"The problem is the hostages," said Lieutenant Colonel Thomas Wu. He was the junior officer in the room, although physically the most imposing, and was commanding the Delta Force boarding party.

The problem was *the hostages,* Mark thought. Assuming that the ship was locked down, it would take time to force open the airlocks, and once they started to do that, if not sooner, the pirates would be alerted. And the easiest way to control the hostages was to lock down the ship. It would take more time for the boarding party to get from the airlocks to the passenger areas, time which could be increased by the pirates simply shutting pressure-tight doors. All this time would give the pirates ample opportunity to kill hostages.

Mark looked at a clock on the wall. "Commander Solis should have checked in with the *Cydonia* two hours ago," he said. "If they were able to get the radio."

Morehouse looked up from the tactical display, which was showing a schematic of *Cardinal.* "Where on the ship are they calling from?"

Wu pointed to an area on the schematic. "They need to access the antenna junction room here on Deck Five."

"And they are being kept on Deck One?" Morehouse asked.

"Yes, ma'am," Wu replied.

"So, they can move around the ship without being seen?"

"Somewhat," Wu replied. "Not every area is covered by security cameras or alarms."

Morehouse looked at the schematic again. "Okay. The problem is that the pirates in the pilothouse can lock down doors and airlocks, forcing us to cut our way in. Yes?" Mark and Wu nodded affirmatively. "But these doors can be opened locally?"

"Some of them," Mark said.

"And all of them can be bypassed locally from the right location," Morehouse stated.

"Presumably," Mark answered. "We can validate that on the *Bluejay*." He looked at Morehouse. "If you're thinking what I'm thinking you are, Solis is not going to like it."

"She'll like being dead or a slave on Mercury even less," Morehouse replied. "What's the time delay to *Cydonia*?"

"Nine minutes," Mark replied.

"We need to draft something and get the hostages up to speed," Morehouse said. She sighed heavily. "Assuming they got the radio, which looks increasingly doubtful."

ValuTrip Cardinal

Kelly

"I am not fucking him," Kelly said. *How many times do I need to say this?*

"Don't want you to," Maria replied. They were on-shift in the laundry, standing next to a very industrial-looking and surprisingly noisy clothes dryer. "Just want you to think you want to fuck him."

"And when he realizes he's not getting any nookie, then what?"

"He won't."

"Oh?"

"So, here's the plan." Maria glanced over her shoulder. The guard was not paying them any special attention. "Go to sickbay. Tell them you're having your period and need some meds." Maria leaned in. "Then, on your roving shift..."

***

As expected, Bruno the Green-haired Creep showed up during her rounds, this time as she was exiting one of the grow-houses. "Hey, Sunshine," he said. "Have you done some thinking about my offer?"

The son-of-a-bitch really thinks he can flash me a smile and my panties are going to melt. "Yes," she replied, not having to fake the tremor in her voice. "I will need a friend." She stepped closer to him, willing herself not to vomit. "But I have a confession. I've never been...well...with a man."

The dumb lug fell for it. "That's okay," he replied. "I'll be gentle."

"Thanks." She leaned into him. "Can we stop at the duty room? Pick up a bottle of something."

"Whatever you like, dear."

"You pick. I don't drink." *Well, only since I got hijacked by fuckers like you I don't.*

"I'm not much of a drinker," he said.

"Well," Kelly said, rubbing the back of his hand with hers. "I just told a little fib there. I have had an occasional drink. I'm sure we can find something."

"Sounds like a plan."

***

Kelly had never had Port, but she'd heard it was sweet, and there was a bottle of Traskers Super Aged—supposedly expensive stuff—sitting on the shelf in a ripped-open bag. She figured if she was going to risk getting raped by Bruno she might as well try the good stuff. They had retired to his cabin in what was formerly the first-class section. They ran into another female prisoner in the hallway, who gave her a knowing smile and a nod. *Yeah, and if this goes really sideways, I'll be branded a collaborator.*

"Is this supposed to be cold?" Bruno asked when they got inside.

"I don't think so," Kelly replied. "Least, never see it over ice on videos. Can I use your toilet?"

"Sure." He leered. "Maybe leave your clothes in there."

Fuck you very much. Kelly went in and closed the door. She actually did have to use the facilities—nerves—but that only took a minute. When she was done, she took a deep breath, peeled down to her panties and palmed the packet

Jay Jay had given her. They'd told her the white powder was a pair of ground-up sleeping pills and was enough to knock out a horse. Kelly had never actually seen a horse but had heard they were big. "Let's hope this is enough."

First class cabins came with a built-in couch and a bed, which in this cabin hadn't been made in days. When she came out Bruno was sitting on the couch, his shirt off, revealing quite a bit of greenish chest hair. "I..." Kelly said, covering her mouth. She realized she'd left the key on and it was dangling between her breasts.

"Yeah," Bruno replied, glancing down. "One of my grandparents got gen-modded. I inherited it."

"Is it, all the way?"

"You'll find out," he said in what he surely thought was a suave tone.

Unfortunately, I will. "The wine?"

"Behind you."

Kelly turned around to the tiny sink, barely big enough to wash your hands in, and the equally tiny counter. The bottle was there, opened, and two juice glasses. She dumped the powder into one glass then poured the Port.

"Those are not the panties we issued," Bruno said.

"They didn't completely clear out my cabin," she said over her shoulder. She walked to Bruno with the drinks and handed him the glass with the powder in it. "Here you go."

He took a healthy sip. "Kind of sweet."

She took a more moderate sip of her drink. "Yeah." *So now what the fuck do I do?*

"You don't have to be nervous."

"If you say so." She clicked his glass with hers. "Toast."

He took another healthy swallow, then looked at the glass contemplatively. "Got a bit of a kick to it."

"Yeah," Kelly said, truthfully. She climbed on his lap and his free hand wrapped itself around her bare breast.

"Nice," he said, his voice starting to slur. *Thank God Jay Jay gave me something that works quick.*

She clicked her glass to his. "Tell me something," she said, faking a sip of her Port. "Why is it so damn hot on this boat?"

"Language," he said, putting a finger on her lips. *At least he's not pawing my breasts.*

"It's hot because of language?"

"No, it's hot because we're inside Earth's orbit."

"We going to Venus?"

"Mercury." He downed the rest of his drink. "Let's get those panties off."

Let's not. She stood up and worked on his belt buckle. He attempted to assist, but mostly didn't hinder, her efforts to get his pants off. *Son of a bitch, it's green all the way down.*

"Bed," he said, his pants around his knees. Then his legs gave out. Kelly pushed him onto the bed with an effort.

"Sleep well, Mister Green," she said.

***

"You got the keys?" Hank said, rubbing sleep from her eyes.

Kelly held up a dozen pieces of metal. It had taken her a bit to figure out how to work the machine, and she was concerned that the noise would attract attention, but it hadn't.

"Good. Now get back up there."

"What?"

"He needs to wake up next to you," Maria said, walking up behind Hank and wrapping an arm around the other woman's bare stomach. "And you need to tell him what an impressive hunk of burning manhood he is."

"And what if he wants an encore?" Kelly asked, feeling a bit ill.

"You'll figure something out," Maria said.

"And I'm supposed to be the asshole!" Hank said, punching Maria in the shoulder. To Kelly, she said, "Be sick to your stomach. After all, you're not a drinker."

Maria chuckled at that and said to Hank, "Come to bed. We go tomorrow for the radio."

***

Kelly jerked awake with a start. Some woman in a dress with a pistol in a shoulder holster was yelling for Bruno.

"What time is it?" Kelly blurted out. She'd sworn she'd set the cabin's alarm to be up early. She was getting used to the gravity, but still found herself sleeping more.

"Time for Bruno to be on goddamned watch!" the woman said. "Where is he?"

"I don't know!" It wasn't like there was any place big enough to hide him. Then the toilet flushed. *That answers that.*

"What's that key?" the gunwoman asked.

Kelly looked down at the key. "Mister, er Mister Bruno gave it to me." From the surprised look on the woman's face, that was not supposed to happen. *Oh fuck.*

Bruno walked out, bare-assed and proud of it. The gunwoman gave him a glare while fighting back a smile. *Apparently, she didn't know his hair was green all the way down either.*

"You rang, Your Excellency?" Bruno asked.

"Your Grace," the woman corrected. "And what in the fuck are you doing?" she barked. "Your watch started half-an-hour ago!"

He grinned and winked at Kelly. "Isn't it obvious?"

"What's obvious is you're not on watch!"

"Hey! You had a girlfriend!"

"You mean the bitch I slapped around and choked out?"

So that's how Hank got those bruises. Kelly took a deep breath. *He's the boss, I'm just a girl he grabbed up. Keep calm and act dumb.*

The gunwoman looked at Kelly. "Why, Miss Sweet Boobs, did Guard number," she looked at Bruno.

"Thirty-seven," he said, stepping around the woman to grab his pants.

"Why did Guard number thirty-seven give you a key?"

"Well, Your Grace," Kelly said, not having to fake being scared. "Mister...Bruno"—she looked at Bruno—"sorry, sir, don't know your last name...he pulled me out of the food line."

"She's checking CO2 levels," Bruno said. That shit-eating grin. "Among other things."

"Mister Bruno suggested I might want a friend," Kelly added. *And this friend would feel a hell of a lot more comfortable if I were anywhere other than here.* The alarm started to beep and Kelly went to shut it off. *I must have set it for the wrong time.*

"Friends are okay, I guess," the gunwoman said, "but tell me about this CO2 level thing?"

Kelly waved toward the couch. "They gave me a clipboard and told me to check CO2 levels."

"Fine," the gunwoman said, holding up a hand. "Would you mind putting on some damn clothes?"

"They're in the toilet, Your Grace."

The woman waved in that direction. "Is that a Martian accent I hear?"

"Yes, Your Grace."

"You got a name?"

"Kelly Rack, Your Grace."

"Good. Now go get dressed!"

Kelly got out of the bed as quickly as she could and into the toilet. She heard the woman grilling Bruno about the 'CO2 bullshit.'

***

Bruno had said that the 'CO2 patrol' had been Otarski's idea. So now Kelly, Otarski, and Bruno were in the First-Class lounge, standing in a row at one end of the small dance floor. Commander Zero was there, and several off-duty guards. The gunwoman sat down at the piano.

"What's up, Victoria?" Zero asked.

"What's up is we're going to figure out why we got a goddamned prisoner wandering around with a Level One key," the woman, Victoria, replied.

"Oh," Zero said. "Not what I got from your initial call."

"And what did you get from my initial call?"

"That Saint Bruno here had fallen in love and overslept."

"Well, that too," Victoria replied. "Mike, I expect more out of you. People are getting sloppy." She waved her arms around. "Too many of your guards have found themselves benefriends."

"Where we're going—"

"Not now," Victoria cut in. "And we're not where we're going yet, are we?"

"No, ma'am, we're not." Zero wiped sweat off his brow. He glanced at a vent in the ceiling. "And it's just going to get hotter."

"That it is," Victoria said. Clearly, she was in charge, not Zero. Victoria looked at Kelly and the others. "Let's start at the beginning. Whose brilliant idea was it to put a prisoner on this make-work detail?"

Bruno, sweating even more than usual given the heat, pointed at Otarski. "His. He even asked for a crewmember."

"No," Otarski said. "Bruno asked me what O'Brian did and I told him. We got talking about the *River of Stars.*"

"I'm familiar with that wreck," Victoria said. "They had a lot of problems—CO_2 levels were just one."

"Well, if you look at it, we're in a similar situation. When was the last time somebody was in the furniture shop, for example?" Otarski said. A pale and tired-looking man, sitting slumped at a table behind her, grunted.

"You want to say something, Mr. Beale?" Victoria said.

"Usually, all manned spaces get inspected at least daily," the grunting man replied.

"Go on," Victoria said, gesturing at Otarski.

"So anyway, Bruno said he didn't want a crew member wandering around. I said you needed somebody who knew what they were looking at and suggested a Martian." Otarski gestured at the girl. "I'm not sure how Kelly's name came up, but we pulled her out and put her on it."

Victoria looked at Kelly. "What's your story?"

She took a deep breath. *Stick to the story.* "Those two pulled me out of food-line and gave me a clipboard," she replied, pointing at the others. "I did what the man with the gun told me to do, Your Grace."

"And whose idea was it to become Bruno's fuckbuddy?"

Most assuredly not mine, Piano-Lady with Gun. "He said he'd be a friend and that I needed a friend."

"Oh, you'll have more friends than you can shake a stick at, little girl, with an ass like that." Zero said. This earned him a glare from Victoria at the piano.

"And you, Bruno?" Victoria asked.

"It was Otarski's idea!" He looked bashful. "I mean the CO2 thing. As far as the cabin..."

"I get the picture," Victoria said, holding up a hand. She looked around. "Where's Sky?"

"Here," a woman called from the back. "What can I do for you?"

"Need to hear what you've seen on your cameras."

Oh shit. Was there a camera in the office? Did she see me copying keys? Kelly felt weak at the knees, and it wasn't because of the heat.

"You rang?" A woman, presumably Sky, sauntered up, a fried chicken leg in her hand. She was white with greasy hair and a swivel-chair spread.

"You could use a shower," Zero said to her, wrinkling his nose.

"If I get time before Jose has to go on shift, I will," she replied.

"So," Victoria said to Sky. "Did you see this prisoner wandering around the ship?"

"I did," she said, talking around a bite of chicken.

Just how much can you see, Sky?

"And you didn't call it in?" Zero asked.

"Call what in?" she replied. "I saw one of us directing a prisoner to do work. How was I to know it wasn't approved?"

"Sky," Victoria asked, "did you pull the access logs?"

"Of what?"

"Of the doors?"

"No point," Sky said.

"What do you mean, no point?"

"I mean, it won't tell us anything," Sky said. She pulled out a key from her pocket. "We dropped the access band system. We're using keys. The system has no way of knowing which key was used for which door."

Well, that's a useful bit of news. Kelly looked around. *Keep arguing among yourselves. Don't look at the little prisoner.*

"So, we have no idea where this girl was," Zero said.

"Nope," Sky said. "We done?"

"Yeah," Victoria said. She turned and looked at Zero. "Step into my office please." The two of them went to a booth in the back, joined by the guy she'd called Beale.

Victoria

"Let's get to it," Victoria said.

"You don't seriously believe Otarski?" Beale asked.

"If bullshit were music, he'd be a brass band," Victoria replied. "But damned if I can figure out what his angle would be."

"Get to the armory?" Beale asked.

"We cleaned that out days ago," Victoria said. The gun Victoria was carrying in her shoulder holster had come from there. She looked at Mike. "You don't seem concerned."

"The only thing I'm concerned about is Bruno missing a watch because he got laid," he replied with a shrug.

"Well, we can fix that," Victoria replied. "Have the Martian show Bruno what to look at and then get her off that detail. And tell him to keep his dick in his pants."

"Copy that," Mike said.

"Good. Now, move out."

It is so hard to find good help. The group stepped away. *I wonder what other fuckery's going around that I don't know about.* She gritted her teeth. *I guess I'll have to make some inspection rounds.*

Kelly

"Were you scared?" Spider asked.

Kelly's stomach heaved but nothing came out. She'd stayed more-or-less calm during the yelling match in the lounge. The shakes had hit after they left. She took a sip of water from the cup Spider handed her. "Shitless. Scared shitless," she said, glad that privacy laws meant no cameras in cabins.

Spider was half-holding her, half-hugging her as she knelt on the floor in the cabin's tiny bathroom. She tried to shrug him off, but it came off as a shiver.

"Maybe I should lay down," Kelly said.

"You sure you're done?"

Not really. "Yes."

Spider helped her to her feet and into the main cabin, where Hank was sitting impatiently. She crashed into the bottom bunk as Spider went back into the bathroom.

"You owe me a report, soldier," Hank said.

"Eat shit and die, Commander Fucking America," Kelly replied.

Hank smirked. "That's better than puking, I guess." Spider returned and placed a wet cloth on her forehead. Kelly summarized her meeting with the Head Pirate, ending with, "I thought the bitch was going to kill me."

"You're sure she was in charge?" Hank asked. "I mean, the Piano Lady?"

"Yes, fucking goddamn it," Kelly said, tiredly. "The bitch was in charge, and was treating the piano like it was her damned throne!" She smirked. "Oh, and she sends her regards. Maybe you should see if she needs you to keep her bed warm."

"That's not going to happen," Hank said.

Of course not. "Look, I got your goddamned keys, Bruno thinks he's a superstud, and I didn't have to suck anybody's dick for it or get my brains sprayed across a bulkhead. Say thank you and fuck off, please."

Several emotions played across Hank's face, anger among them. Concern ended up the winner. "I'm sorry. I really am. I've asked a lot from you, but nothing you couldn't handle." Hank stood up. "Like you said, we all got handed a shit sandwich and have to take a big bite of it." The woman left the room.

"Thank God she's gone," Kelly said.

"She's trying," Spider said.

Is she? Kelly glared at him. *He needs to believe.* She felt her anger fade. "I know, damn it. Doesn't make it any easier."

"You hungry?" Spider asked.

"No," Kelly said, and the orders to assemble for evening meal were being played on the announcing system.

"I'll see if I can bring you something," Spider said. "For later."

"I doubt I'll want anything."

***

Kelly woke with a start. "What time is it?"

"1935 hours," Spider said. "You were asleep when I got back, so I left you."

"Now I could eat," Kelly said, wishing she'd gone to dinner.

"Figured you would," Spider said, rolling out of the top bunk. "I smuggled in some food." He produced a peanut-butter and jelly sandwich and a ship-grown apple.

"Hot damn," Kelly said. "You didn't have to do this."

Spider shrugged. "We're a team, remember?"

Kelly ate both ravenously, washed down with tap water.

"All I could smuggle," he said when she finished. "Well, almost." He smiled and produced two pocket-sized bottles of booze—the kind that was stocked in hotel room mini-bars. "No point in tunnel-ratting if you don't get some cheese."

"You risked your life for booze?" Kelly asked.

Spider shrugged. "Man does not live on bread alone."

"We should split one," Kelly said. "After we get back from tonight's run for the radio."

"Split my ass," Spider said. "But yes, business then pleasure."

***

"Not very impressive, is it?" Kelly said.

"Looks shockingly like the unit we had in the captain's lifeboat on my old ship," Hank replied. She knelt down and opened the small, suitcase-sized plastic case. The radio was built in, and the top of the case had laminated instruction cards. With Stan the Maintenance Man's help, they made the connection to the directional antenna.

"We sure they can't hear us when we go out?" Hank asked.

Stanley shrugged. "I'm a plumber, not a radio tech. But that's a directional antenna facing aft, so it makes sense to me."

Pretty fucking slim chances, Kelly thought. But they had posted lookouts at both approaches to the room, so if somebody came running, they had a chance to scatter. "No names," Kelly said. "In case they hear."

"I thought of that," Hank said dryly. She turned on the unit, then picked up the handset. "Fox Charlie, this is Victor Charlie. Do you read? Over."

Fox Charlie, the Martian ship, was supposedly five light-seconds behind them, so it would take ten seconds for any reply. It was a long ten seconds.

"Victor, this is Fox actual. We read you five by five. Am I speaking to Victor actual? Over."

Hank keyed the mic. "I can relay. Over."

Kelly looked at Hank quizzically. "In case our friends are listening," Hank said.

Ten seconds later came the reply. "Roger. Please relay to Victor that they have been recalled to active duty, and per POTUS are now in command. Over."

"That's the second time I've heard potus," Kelly said. "What's a potus?"

"Acronym, for 'President of the United States,'" Hank answered. "At least they're taking this shit seriously." Hank went back to the mic. "Wilco. Break, be advised that we command very little here. Over."

After another long delay, longer than speed-of-light, the Martian commander of the frigate *Cydonia* started to talk. "Victor, that last was not mere ceremony. I've been in contact with the task force coming to get y'all. They advise that they will need active assistance from your forces to retake the ship. I repeat, active assistance, so you are authorized to draft whoever you need, Martian or American. How copy? Over."

Hank rolled back on her heels. "What the fuck are they smoking?" she asked. "Active assistance? We're fucking running around at gunpoint. What the fuck do they expect us to do?"

Kelly felt a weight in her gut. "Doors."

"Huh?" Hank said.

"Doors," Kelly said. She pointed vaguely toward the central passageway. "All these doors that are closed. All the airlock doors on the hull. If they have to fight or cut their way through them, it will take forever."

"Then we'll need a bigger committee," Hanks said. She keyed up the mic. "Victor copies. We look forward to assisting with your plan. Over."

Stan looked at Hank. "We need to talk."

"Later," Hank said. "Right now, we got to move before they notice that the camera is down."

"Okay," Stan nodded. "But it ain't going to be easy."

***

Kelly stifled a yawn. "We're going to need to open doors for them," she said, summarizing for Maria the conversation Commander America had with the CO of the *Cydonia*. Hank had gone to another cabin to confer with Stan and Cody the Cop.

"I figured that," she replied. "Which means we're fucked."

"How so?" Kelly asked. "We got keys."

"We got Level One keys," Maria said.

"So?"

"So, we need Level Four keys and a way to override Central Control," Maria said.

"Huh?"

"*Fantasia.*" Kelly gestured for Maria to go on. "Different keys have different access levels, to prevent somebody from getting access to sensitive areas. Level Four keys are what we need to open any pressure door that could potentially vent the ship."

"Like the doors we went through to board the ship." Kelly sighed. "Let me guess—they were in that cabinet in the Ship's Office that got busted into."

"That or on people's hips," Maria said. "And it gets worse."

"How?"

"Those doors are motorized. All the key does is give access to a local control panel. Once the door opens, Central Control gets an alarm, and they can override remotely."

"Can we bust open the covers to the panels?"

"Sure, if you want to stand there and bang on them while on video camera," Maria said. "And even if you do, they can command the doors closed."

"All this skulking around was for nothing?"

"Well, at least you found out where we're going," Maria said.

"You didn't seem to be very happy," Kelly said.

"It's the most lawless place on the Solar System," Maria said. "They got actual slaves there."

"I don't believe it."

"Believe," Maria said.

"Why doesn't somebody stop it?"

"The Treaty of Copernicus," Maria said. "Earth and Mars agreed to not claim 'any planet inside the orbit of Earth.' At the time, Mercury was basically uninhabited."

"Now it's inhabited?"

"Yeah. And anybody with a military large enough to do anything about it is prohibited from intervening." Maria's eyes watered. "We get there we're on our own."

Chapter 17

Kansas City, MO

Ray

Ray tried and failed to stifle a yawn. "I can never sleep on planes," he said by way of excuse.

"Neither can I," replied their lead technical agent, Don Horvath. "That's why I don't fly."

"I didn't have a choice on this," Ray replied. He gestured to Don's desk, cluttered with keyboards, monitors, and miscellaneous junk. They'd worked together since Ray had joined the FBI, and he'd never seen Don's desk anything other than covered with stuff. "Is that getting the message feed from *Cardinal*?"

"Yes, and several other interesting feeds," Don replied. "Our Alaskan friends really are sending us everything."

"They seemed concerned about getting bombed."

"We should just do that anyway, then take back the joint."

Ray nodded noncommittally. His understanding had been that the Alaskan succession had been a mutual thing, and he'd seen nothing up there worth getting anybody killed—American or Alaskan. "I assume you'll send the other interesting stuff on, but for right now we've got a rocket racing to Mercury with hostages. What do you have for me?"

"Two things. First," he sent a file to Ray's handheld.

Ray skimmed it. "Talk about incriminating evidence." It was a message asking the recipient to kill somebody. "Who's the target?"

"The CFO of ValuTrip. The real point is the recipient." Ray gestured questioningly at Don, who smiled. "The hitters you took out at the Malan house."

"Oh shit!" Ray gasped. "The hijackers don't know they're dead."

"Yeah," Don said. "It's a test. If somebody from law enforcement is listening in..."

"We're supposed to react to it."

"And they see us react, and know we got them bugged." *Which means they've got somebody on Earth and on Mars watching us. Wonder who?*

"Exactly." Don sent up a second message. "This one went to somebody who works for Martian Customs."

"Same idea?"

"I think so," Don said. "So, I deleted it from the file we're giving to their Federal Police."

"Good," Ray said, breathing a sigh of relief. "You said two things. What else?"

"Traffic analysis," Don said while waving a list from one of his monitors into the air between the two men. "I sent the file to your terminal. You can drill down as deep as you want—nothing they are sending is even commercially encrypted."

Ray looked over the display. There were twelve active accounts—three hostages and nine with numeric user IDs. "Anything jump out to you?"

Don gestured at the list. "That's sorted by message volume. The first account is getting mostly automated news updates. The second is getting ship-specific stuff—maintenance updates, navigational notices, etcetera."

"Anything with a personal twist?"

"The number six account is getting what looks like updates from a US bank."

"Number six just jumped to number one with a bullet on my list." Ray stood up. "Thanks."

***

The bank account emails were in plain text, and came from Spacers' Bank of Branson, Missouri. No name, just the last four digits of account numbers. But one of them showed a large deposit designated 'payroll.' Ray grunted and took a walk to the second-floor research area.

There he learned that Arlena Malan had been a principal in a failed bank which was bought by Spacers' Bank. He also learned that one Lawrence Flashman, ship security specialist on ValuTrip *Cardinal*, had his salary direct deposited into that bank. Having a ship's cop on your side would be handy for a hijacking. He also decided to put in a call to Mark Nagata—if ValuTrip had one mole, they might have another.

***

"Thank you for seeing me," Ray said, settling into the too-soft armchair in Cami Niland's lush office at ValuTrip. It was nearly four-thirty PM, and Ray was hoping he could expedite this meeting before people left for the day.

"I literally have nothing more important on my plate than solving this," Cami replied. She looked tired and stressed. "My board is baying for somebody's blood, and when it comes out where *Bluejay* really is, they'll shit."

"Which brings me to the problem," Ray said. "We've gotten some information about who potentially hijacked the ship."

"Great. How can I help?"

"What do you know about Lawrence Flashman? He's listed as one of the security officers on *Cardinal*."

"Not much. Why?" Cami asked.

"We think he's one of the hijackers."

Cami's face went through several expressions, settling on weariness. "Every time I think it can't get worse, it does."

"Well, my concern is who hired him."

"You don't think Denise is in on this?" She presumably meant Denise Ricardo, ValuTrip's chief of security. She was with the rescue task force—Ray had sent a message to Nagata and gotten an acknowledgement, so presumably a similar conversation was happening on *Bluejay*. "I don't know."

"I have a hard time seeing her as in on this," Cami said. "She's been with the company for several years now."

"Almost five," Ray said. "Whereas Flashman was hired a year ago." Shortly after Frank Malan, the booking agent, in fact, but Ray decided to keep that to himself.

Cami stood up. "Well, I didn't hire him, so let's find out who did."

***

"God, do I love corporate America," Ray said, rubbing his eyes. His stomach growled, reminding him that it was well past dinner time.

Cami Niland walked into the conference room they had commandeered, carrying a tray. She set it down on the table and lifted a metal cover off a plate. "I had our cook make something. I hope you like your cheeseburgers medium."

"As long as it's not still mooing, I'll eat it," Ray said. He opened the can of pop on the tray and poured it into the glass. "Thanks."

"Anything?" Cami said, settling into a chair opposite him.

"Nothing so far," Ray replied. "I mean, he applied, went through the background checks, and started working."

"May I?" Cami said, gesturing at his tablet. Ray waved assent while taking a bite of his cheeseburger. It was tasty. *Must be nice having your own corporate chief.*

Cami skimmed the file, then frowned. She typed a message on her personal device. A short time later, a mousy woman walked in, who Cami introduced as Tammy Sullivan from HR.

"Who's AVM Services?" Cami asked of Sullivan, her voice noticeably calm.

"Sorry?" Sullivan asked.

"AVM Services. The people who did the background checks. Who are they?"

Sullivan's brow was dotted by sweat, remarkable in the cool office. Some aspect of her face told Ray she had something to hide. He set down his cheeseburger.

"AVM Services?" Sullivan said. "I'll have to check—"

"Don't bullshit me, Tammy," Cami interrupted. "Who..."

Sullivan started to cry and back out of the room. Ray and Cami stood up. Cami was quicker, and marched over to Sullivan, grabbed her collar, then slapped her face, hard. "Ditch the waterworks. Who is AVM Services?"

"Arlena Malan," Sullivan said, rubbing her face. *That was going to leave a mark.* It was also not an FBI-approved interrogation technique, but Ray had occasionally wanted to do the same.

"Frank's wife."

"When did we hire her?"

"We just used her for overflow," Sullivan said, whining. "H & K got so backed up sometimes..."

"So, we hired some freelancer off the street for background checks?" Cami looked ready to strike again, and Sullivan winced.

"Frank said they were having financial troubles, and asked if I could throw some business her way."

"Even worse!"

"Who else did Malan screen?" Ray asked. "I'll want a list. Also, who hired Frank?"

"I did," Sullivan said. "He went to my church."

"Please tell me H & K did his background check," Cami said.

"Of course," Sullivan said.

Background checks were helpful, but there was always a first time for somebody to go bad. Like when they were having financial trouble because a bank they were heavily invested in went bust. "I noticed that Flashman had a note on his file about 'find a friend.' What's that?"

"A referral program we ran. Find a friend to work for us and get thousand-dollar bonus," Cami said. "Frank referred Flashman."

Shit. "I'll want a list of everybody he referred," Ray said.

"Now," Cami growled. Sullivan scampered out, and Ray returned to his burger. Cami made a call on the conference room phone, and a security officer came to the conference room shortly thereafter. Cami instructed him to 'sit on' Sullivan.

***

Cami looked mad enough that Ray was glad she wasn't carrying a gun. *Least I hope she's not—Missouri will let any idiot pack.* Sullivan—accompanied by the security officer—was sitting at the conference table, looking at Ray over the remains of his burger. Sullivan was sporting a growing red spot on her face that matched nicely with Cami's hand.

"So, every fucking time Frank referred somebody, H & K *just happened* to be backed up and you had to go with AVM?" Cami asked, a note of danger in her voice.

"Well, not every time," Sullivan said. "But when Frank came to me with a referral, he'd always mention how his wife needed the cash."

"Therefore, you just decided to give her the business?"

"We went to the same church," Sullivan whined. Ray bit his tongue. *If I had a nickel for every time somebody's buddy from the church fucked them over, I'd be rich.*

"You do realize you're fired, right?" Cami said.

"Not until—" Ray started.

"Fine," Cami said. "But she's not going to be in this building."

"She can hang out at our Garden City office," Ray said. Garden City was a town of thirty thousand or so in the middle of western Kansas, and the FBI maintained a short-term safe house in town for witnesses. The small town was perfect for hiding people. "It's very quiet there."

"Good," Cami said.

Ray nodded at the FBI agent he'd called. "Take her there directly."

"What about my clothes?" Sullivan asked. "And my cats?"

"They've got a few things at the safe house for tonight," Ray said.

"Joey will go to your place," Cami said, gesturing at the security officer, "and pick up the cats. He can pack some things for you as well. He'll take them to the FBI office in Garden City and they'll get them to you." Cami stretched, looking old. "You'd better get moving," she said. Ray nodded, and the FBI agent touched Sullivan's elbow. They left.

"She just cost us a billion dollars," Cami said to the closing door. "And if the zoomies fail on the rescue, she wrecked the whole company."

I'm sure the Space Force is thrilled to be called 'zoomies.'

"Worrying about lawsuits at—"

"I'm the CEO," Cami snapped. "That's what I'm supposed to worry about."

Ray looked at the list they'd generated. The Malans had hired and screened seven people. Five, including Flashman, were on the *Cardinal*. Two were groundside and being picked up by FBI agents on Ray's orders.

Ray's phone rang. It was Special Agent in Charge Fetterer. "I thought you had trivia tonight?" he asked. She had a weekly trivia game at a bar and didn't like to be disturbed.

"I saw the request for the Garden City safe house and thought I'd call in on my break," she replied. "That and I got an interesting call."

Ray filled her in, ending with, "I sent another message to Nagata."

"Great," Fetterer replied, the distaste clear in her voice. "I swear, the 'he went to church with me, he had to be okay' excuse just gripes my ass."

Ray shrugged, which was probably not visible on her small handheld screen. "That's why I don't go to church."

"Yeah, right. Well, obviously the Malans weren't the ringleaders of this circus. Sweat the suspects and see what they say."

"Will do."

"One other thing."

"Ma'am?"

"I got a call. Somebody's been asking the Air Force where the *Oklahoma* really went."

"Shit," Ray said.

"Yeah. Air Force is looking for a leak and the local FBI's talking to the questioner."

"I assume you told our techs to not let any news of this get to the ship?"

"I did. I'm worried though—there are codes we may not be able to break, including messages that aren't sent."

"Got it."

"Get me the ringleader of this circus, fast."

"Will do."

Chapter 18

ValuTrip Bluejay

Mark

Mark wiped his brow. *Bluejay's* HVAC was working better than *Oklahoma's*, but now that they were well inside Venus's orbit, solar loading was significantly more than the ship had been originally designed for. *At least we rigged sunshades.* Per *Cydonia*, the ship they had trailing *Cardinal*, she hadn't, meaning that the hostages and pirates were sweating buckets over there. *And if we can't figure out a way to get on the ship faster, all our sweat is for nothing.*

"Twenty minutes," Tom Wu said, leaning over the schematic of the *Bluejay*. That was how long it had taken them to get to the passenger decks in the last drill. "If we could just get the airlocks to move faster," he said, glancing at the other Martian in the room, Leading Lieutenant Art Peterson.

Everything is taking too long! Using the *Bluejay* as a guinea pig, they'd seen how close to the target they could get a ship before it was detected. In optimal conditions, that had proven to be five thousand kilometers. The American assault craft, small and highly stealthy, could get closer, within one thousand kilometers. Covering that distance would take around ten minutes.

Then they had to get inside the ship. That meant getting exterior airlock doors opened, as well as two sets of interior pressure doors. Doors could be forced, but that took time.

"Airlock doors only cycle so fast," Peterson replied with a shrug. "And if we can't get the hostages to get those doors open, we'll have to bypass them manually from outside."

Which took time, Mark thought. *Time we don't have.* Mark glanced at his fellow Martian.

The American Delta Force team was good, but it had quickly become apparent the force needed more shooters. Mark had started drafting anybody with zero-gee experience, pulling both USSF security forces from their ships and Marines from the Martian vessels. Peterson had been slated to relieve the XO on the RMS *Eric T. Reynolds*—one of the Martian destroyers in the task force. Partially because he wasn't immediately needed, and partially because he had a Marine background, Mark had drafted him to command the combined Martian marine contingent.

"The only way to move them faster is to blow them, and with pressure behind them, that means we're fighting a hurricane." This was from the last person in the room, Major Tony Taguba, USSF. He was lead security officer on the USS *Kentucky*, and commanding the USSF security troops on *Bluejay*. The doors he was talking about blowing were outer airlock doors which opened to vacuum.

"Well, actually, the way to get them to cycle faster is to have them open and depressurized when we get there," Peterson said. "That's five minutes."

"Which is still fifteen minutes," Mark said, his words coming out more sharply than he intended, "and at least five minutes too late." Even fifteen minutes would give the pirates plenty of time to either depressurize the passenger spaces or just start shooting people. "And we can't get the passengers to open them, unless we want the pirates to see what's going on."

Peterson's handheld comm beeped. He glanced at it, reading a text message. "We may have a solution to the airlock problem."

"Oh?" Mark asked.

"Chief Shadout and Master Sergeant Mapes have something to show us."

Mark shrugged. "I'm all for a field trip."

***

Shadout and Mapes were a study in contrasts. Agnes Shadout, the Martian Chief Astronaut, was a tiny woman. Larry Mapes, the American Delta Force operator, was gigantic and looked like he picked up locomotives for a hobby. The two of them were standing in a passageway just off the main passenger lobby. They were among the senior enlisted personnel on the ship, and well aware of the problems facing the rescue team.

Shadout started. "The big problem with getting the exterior airlocks open is getting prisoners to them, right?"

"Correct, Chief," Wu said. He glanced at his subordinate. "Larry, this going somewhere?"

Mapes looked hurt. "Always, boss," he replied. "Why can't we get hostages to the airlocks?"

"Security cameras and alarms," Wu said. "And?"

"Give me a boost, big guy," Shadout said. Mapes picked her up like a grocery bag and held her up to the ceiling. She popped a ceiling tile, scrambled into the overhead, and disappeared. A short time later the door opened from the inside. "Gentlemen and Larry, if you please."

Mapes waved the officers into what appeared to be mostly a janitorial closet. There was, however, an electrical distribution panel on one wall. As the officers crowded around, Shadout opened the panel and tripped two main breakers. The lights went out in the hallway and an instant later everybody's handheld beeped.

Mark answered his first. "Nagata."

"Sir," the voice came, "we just lost all video monitors."

"Yep," Shadout said. She reset the breakers. "Ask him now."

Mark did so, and the report came back that the monitors were coming back on.

"Well dip me in shit," Taguba said. "Talk about a single point of failure."

"Not considered a critical system," Shadout said.

Mark looked up. "That wall doesn't go all the way to the bulkhead."

"No sir," Shadout said. "It's just a privacy partition." She tapped at the wall. "Single layer of fiberglass, so it wouldn't stop a determined attack anyway."

"It's just to keep out nosy passengers," Taguba said.

"But the bottom line is," Mark said, "if they can get somebody in here, they can drop all video."

"And while it's down," Wu said, "they can have people run to the doors we need open and work on them locally."

"But when cameras come back up," Peterson said, "the pirates will know what's happening."

"Yep," Wu replied. "So, we need to time our attack such that by the time they get their shit in one sock we're onboard."

"And there's no way to really practice this," Mark said.

"No sir," Shadout and Mapes said in stereo.

"Fuck it's thin," Mark said. He gestured at the closet. "This doesn't stop them from starting to shoot hostages—"

"Which if the terrorists are confused or scared is the first thing they'll do," Wu finished.

"We can make that a lot harder, sir," Mapes said.

"Oh?" Mark replied.

"Probably easier shown than explained, sir," Mapes replied.

"Lead on," Mark said.

"Son of a bitch," Mark said, after the show-and-tell from Shadout and Mapes. "This just might work."

"We still have to convince the President," Wu said.

Chapter 19

Kansas City FBI Office

Ray

"The piano player?" Ray asked. "The piano player is the Head Pirate in Charge?"

"That's what the report says," Special Agent Fetterer replied. She gestured at her system. "Hot off the latest intel from *Cardinal*. Apparently one of our resistance people got pulled into a meeting."

"Wonderful," Ray replied. "How did the piano player get to be king of this?"

"Queen," Fetterer said. "And that's a damn good question. Maybe you can ask your other two perps? They said anything yet?"

She was referring to the two Earth-side employees referred to ValuTrip by the late Frank Malan and screened by his equally-late wife's background checking firm. *A firm that had no customers other than ValuTrip.* "The Pickett woman only seems to know of Frank, and I think she's frankly too dumb to be in on a conspiracy." She was an assistant booking agent, and Frank used her in a purely clerical capacity. Her knowledge began and ended with inputting data Frank gave her.

"And Campallo?"

Ray shrugged. "So far he's lawyered up." He was responsible for the cargo portion of the ship. Passenger ships didn't carry a lot of cargo, but they could carry enough to make it a profitable sideline.

"I've got an idea about getting him to sing," Fetterer said.

***

Ray walked into the interrogation room, followed by his boss. They were accompanied by a trio of Martian Navy personnel in uniform—two burly men and a slender female Lieutenant.

"Brian Campallo," Ray said. Brian, a thin and squirrelly man, looked up from the metal conference table.

"Talk to my lawyer," Brian replied, cocking a thumb at the lawyer in question. Ray had done some checking on her, as she wasn't one of the usual lawyers he saw. Her name was Nicki Zipser, and she was mostly family law, but had been smart enough to have her client say nothing.

"Actually, Brian," Ray said, "we're done with you."

"I'm free to go?" Brian asked.

"From the FBI's perspective, yes," Ray said.

"From ours, no," the Martian Lieutenant said. "Under the authority of the Treaty of Copernicus, Article Five, I am arresting you for piracy." She nodded at the men. "Cuff, gag and hood."

Brian pushed back from the table as the two men stepped rapidly around it. Before Campallo had much more than a chance to squeak, the two guards had him on his knees, handcuffed, a gag in his mouth and a black hood over his face.

"Are you going to let them do this?" Zipser asked.

"Do what?" Ray asked, not bothering to hide his smirk.

"Manhandle him like this! He has rights!"

"We can't hold him," Ray said, "since he's not cooperating, so the Martians are taking him. How they handle arrests is their business."

"This is bullshit," Zipser replied. She got into the face of the Lieutenant. "When's his arraignment?"

"We've convened a court-martial on RMS *Victorious*," she replied. "They're waiting for the accused."

"Court-martial?" she said.

"Under Martian law, piracy is handled by the military," the Lieutenant replied. "Which means court-martial. Admiral Teng, Commander Force E, is the convening authority, and Fleet Captain Gabay is presiding." She gestured at her guards. "Let's go. You know H.M. isn't patient."

"H.M.?" Fetterer asked, her face impressively blank.

"Horace Marcus Gabay, but most people call him Howling Mad," the Lieutenant replied.

"Now, just hold it," Zipser said. "He gets a lawyer, right?"

"If you're willing to come, yes," the Lieutenant replied. "Otherwise, no. I should point out that the penalty for piracy is death."

"After appeals, of course," Zipser said, a look of concern on her face.

"Admiral Teng does have the option to hear appeals, yes."

Ray found the look of horror on Zipser's face priceless. The lawyer looked at Ray. "You can't let them do this. He's a US citizen."

"I'm sorry," Fetterer said. "We can't hold him, and we have to honor our treaty commitments."

"I'll get an injunction," Zipser said.

"I have a tiltrotor inbound and a rocket at the spaceport," the Lieutenant said. "I'll be on *Victorious* before you get to the courthouse."

A tiltrotor aircraft was dimly audible outside. Campallo started to vigorously grunt around his gag. Zipser smiled wanly. "Agent Fetterer, surely we can work something out."

Fetterer sighed theatrically. "Lieutenant, can we have a moment?"

"Bird's still a few minutes out," she replied. "I'll be waiting for it."

***

Ray walked outside to the parking lot. The tiltrotor was sitting there, and a gaggle of Martians were loitering about. He walked up to the Martian Lieutenant.

"Nice little performance you put on in there," Ray said. He stuck out his hand. "I'm Ray Volk. You are?"

"Elena Mirronoff," she replied. "Performance? There was no acting. There really is a court-martial convened. The officers, other than Gabay, aren't sitting around waiting, but they've been named and filed the paperwork."

"You think he'd really get the death penalty?" Ray asked.

"In an Earth minute," she replied. "He'd be shoved out an airlock by the end of the week."

Ray shuddered. "Hell of a way to go."

"Actually not. You pass out in fifteen seconds, and then die." The Lieutenant gestured at the FBI building. "Surely you didn't come out here for small talk."

"Well, those cheap seats in interrogation do hurt my ass. But no, I do have something for you." Ray produced a photocopy. "Here's the container number and shipping agent y'all need to take a look at."

Elena took the paper. She glanced at it and waved over one of her knee-breakers, who took the paper into the tiltrotor. "23rd Century, and we're still looking at handwritten confessions."

"Juries find them much more believable."

"I guess so," Elena replied. "So, my astronaut there wants to know if you're interested."

Ray shrugged. "Which one?"

She pointed at the slightly shorter of the two. "Just for the record, I don't usually run a dating service for my troops."

"Well, then," Ray said, "thanks for the referral. I'll handle it from here."

"Good."

Ray walked up to the Marine and they introduced themselves. "So, you think you'll get a chance to actually visit KC?"

"I'm detailed to our embassy in DC," the Marine, Ralph, replied. "I get leave and there's flights every day."

"That there are," Ray said. He handed Ralph a business card. "Give me a call when you get a chance. I can show you around town."

"Thanks," Ralph replied, looking at the card. "Old fashioned."

"I deal with a lot of crooks. Exposing electronics to them is a great way to get hacked."

"Sounds interesting." Ralph flashed a smile. "Although I'd assume you had top-end security."

"Yeah, maybe. Except it would have to be from the lowest bidder. Besides, some of the people I deal with are trying to stay off the grid."

"Yeah, didn't think of that." Ralph flashed a very winning smile. "I'm looking to be a cop after I get out of the service. Maybe I can get some advice?"

"Maybe," Ray said. "Call me."

"I will."

***

The sound of the tiltrotor was fading by the time Ray got back to the interrogation room. Campallo and his lawyer were sitting at the table. The lawyer was nursing a paper cup of coffee while Campallo was staring at a blinking cursor on a holo display.

"Writer's block?" Ray asked. "I'm sure we can get that tilty-bird back here."

"Fuck you," Campallo said.

"You're the one who's fucked," Ray replied. "So, who's in charge here on Earth?"

"We told you that," Zipser said. "He doesn't know."

"Well, if he doesn't know," Fetterer said, "then what value is he to us?"

"You're not going to give me to those apes?" Campallo asked, all trace of bravado gone.

"Full cooperation means full cooperation," Fetterer said. "So, like Agent Volk asked, who's calling the shots on Earth?"

"I thought Malan was the boss," Campallo wailed.

"Well, somebody had him capped," Ray said, "so let's try that again." Ray noted Fetterer's glare, but he waved her down.

"Look," Campallo said, leaning across the table. "Frank recruited me. I don't know nobody else."

"Oh really," Ray said. He called up a few pictures on the room's very durable-looking wall-mounted data display. "Any of them look familiar?"

"Yeah," Campallo said. "The woman, lower right."

Stevens, the piano player. "Where'd you meet her?"

"She played piano at the Holiday Inn by the new spaceport. Frank and I met there."

"You talk to her about the hijacking?"

Campallo scoffed. "Hell no. Didn't talk to her about anything. I just remember her because she was hot."

She probably was if your taste went to women. One of the other photos was of Flashman, the crooked ship's cop. Ray highlighted it. "What about him?"

"Nope."

"Then who ordered a hit on the Malans?" Ray asked.

Campallo looked genuinely stumped. "Well, Frank was talking about the banker."

"Go on," Ray said.

"Yeah," Campallo continued, "he was always talking about a banker. I guess somebody had to front the money to pay for the goons to take the ship."

"Any idea who this banker was?" Ray asked.

"No. Honestly. All I can remember was that Frank had lunch with him every Tuesday."

"My client is fully cooperating," Zipser said.

"Your client better hope we can figure out who the Tuesday luncheons were with, or I see a tiltrotor in his future," Fetterer said.

Ray and Agent Fetterer stood up. "Take him to holding," Ray said.

"Is my client going to get arraigned?" Zipser asked. "I have some ideas on bail."

"Your client is going to stay in FBI headquarters until I decide otherwise," Fetterer said. "Either that, or Martian custody."

"Your holding cell is fine by me," Campallo said. "Although I would like a shower."

"We'll work something out," Ray said over his shoulder.

He walked out of the room and down to his desk where he'd left his handheld. The tech people had uploaded Frank's calendar to the evidence system, so it was only a few keystrokes to see what Frank did on Tuesdays.

Son of a bitch, Ray thought pushing back from his desk. He called Fetterer. "You're not going to believe this," he told her. "Frank Malan had lunch every Tuesday with Denise Ricardo, ValuTrip's head of security."

"Fuck!" Fetterer replied. "And she knows everything about the rescue effort."

Chapter 20

ValuTrip Bluejay

Mark

Mark looked around the sitting room of his cabin. When they had chartered the ship, the senior officers ended up getting first class cabins. Although small by ground-based standards, the sitting room was quite nice. There was a knock on his door. Mark opened it to admit Denise Ricardo. Colonel Ricardo, now—freshly recalled to active duty. He had her sit on the built-in couch on one wall.

"Let's get right to this," Mark said, planting himself in the armchair opposite her.

"Sure," Denise replied, a look of puzzlement on her face.

"Ray Volk, back on Earth, has had something of a breakthrough on the hijacking."

"Good," Denise said.

"Apparently Frank had lunch with the real head of the operation on a weekly basis." Mark left it at that, wondering how Denise would react. Her snort was not what he expected. "Something funny?"

"Frank never ate lunch," she said.

"Oh?" Mark replied. "Our source said he had lunch with you."

Denise shook her head, still smiling. "We attended a lunch meeting. Frank didn't eat."

Mark frowned. "A quibble. With whom else did Frank attend lunch meetings?"

Her smile faded. "To my knowledge, nobody. And our lunch meeting was with the Rotary Club of Overland Park Space Professionals. We have around twenty members, although not all of them are at every meeting."

Thank God I didn't listen to Morehouse, Mark thought. The General had wanted to 'sweat' Ricardo on the *Oklahoma*. "How interesting. Earth doesn't seem to know either of you were in Rotary."

"They wouldn't. I just joined a month or two before the hijacking—my official installation was the day before *Cardinal* went missing. I was planning to run out and get a frame for my membership certificate when the shit hit the fan."

"And Frank?"

"We have a policy—only three personal items per cubicle." Denise shrugged. "Don't ask me why—somebody must have made a stink to HR in the past."

If Frank was limited as to the amount of personal stuff he could display, maybe Rotary didn't make the cut. "Well, we're back to square one, then."

Denise made a face. "I don't know. One of our members seemed a bit, well, off."

"Oh?" Mark raised an eyebrow.

"Yeah. Wilma Simmons. Has one of those vague 'import-export' type companies. Frank seemed nervous around her, and I know they've had a couple of private meetings before or after the club meeting."

"Not much to go on," Mark said.

"It's all I've got." Denise stood up. "Anything else?"

Mark grimaced. "You'd better sit down." She did, clearly puzzled. "General Morehouse is, well, very concerned about you."

Denise shook her head sadly. "Damn ring-knocker." At Mark's puzzled expression, she continued, "Ring-knocker. Always waving their Air Force Academy class rings around as if their shit didn't stink. I was ROTC, myself."

Mark was learning vastly more than he cared to about the internal politics of the US Department of the Air Force. *I guess that was part of the gig,* he reminded himself. His original posting was as a guest instructor at the US Air Force Academy. "Be that as it may," Mark said, "let's keep this discussion under our helmets."

"Hats, you mean."

"Whatever."

After Ricardo left, Mark queued up the ship's external communication system. They had set up an encrypted channel, which he used to call Ray Volk. It was evening both on the ship, which followed Colorado time, as well as in Kansas City. The system was able to locate Volk at his house. Speed of light delay to Earth was only a few seconds—awkward but not ridiculous.

"Ray," Mark said. "I talked to Ricardo. I don't think she's involved, but she gave me somebody I need you to look at." He summarized his conversation with Ricardo, then waited for Ray to digest and for his reply to come through.

"Yeah, I'll get on that. Hey, how's the rescue plan going?"

Mark opened his mouth to reply and noticed Ray was grinning at something off-camera. "We're working on it—some of the Special Forces-types have some ideas. What's so funny?"

It was a long pause before Ray replied. "Oh, I met a dude today and he texted me back. Seems interested."

"Glad to hear that," Mark said, feeling relief. *I'm glad he's moved on.* "Good hunting."

After another long pause, Volk replied. "Thanks. You, too."

Kansas City—FBI offices

Ray

"I think Nagata's a bit pissed," Ray said after recapping his conversation from last night.

"As he should be," Fetterer replied, looking at him across her scrupulously clean desk. "That's the sort of basic homework we should have done."

Ray nodded. "True, but the connection to Ricardo seemed pretty obvious."

"Yes, too obvious. That's the point. I wonder who invited her to join the club?"

"Guy's the only Rotarian I know that doesn't have Rotary shit in his office," Ray said, referring to Malan and feeling a bit defensive.

"Be that as it may," Fetterer continued. "What do we know about this Simmons person?"

"Not much," Ray allowed. "I pulled what information I could from the club's database and ran it against our records." Ray shrugged. "Nothing pops out. She's near retirement age, but never had anything more serious than a traffic ticket."

"Wait," Fetterer said. "She's how old?"

"Seventy."

Fetterer pulled up something on her data pad, then showed it to Ray. "That's Simmons. She look seventy to you?"

It was a picture from the club's newsletter, showing Simmons as having won some kind of internal raffle. "No, that gal looks barely old enough to buy beer." Ray got up. "Looks like I'm going to go talk to Simmons."

Overland Park, KS—Royal Office Suites

The business address—the only address listed on the club contact sheet provided to Ricardo—for Wilma Simmons proved to be on the fourth floor of a mid-rise building a block away from ValuTrip's headquarters. Decorated in an anonymous corporate style, it was a shared office suite— individual tenants rented a four-by-four-meter office and had access to some shared amenities.

One of the amenities in this case was a youngish man with blue-streaked hair working as the receptionist. "I'm sorry," he said. "I'm not authorized to give out that information."

Ray held his badge closer to the man's face. "I'm investigating a murder. Surely you can tell me if Wilma Simmons is in or not?"

"Sir, we at Royal Office Suites pride ourselves on customer discretion."

"There'll be a lot less discretion if I come back here with a SWAT team," Ray growled.

A young woman, trim, with short brown hair walked out of the door behind reception. She'd cut her hair but that was definitely Wilma Simmons. "Calling it a day, Joe," she said to the receptionist. Then she glanced at Ray. "You don't look very happy."

"Actually, I am," Ray said. "I was looking for you."

"Can this wait?" Simmons replied. "I'm leaving for the day."

"Not really," Ray said. "Miss Simmons, I'm Special Agent Ray Volk, FBI, and I'd like to ask you a few questions."

"Regarding?"

"Frank Malan and his wife."

Simmons frowned, pasting a genuine look of sadness on her face. "I was at his funeral. Very sad. I don't know what his kids are going to do."

Financially, since Malan's insurance was paid up, they would be fine. Emotionally, who knew? At least they had both been away at the time of the murders. "It is sad. Do you have time to answer some questions?"

Simmons looked at her watch. "If we keep it brief."

"I'll try." Ray gestured. "Your office?"

"Yes."

***

Simmon's office proved to be a small interior space, furnished with a single wooden desk, two matching (and not terribly comfortable) wooden guest chairs, and a black swivel chair for Simmons. The desk was dominated by a black metal stand with a 3-D display bolted to it.

"I alternate between sitting and standing," Simmons said, running the device up while settling into her chair. "Keeps the blood flowing. Want a coffee?"

"I'm good, thanks," Ray said. "So, how well did you know Frank Malan?"

Simmons shrugged. "Business acquaintance. Why do you ask? I was told that they were killed as part of a home invasion."

"We're trying to figure out why that particular home was targeted," Ray said. "Why don't we start with when you two met?"

"That's easy," Simmons said. "The Friday after Thanksgiving—not last one but the one before."

"Go on."

"I was in the office here. I think I was the only one—even Joey was off. I had a burning need for an optimizer and Frank cold-called me."

"Sorry, I'm a cop, not a spacer. What is an 'optimizer' and why did you need one?"

Simmons leaned back in her chair. "In the cargo business, ships make money by maxing out capacity. Optimizers are hired by shipping companies to help fill odd-sized holes in their cargo holds."

"I thought everything went by container?"

"Most of it does, but unlike ocean or rail shipping, container mass is important as well. So, if your ship has say, ten thousand kilograms spare mass and one hundred cubic meters of space, you're looking for a different cargo than if you have one thousand kilograms and one hundred cubic meters space."

"So that's the 'what.'" Ray left the 'why' in the air and suppressed a smirk, thinking he'd managed nicely to turn that question around on Simmons.

"I'm mostly in the business of what we call personal shipping," Simmons said. "An individual, usually high-net-worth, orders something from one planet and wants it shipped to another. Art, collectables, furniture, you name it. If it's not alive, explosive or corrosive I've shipped it."

"So, if, for example, I wanted this desk sent to Mars, you'd be the person to see?"

"Exactly." Simmons glanced at her watch. "In this case, I had a statue on Iapetus that needed to get to Earth by a certain date to make a cross-shipment to Mercury. Frank just happened to have a slot from Iapetus."

"How convenient."

Simmons shrugged. "Sometimes you get lucky."

Luck or planning? "How does one get into your line of work?"

Simmons smiled. "Looking for a career change? Besides, I thought we were talking about Malan."

Ray shrugged. "I won't be in the FBI forever. And yes, we were talking about Malan. But like I said, somebody picked his house for a reason, and I keep thinking that if I understand more of what he did for a living, I'd get a clue as to why."

"And understanding how I work helps?"

Ray faked a bashful smile. "It might."

"I really think you should be looking at his wife," Simmons said. "I understood she had a job at a bank. But to answer your question, my business really consists of contacts. People who need stuff shipped, people who can ship it, and knowledge of how to clear customs. I had a partner who had all of those contacts, while I did the actual legwork. When he died, I inherited the business."

Simmons stood up. "Now, I really should be going. I have tickets to a play."

Ray kept his seat. "You don't look a day over thirty."

"Thanks," she said, puzzled.

"Yet our records show you're seventy-one. I'm confused."

A look of anger flashed over her face. "I have the same name as my grandmother. Some knucklehead in the government got our records mixed up. It's been a mess for going on two years now." She pushed in her chair. "Now, I really must be going."

That's a bullshit excuse, but I can't arrest her for it. At least not yet. Ray stood up. "Well, thanks for your time." As they walked out, Ray sent her his card. "Please, call me if you think of any reason why anybody would want to hurt Frank Malan."

"I will," Simmons said as they arrived at the reception desk.

"Catching a flight?" Joey asked of Simmons.

"Not tonight, no," she replied.

"You do a lot of flying?" Ray asked.

"In spurts," she replied. "Like, earlier this week I was up in Alaska."

"Oh?"

"I have a sick friend there," she said, offering her hand. "And I really do have a play to attend."

"Enjoy," Ray said, taking it. "Where are you parked?"

"Car's picking me up out front."

"Then we're going the same way." He followed her into the elevator. When the door closed, he decided to take one more shot. "Does the name Victoria Stevens mean anything to you?"

"No. Should it?"

"According to our admittedly inaccurate records," Ray said, smirking as the door opened. "You have a condo in Olathe, Kansas. She has the unit next to you."

"Yeah, I'm not the most neighborly person," she said, striding out into the lobby. She stopped. "Do you have a picture?"

Ray pushed one up from his phone. She looked at it, then said, "Maybe I saw her around. Can't say I talked to her." She glanced again at her watch. "Sorry, got to go."

Ray watched her walk out. *Oh, she's good.*

Chapter 21

FBI Headquarters, Kansas City

Ray

"Morning," Ray said, walking into the conference room attached to his boss's office. The *Cardinal* task force had gathered for the morning meeting and were sitting around the table. Ray pulled up a chair next to Amanda Taps, one of their investigators. There was a newcomer there as well, whom nobody introduced. Ray yawned, thankful he'd brought in a cup of coffee.

"You look like you had a long night," Fetterer replied. "New boyfriend, or rekindling an old flame?"

"Neither. Case work."

"Apparently important?"

"Simmons is a next-door neighbor to Victoria Stevens. And just flew up to Alaska to 'check on a sick friend.'"

Fetterer arched an eyebrow. "How special. You call the ABI?"

"I did. They're pulling their records."

"What else?"

"Simmons isn't her real name," Ray said.

"Which we knew," Fetterer replied. "So why isn't she in cuffs?"

"She had a story about a data mix-up between her and her grandmother," Ray said. "But when I checked there was no indication she'd filed any paperwork to correct it." Ray pointed to a dark-skinned guy in a bad suit sitting to Fetterer's right.

"Colonel Sam Newitz, USAF," he said in a deep bass voice. "Air Force Intelligence."

"You were telling us about Simmons," Fetterer said.

"Her 'grandmother' got out of the Space Force, filed two tax returns listing a non-US employer called Greenwater, and then disappeared. All this was fifty years ago."

"Ma'am," Newitz said. "We should probably take this in your office."

"Colonel," Fetterer said, "I've been running investigations since you were peeling potatoes in boot camp. I've noticed that keeping investigators in the dark is a piss-poor way to run an investigation."

"My superiors—"

"Are not mine." She glared at him. "Are you going to spill the beans, or should I?"

Newitz visibly swallowed hard. "Might as well." To Ray, he said, "Greenwater is a mercenary recruiting firm. Their main client is the Mercurian military."

"Go on."

"About a third of the Mercurian military is mercs," Newitz said. "US, Canadian, Mexican—North American Treaty members. They are concentrated in skilled jobs, like the Space Force."

"And we're concerned that some of our military might call their buddies on Mercury and tell them about this operation?" Ray asked.

"Which is a problem why, Colonel?" Fetterer asked.

Newitz looked like he'd eaten a bad egg. "The Mercurian government is corrupt and easily bought. It's not impossible that elements of it are involved in this hijacking. More likely, they know who is and would tip them off if they could."

"Well, it looks like our Wilma Simmons is using the identity of a former merc," Ray said. "And judging by pictures, possibly a relative."

"How'd she get into the US without tripping a warrant?" Newitz asked.

Ray shrugged. "Probably used Mercurian ID, then slipped back into the US identity. The IRS stuff is so old it only shows up on a detailed search."

"Which we only run if we think we need to," Fetterer said. She looked at the rep for the technical group. "Drop a net on Simmons. Every erg of electronic transmission coming out or in, I want to know about it, Amanda. What did you find in Stevens' condo?"

"We weren't supposed to search that," Newitz protested.

"Which is why Amanda has a gas company uniform," Fetterer said.

"I didn't need it," Amanda replied. "Place is for sale. The realtor took me on a tour. Completely empty—not a stick of furniture or scrap of clothing."

"Wonderful," Fetterer said. "Did you get to Flashman's?"

"Yes," Amanda replied. "Got a lot of attitude from his high-drama stripper girlfriend."

"Most strippers are high drama, Ray's aunt being the notable exception." Fetterer said.

"And you're the other exception," Ray said.

"At the time, I was not," she said. "Your aunt got me straightened out. Hell, she got me into college. Been a long time since I thought about dancing." She chuckled. To Ray, she said, "Ask her how Bam Bam is doing. Tell her the Ice Queen wants to know."

"Now that we've cleared that up," Newitz said, "Amanda, you were telling us about Flashman."

"His girlfriend was giving us a lot of drama," Amanda said, clearly having a moment trying to process the idea that her ancient and strait-laced boss had once been a high-drama stripper. "But we were able to get some looks. Nothing of interest."

"She gets the full electronic net," Fetterer said. "Maybe her golden hoo-ha is calling Flashman."

"Ah, ma'am?" this was from Mike, one of the tech guys. He was referring to something on his ocular.

"Yes?" Fetterer said.

"Simmons flies to Denver on a regular basis, like every other weekend. Including this one. Leaving on Fridays. As in today."

"Shit!" Newitz said with emphasis.

"A little help?" Ray asked.

"US Space Force Command is based in Colorado Springs," Amanda said. "Just down the road."

"What, we think she's just going to waltz into HQ and ask, 'hey, fellas, know anything about a rescue mission?'" Ray said.

"No," Newitz replied, "but there are literally dozens of people at Colorado Springs who know, who have to know, the details of this mission," Newitz said. "And probably dozens more who know enough that Simmons could piece the plan together."

"I guess I'm going to Denver," Ray said.

***

On the way to the airport, Ray's handheld buzzed, signaling an urgent message. It was from Mark Nagata. "Per Colonel Ricardo, Frank Malan and your subject Wilma Simmons both knew pianist/head hijacker Victoria Stevens. They met regularly while they were on Earth in Kansas City."

Yeah, this 'Wilma Simmons' is definitely in this up to her eyebrows. And if she lets the pirates know we're coming, the only advantage we've got is shot to shit.

Chapter 22

Centennial, Colorado

Ray

Ray scratched himself. "Join the FBI, see the country," he said to nobody in particular. He was in an FBI van, parked in the parking lot of a generic apartment development in Centennial, a suburb of Denver. The van was painted and decaled to look just like a local utility van, and in the large parking lot of the development would draw no attention at all.

"This is part of the country," said his counterpart, a local FBI agent named Taylor. Or was it Troyer? Ray wasn't sure. She was very nondescript—medium height and build, with sensibly-cut strawberry blonde hair and flat shoes.

"Yes, Centennial, Colorado is part of the country," Ray said. He gestured at the video monitor, which showed the generic parking lot. "Not a particularly scenic part."

Wilma Simmons had arrived at the airport on her discount airline, marched into baggage claim and locked lips with a tall blond man, casually dressed in jeans and an Air Force T-shirt. After a couple of sloppy kisses, the amorous couple had adjourned to the blond's car and driven directly here, where at two AM they were presumably finally asleep.

The phone in the van rang, and Taylor/Troyer answered it. "Got a name," she said. "Scott Hancock, Captain, US Space Force."

"Finally," Ray growled.

"It gets better—he's assigned to a communications office groundside."

"So, he'd know where our fleet was?"

"Presumably, since he or his unit needs to talk to it."

"And he's having pillow talk with somebody who's involved up to her eyebrows in the hijacking," Ray said.

"Should we pick her up?"

"For what? Do you see probable cause for an arrest?" Ray banged his hand against the van's wall. "Besides, if we do, just picking her up might tip off the hijackers."

***

A short time later, Ray was in the passenger seat of a government-issue car with Colonel Newitz, who was manually driving it down the highway. "You wanna put it in auto, Colonel?" Ray said, trying to prevent his nervousness from creeping into his voice.

"No," Newitz replied, passing a car. "It's against my religion."

"Really?" Ray asked. "What religion is that?"

"No," Newitz said. "I just like driving."

"Well, I don't like dying, so could we please put it in automatic?"

"My car, my rules. Besides I paid extra to get this full-sized steering wheel instead of those dinky side-mounted dials."

Great. I'm riding with a crazy spy. "What's your plan?" Ray asked.

"We're going to talk to his boss."

Buckley AFB, Colorado

Ray yawned, not caring who saw him. *I'm getting too old for this up all night shit.* Colonel Newitz, walking ahead of him, stopped to salute a statuesque blonde female in a Space Force dress blue uniform. After the blonde returned the salute, Newitz made the introductions.

"General," Ray said, offering his hand.

"Elizabeth Ostrander," she replied. "But you can call me Brigadier. It's Saturday, my daughter graduates from college tonight, so this damn well better be important."

"Did you brief the General?" Ray asked Newitz. "Fully?"

"Didn't have time," Newitz said. "But she does know about the *Oklahoma's* mission."

"In broad strokes," Ostrander replied. "Let's hold the rest of this until we're inside."

Once in her office she planted herself behind her desk and glared at Ray. "And what exactly do you want from me?"

"It's imperative, ma'am," Newitz said, "that no word of our rescue effort leak to the pirates. Either via whatever intelligence network they have organically or via the Mercurian Secret Service."

"And we think they have an 'organic intelligence network'?" Ostrander said with air quotes.

"Captain Scott Hancock is having, well, romantic relations with somebody we think is affiliated with the hijackers," Ray said. "We really need to find out what he's already told the hijackers and control further messaging."

"Well, that's pretty damn organic." She leaned back in her chair. "They call him 'Hardcock' because he would bang a goldfish if he thought it would fit," Ostrander said with a sigh. She held up a hand. "I make it a point to know my officers. I do like to think that they have the smarts not to say things they shouldn't."

"But we can't take that chance," Ray said.

"No, we can't," she replied. "I'll get him in here." She gestured at the door to her office. "Please wait outside."

***

Youth is wasted on the young, Ray thought, watching the twenty-something Hancock, dressed in casual civilian wear, T-shirt and shorts, walk through the General's waiting room. The kid didn't look at all worse for the wear of a late night of athletic sex.

Hancock did shoot Ray and Newitz a quizzical look as he knocked on Ostrander's door. She opened it, and beckoned everybody in. Ray and Newitz took seats on either end of Hancock, all in front of Ostrander's desk.

"Agent Volk, FBI and Colonel Newitz, Air Force Intelligence," Ostrander said, pointing. "They have the highest security clearances, actually higher than mine. Thus, I want a frank and full answer. We're concerned that information about the 30th Space Wing's current mission may have leaked out. Do you have anything you want to tell us?"

Hancock shot Ray a puzzled look. "No, ma'am," he said to Ostrander.

"Don't bullshit me, Captain," Ostrander replied.

"Ma'am," Hancock replied, a pained note in his voice. "I know how to keep a secret." He glanced again at Ray. "Why are you asking me?"

"What do you know about your girlfriend Wilma Simmons?" Ray asked.

"She's a freight forwarder out of KC," he said. "We're friends."

"How did you meet?" Ray asked.

"SeaTac in an airport lounge. Our flights got cancelled because of a hurricane, and we ended up sharing a room." He smiled. "We had a great time."

"I'm sure you did," Ostrander said. "You have a way of making the best of a situation."

Hancock looked at Ray. "You don't think..."

"We do," Ray said. *Sorry kid.* "So, we really need to know."

"I swear to God, I've told her nothing confidential." He looked at Ostrander. "Really, ma'am. No shop talk at all."

There was an uncomfortable pause. Finally, Ostrander said, "Captain, wait outside."

He left. When he was gone, Ostrander said, "I believe him."

"Well, I believe Simmons is involved in this," Ray said.

"She might be," Ostrander replied. "But I got to tell you, besides my unit—and not all of them, mind you, but a few— there are probably fifty people who know where the 30th is.

There are probably another fifty who know they're not where they are supposed to be."

"Be that as it may, ma'am," Newitz said. "How many of those people are sleeping with somebody who's involved with the hijacking?"

"That we know of, Colonel, just one." She leaned back in her chair. "Ideas?"

***

"Captain Hancock," Ostrander said. The unfortunate captain was standing in front of Ostrander's desk, having been pointedly not offered a seat. "Your girl-toy is going to ask you about the 30th. I'm sure she'll bring up some gossip she heard from somebody else."

"So, I should deny it?" Hancock asked.

"No, confirm it," Ostrander replied. Newitz glared at her, and she waved him off. "What you're also going to tell her is something she can't have heard from anybody. You're going to tell her 30th Wing is heading to the asteroids."

"Big place, ma'am," Hancock said.

"It is," Ostrander said. "Which is why you'll tell her the target is 243 Ida. You'll also tell her that we think the CIA hijacked it."

"Ma'am, why would the Central Intelligence Agency hijack a spaceship?"

"Committee for Independent Asteroids," Ray said. To Hancock's puzzled look, he said, "I just heard of them the other day myself."

"Originally they were a separatist movement," Newitz said, "opposed to Martian control of the asteroids. Nowadays more like the Mob than freedom fighters, but occasionally they sponsor some political terrorism."

"Would stealing a ship be up their alley?" Hancock asked.

Not from what I've been told, Ray thought. But what the kid doesn't know won't hurt him. "Money's money."

"Copy that, sir," Hancock replied. "But why are we telling her this?"

"We want to see who she calls," Newitz said. "And it's important that you sell her on this. Understand?"

"Yes sir," Hancock replied. To the general, he asked, "Anything else, ma'am?"

"No. You're dismissed," she said. He saluted and left. She looked at Ray. "I hope he's her only source, but I wouldn't bet on it. Keep digging."

Ray could tell when he'd been dismissed. "Yes, ma'am," he said standing up. Newitz took a second to follow that lead.

***

"Well, looks like we patched our leak," Newitz said.

"Maybe," Ray said, walking out to the car. "It doesn't help me much, though."

"How so?"

"I'm trying to build a case on Simmons as part of the hijacking, remember?" Ray waved his arm. "I still only have suspicions."

"You'll have more soon," Newitz said.

"How so?"

"We put a tap on her communications," he said. "When she sends out the message..."

"I still can't use it, because the US military can't spy on our citizens."

"We can if it's a counter-espionage mission," he said.

"Which means she'd have to be working for a foreign government."

"Well, it's reasonable to assume that she's working for the Mercurian Syndicate," Newitz said.

"Is it?" Ray asked. "From the little research I've done they seem much more interested in cash than stirring trouble."

Newitz shrugged. "I didn't say she was working for them. Just that it would be reasonable to assume that."

We just need to convince a judge it was reasonable to suspect her of being a foreign agent, not that she is one. "Got it."

"Where to?" Newitz said.

Ray had put his ocular on, and it was identifying the rental car he'd ordered. "You can do whatever. I'm taking a car to the local FBI field office." A proper car that drove itself.

"I could give you a ride and save the government some money."

"Thanks, but I'm good." *Except we still don't know how much information leaked out.*

***

In the rental car, Ray played his latest message from Mark. Speed of light delays were increasing dramatically, making real-time conversations difficult. Mark, speaking on behalf of the fleet, was trying to figure out how much the Mercurian military knew about what was going on and what level of involvement, if any, they had. Ray still had no answers, which made his personal question at the end of his reply even more awkward.

"Hey, Captain," Ray said. "I've been texting a cute Martian Marine, but about half of his replies come back with alphabet soup instead of words. Got any advice on how to translate Marine jargon?"

ValuTrip Cardinal

Victoria

"What's the soup?" Victoria asked, walking up to the buffet line they'd set up in the piano lounge.

One of Helen's boys, sweaty and flushed, looked at her. "How can you eat soup in heat like this?"

Cut the kid some slack. He's a Martian. When she'd first arrived on Earth, she thought she'd never be warm again. "I'm hungry, that's how."

"It's homemade," Helen said, coming up to take over from her boy. She gave Victoria a cup of it. It was noodles which were leftover elbow macaroni from last night's pasta dish mixed with cut-up hot dogs in a chicken broth. Weird looking, but it smelled good. She took the cup and went down the line, loading her plate up as she did.

She'd eaten at a keyboard before, but it was awkward, so she took a seat at the bar instead. A prisoner behind the bar set a glass of water in front of her. "Sorry, ice machine isn't keeping up very well."

Victoria took a sip of water then stopped. "You. Prisoner. Come here."

The prisoner, an older balding, white dude, walked over. "Yes ma'am?"

"What are you doing here?"

"Working, ma'am." He gestured at Mike. "Commander Zero assigned me."

She gritted her teeth. *Goddamn it! This place was supposed to be off-limits to prisoners!* "Okay," she said. "Carry on."

Skye, their video surveillance person, strode into the room. She grabbed a plate and took a seat next to Victoria. The woman could definitely use a shower. She was their only person in the video surveillance room, and was basically living there. She only came out for brief periods to eat and use the facilities.

"Who's in video?" Victoria asked.

"Juan's spelling me," she replied, talking around a biscuit.

"How's it going?"

"This heat sucks," Skye replied. "Five cameras went down last night."

"They back up?"

"Yeah. Lou got to them." Skye had set a ship's handheld down on the bar next to her. It buzzed and she put the call on speaker. "Yeah?"

"Camera 15-6 is down." She recognized Juan's distinctive accent.

"I'll get Lou on it," Skye replied.

"No, I'll go, after I finish this," Victoria said. "Where is it?"

"Third deck. Access to crew's quarters."

***

The camera in question was mounted on the ceiling in a position to cover one of the doors leading into the crew's quarters. Victoria had brought a small folding stepstool, which she used to reach the camera. It was mounted in a tamper-proof case, which required a special screwdriver to unscrew.

Well, it was supposed to require a special screw. The screws were missing, and all she had to do was turn the mounting forty-five degrees and it came off easily. The problem was also immediately obvious and not heat-related. The camera was wired into a network for power and data, but the wire had been unplugged. "What the actual fuck!"

She called Skye. "15-6 should be up."

"It is."

"Anything else down?"

"Not right now."

And what the fuck does that mean? "Define, 'not right now' please."

"I mean, individual cameras go up and down like all the damn time."

"You mean they stay down until Lou fixes them?"

"No, sometimes they go down and stay down, other times they come back up."

"Is that normal?" *I hired you for this because you had this exact same job on another passenger ship. Use your fucking expertise, bitch!*

"One or two, yeah," came the reply. "Does seem like there've been a lot more down recently."

***

"Explain to me, Lou," Victoria said, back in the piano bar, "what you've been doing to fix the cameras."

"Plug them back in," he said, a cow-like look on his face. Not for the first time she wondered if he was high on something. He was one of the people who'd been smuggled aboard on the cargo container. He'd briefly worked as an Able Spacer on an in-system cargo ship, then 'became unemployed.' *It was hard to find good help.*

"And you weren't surprised to see them unplugged?"

He shrugged. "I figured vibration did it."

Beale's constant jacking the engines on and off, part of his master plan to confuse any tracking system, was introducing a lot more vibration to the ship. The ship came under thrust again, causing Lou to sway a bit and her to lean back against the piano. "I thought that the cameras were supposed to have special screws on the covers."

"Supposed to," he said with a grin. "Most don't." Her face must have shown her displeasure, because his smile fell. "Like that from before I got here."

And you didn't think to mention that to anybody. Just like that fat bimbo Skye didn't report cameras dropping like flies. Victoria glared at him. *I ought to just shoot the both of them.*

There was a commotion at the door to the bar. Victoria looked past Lou to see Helen Grabowski hauling the younger of her sons in. The kid's face was dirty.

"Kids giving you grief?" Lou said.

"Caught him ratting," she replied, cuffing the boy's ear.

"People are doing it all the time!" the kid cried.

That's an odd turn of phrase. "Helen," Victoria said. "Bring him here." She glanced around, making sure that the prisoner who'd been there earlier was gone.

Helen marched up, her young son in tow. "Yes?"

"Son," Victoria said, trying to sound non-threatening. "You said people are doing it all the time. What did you mean by that?"

He looked askance at his mother, who nodded. "I mean, I seen signs in the tunnels."

"Such as?"

"Such as footprints in the dust."

"Our footprints, right?"

"No," he replied. "The soft-shoed ones like we gave the passengers."

Oh fuck. Victoria felt suddenly dizzy. *Forty goddamned Martian high schoolers on this boat. Tunnelling was practically the Martian national pastime!* She clenched her stomach. "Thanks. That will be all."

Helen nodded, gave her son another whack, and dragged him off. She turned to see the prisoner from before walk into the bar, carrying a tub of ice. *This shit stops now!* She got up to where Mike was sitting, gabbing with Ted Beale. "Gentlemen, could I see you in my cabin?"

***

"I swear, if you tell me to 'be calm' again I'll shoot you!" Victoria said, glaring at Ted Beale. *I called you and Mike to my cabin to help, not treat me like a fucking madwoman.* "We're being rat-tunneled! They're taking out cameras!"

"To do what?" Mike asked. "Where can they go?"

"If they get out of line, we depressurize," Beale said.

"Then we got no money," Mike replied.

"I don't know what they're fucking doing!" Victoria said. She jabbed her finger hard into Mike's chest. "And neither do you!"

"Okay, then, lose your shit," Beale replied. "But tell me this—what exactly do you want us to do differently?"

"Move the prisoners," Victoria said.

"Oh man," Mike replied. "Keeping them in the dining room will be a genuine bitch. Place gets hot enough now."

"No," Victoria said, thinking back to a prison movie she's seen. "Move them to different cabins. With different roommates."

"What will that do?" Mike asked.

"Not everybody is in on this," Victoria said. "Not every cabin is set up for people to leave from." *I hope.* "So, we move them." She pointed at Mike again. "And Commander Zero makes a speech about how obedience is important. Maybe punishes somebody."

"At random?" Mike asked.

"Why not?" Victoria said.

"I don't know..." Mike replied.

"I do," Victoria said firmly. "Make it happen. Oh, and I better not see another prisoner wandering around in our lounge."

"Helen was looking for help," Mike said.

"Ask me if I give a fuck," Victoria replied. "That's sacred ground. Got it?"

"If you ask me—" Beale started.

"I did not." She glared at the two men. "I remind you that you need me to get permission to enter Mercurian space. This is my mission, and by God, I'm in charge."

"So would *you* like to make the speech?" Mike asked mockingly.

"No, Commander Zero," she said. "I think you'll do just fine."

"Anything else, Your Grace?" Mike asked.

"Yes. I'd like to take a tour of the fan rooms."

"I'll get on it."

"After we move the prisoners."

***

"Don't they clean this?" Victoria asked. They were standing in a cramped, noisy and dirty room just off of the main passenger cabins. It was dominated by several large boxes with fans running audibly inside of them.

"Occasionally," Mike said. He was acting as guide, with Ron, one of their guards/techs. "But these units are constantly moving air around, so the dirt gets blown in." Mike pointed at a large round duct. "That valve—the one at the end of the duct—goes straight out to vacuum." He tapped on the valve in question. "This motor is normally activated by the life support computer. We've bypassed it, running power directly to it via this cord."

It was a shame we weren't able to get the codes for depressurization from Montoya. We could have avoided this workaround entirely. The cord in question plugged into a gray box which plugged into a standard electrical outlet. "When the remote is tripped, the gray box sends power to the motor and the motor runs, opening the valve." Mike keyed his radio. "5-52-1, now."

The motor rather noisily sprang to life, causing the valve to move. "Now, to actually depressurize, I also need to move this valve"—he gestured to a nearly identical valve also wired to an outlet—"but since I don't we move one at a time."

"How long will it take?" Victoria asked.

"When all the valves open?" Ron asked. Victoria nodded. "Incapacitation in three to five minutes."

"Death?" Victoria asked. Ron seemed reluctant to answer, so Victoria asked again.

"Depends on the individual, but the book answer is an additional five minutes." He held up a hand. "But brain damage starts almost immediately once they pass out."

"So, you can have vegetables in five and corpses in ten," Mike said.

"Let's hope we don't end up there," Victoria said.

"Happy?" Mike asked, clearly hoping the inspection was over.

"For this room, yes," Victoria said. "Let's see the rest."

Denver, Colorado

Ray

Ray jerked awake, his mouth cottony. He fumbled on the light, then found his phone. "Volk," he growled into the device.

"I've got some bad news for you," Newitz said. Ray grunted, and Newitz continued. "One of your junior G-Men in KC got a fingerprint on Simmons."

"And?"

"She's DEA."

If she's in the Drug Enforcement Agency, why didn't she identify herself? "Wonderful."

"Simmons also changed her flight—she's going back to KC early tomorrow morning."

"Send me her service record. I'll meet her at the airport." Ray broke the connection. He looked at the hotel room clock. *Christ. Might as well stay up.*

Denver International Airport

Not many people felt the need to fly on Sunday morning, so the Denver airport's cavernous spaces were largely empty. Wilma Simmons, real name Jennifer Simmons, was sitting in the waiting area of a closed gate, across the empty hallway from the just-opening gate for the Kansas City flight.

Ray sat down next to her. "Morning," Ray said.

"Agent Volk," Simmons replied. "Fancy meeting you here."

Ray showed her the screen of his handheld. "You could have told me."

Simmons handed back the paper. "Deep cover means you don't tell your life story to every Joe with a badge."

"What do you know about ValuTrip *Cardinal*?" Ray asked.

Simmons gestured up at the—thankfully off—video monitors. "Just what I see on the newsfeeds."

"She's been hijacked, and your buddy Frank Malan was involved up to his eyebrows. Five hundred civilians plus crew are hoping that we can pull off a rescue. So, I'm going to ask you some questions, and I want some no-shit answers."

"Go for it."

"How'd you and Captain Hancock meet?"

Simmons stretched. "His unit has some kind of tracking gear in KC that he comes in periodically to inspect or whatever. We met at a bar and hit it off. Now we fly in periodically, we rock each other's world then we go." Simmons glared at Ray. "What did you tell Scott?"

"That we thought you were a spy. That fake bio of yours makes you suspicious."

Simmons turned away. "That explains a lot. After Scott got back from the base, he was cold. We ended up in a fight and I spent the night on the couch."

"Sorry," Ray said, not that he cared. "Who'd you see in Alaska?"

"Nobody," Simmons said. "I booked a flight to Alaska with a connection in Seattle. I 'accidentally' miss my connection and have to spend a night in the airport hotel, which I use to meet my handler."

"We'll confirm that. How did you really meet Frank Malan?"

That merited a smile. "DEA's been seeing an influx of Martian cocaine. When Brian Campallo got a job at ValuTrip, I made it a priority to get my own contacts."

Brian Campallo? The ValuTrip guy in charge of cargo hired by Malan at ValuTrip? Ray held up a hand. "Wait. What do you know about Brian Campallo? I mean, except for the possession bust?"

"That possession bust was supposed to be 'intent to distribute,'" Simmons said with a frown. "Then one of our witnesses for that case accidentally drowns in their swimming pool. All we could make stick was the possession charge."

"And when he got out, Frank got him the ValuTrip job?"

"Yep. Our witnesses' pool was three doors down from Frank's house." Simmons glanced around, then continued. "We think—hell we know—Frank was desperate for cash. That house was hocked to the hilt. We think Campallo paid Frank to get him the gig, and that they were setting up a drug-smuggling operation."

"We're holding Campallo for the hijacking," Ray said. "Big leap from drugs to kidnapping."

"Depends," Simmons said with a shrug. "If he's just providing a customs contact or something, not so much. We do think he's done the occasional human trafficking gig, and he did murder a witness."

"So, he's the boss and Frank's the underling," Ray said.

"The boss is usually last to get whacked, not first." She took a sip of her coffee. "By the way, Campallo's gone missing."

True and Campallo was very much alive. He would also know how to get a good hit team. Ray decided he'd been too fixated on Frank as mastermind. "How did you and Victoria Stevens get to be neighbors?"

"When I first moved to Kansas, I was staying at the long-term place attached to the Marriott. Vickie gave me a lead on a condo for sale by owner."

"And you know her how?"

"She had a temporary gig playing piano at the bar." Simmons smiled. "She's quite fuckable."

"Did you? Fuck I mean."

"Yes, frequently. Why do you care?"

"She's one of the hijackers?"

Simmons' surprise showed. "Really? When did she book a trip to Mars?"

"She's an employee of ValuTrip."

"News to me."

"Frank didn't tell you?" Ray asked.

"Frank was my in to Campallo," she said. "And didn't I say Campallo's gone missing?"

"He's in a holding cell in FBI headquarters at KC."

"Since when?"

"A couple of days ago." To her pending objection, Ray held up his hand. "We haven't arraigned him yet. Special deal—it was either he stayed as our guest, or we handed him to the Martian Space Fleet as a pirate."

"I take it they don't like pirates?"

"They shove them out airlocks without a suit." Ray sympathized with her disgusted reaction. "I suppose you've got some answer as to why your cover ID ties to Mercury?"

"Great-aunt Wilma moved there then disappeared." Simmons favored Ray with a look. "What does Mercury have to do with anything?"

"Never mind. Why did Ricardo hand you over as somebody Malan was scared of?"

Simmons sighed. "The Colonel has bought my cover story, for one, so she thinks I'm drugged up. Second, as part of my efforts to get to Campallo, I had Frank move what he thought was a suitcase of coke for me. It was baby powder." Simmons took another sip of coffee. "The whole operation was a cluster-fuck, and if I hadn't been DEA, Frank Malan would be in jail. I am, so I made it look successful, but Frank could see it was a close thing. I had to stay in character, so I leaned on Frank."

"So, he was scared of you." It was a statement, not a question.

"I'm surprised Campallo didn't give you my name. It would be an easy way to get rid of a competitor."

"Campallo was being hauled off to face a Martian firing squad," Ray said dryly. "Only thing he was concerned about was his skin."

Simmons nodded. "Firing squads do tend to focus the mind." Simmons offered her hand. "Sorry to put you back on square one."

Not nearly as sorry as I am.

***

Ray called Fetterer as the car drove back to his hotel. He told her about the Simmons meeting, ending with, "We need to go back to Campallo."

"I'll take another run at him today after church," she replied. "In other news, I got a call from the tech squad. Late Saturday afternoon, somebody sent a message to our ship."

"I thought they were getting messages all the time?" Ray said.

"They are." Fetterer looked at something off-camera, and mouthed *in a minute*. "But as the tech guys explained to me, message traffic falls off radically over the weekend, and this particular message stood out."

"What was the message?"

Fetterer shrugged, barely visible on Ray's small handheld display. "Ostensibly it was two articles about investing— what stocks to buy, etc. Somebody on our boat's been getting the same type of message twice every weekday."

"Somebody is thinking ahead about their riches when they pull this off?"

Fetterer smiled. "Nice try, but no. I looked at not only this message, but all the messages sent to the same address from the same sender."

"And?" Fetterer's passion for investing was well known in the office.

"No rhyme or reason I could see as to why she would be getting parts one and three of an article on plastics mining in landfills followed by an article on sex tourism in Idaho."

Ray thought that was an eclectic mix, but let Fetterer continue. "Then I saw one of the articles was supposedly from an investing site I follow. Except the article had been subtly altered."

"Code?"

"Apparently. I checked the rest, and the same was true."

Any code can be broken if we have enough time and enough messages. "What did cryptography say?"

"Non-trivial." She sighed. "They talked about book codes and one-time pads."

'Non-trivial' usually meant 'not any time soon.' "Shit. Do we at least know where the messages are sent from?"

"No. They're run through a source anonymizer."

Ray thought for a moment. "But something happened yesterday to trigger a special alert."

"Maybe," Fetterer said. "Maybe the ground spy just got lucky."

True. Without knowing what was in the message, it didn't prove anything. *Hell, it might just be a happy birthday greeting.* Ray scowled. *They were back at square one.* He broke the connection.

A second later his phone rang. This time it was Andrea Huggins. "Somebody was sniffing around for Beale."

"Our radio operator?"

"The same."

"Great. By the way, there's somebody by the same name on the *Cardinal.* Supposedly an American salesman. Wonder if it's any relation?"

"Beale's got a son who was a spaceship officer. The mother was an American."

Well, looks like we identified another hijacker. "So, who was looking for Beale Senior?"

"Emily Rata, or at least that's one of her aliases," she replied. "I'm sending you all of them that we know about."

Chapter 23

FBI Headquarters, Denver

Ray

"Emily Rata is the alias she's been using around here," Newitz said.

They were standing in a conference room at FBI headquarters, looking at a series of images of an attractive brunette. The office was busy, especially for a Sunday.

"You know her?"

"She's an 'independent journalist,'" Newitz said with air quotes. "Well-known in Space Force circles, largely because she's easy on the eyes."

"We'll find her," Ray said. "It's just a matter of time."

"We don't fucking have time," Newitz growled. "The Space Force hits the ship in four days." He glanced at his watch. "Now three days."

"Do you think she knows that they're going to Mercury?" Ray asked.

"She's smart enough that she could piece bits from different sources together," Newitz said. "So, we have to assume the answer is yes."

Another one of the Denver-based agents walked in. "Guys," she said. "Here's the cell phone analysis. Do you want the bad news or the bad news?"

Ray felt his headache getting worse. "Shouldn't there be some good news in there?"

"There should but there isn't." The agent continued. "She spent two hours Sunday afternoon at the residence of one Major Lou Hinkle, USSF."

"Oh, this is sounding fucking terrific," Ray said.

"Hinkle's an engineering officer, and we confirmed that he got a number of messages from the fleet about the high temperature problems they've been having. Messages that his girlfriend might have seen."

"I'm not a spacer, but I suspect 'high temperatures' and 'asteroids' don't mix?" Ray said sarcastically.

"They do not," Newitz said. "You had other news?"

"She ditched the phone in a shitty apartment a few blocks from her condo. We assume she had some kind of go bag there."

"Now what?" Newitz asked.

"Now we call the *Oklahoma* and ask if they want us to pull the plug on pirate radio," Ray said.

"But we control it!" Newitz replied. "We can block her messages!"

Ray pounded the desk. "How? What other messages is that ship getting that we don't understand? What will they do if the radio flow stops?" He shook his head. "The fleet needs to know. I expect this will end up on the President's desk."

ValuTrip Bluejay

Mark

Mark looked at the video feed. It was of General Morehouse's sitting room just off her flag plot. By Martian fleet standards the room was luxurious, but Mark had heard grumbles from Morehouse's staff about how substandard the space was. Apparently, the staff would have preferred *Kentucky's* much nicer one.

Morehouse herself appeared on the feed, clearly having just woken up. The ships were operating on Denver Time, and it was damned early in the morning. "I assume y'all read the message?"

Mark and the other three people with him, Lieutenant Colonel Wu of Delta, Chief Mapes of the Martian Marines, and the giant Master Sergeant Shadout, gave their assent. The message in question was from Earth, announcing that a suspected spy had found out the *Oklahoma's* true destination.

"Lopez needs to make a recommendation to POTUS," Morehouse said, referring to the Commandant of the US Space Force. "She wants our vote."

"We have to assume that the spy has or will soon tell the pirates on *Cardinal* we're on to them," Wu said.

"No shit, Colonel," Morehouse replied, saying what Mark was thinking. "The question is what do we do about it?"

"Nothing, ma'am," Mapes said. At Mark's arched eyebrow, the Chief continued. "With all due respect, so what?"

"So what?" Wu asked.

Mark smiled as it dawned on him. "You're right, Chief." Mark held his hands out. "What will they do differently? What *can* they do differently?"

"Well..." Wu started, then fell silent.

Mark pressed on. "They don't have re-mass to change course. They don't have any additional firepower, and they don't know when exactly we're coming or what our attack plan is."

"They could kill the hostages," Wu said. "Right now."

"They could," Mark acknowledged. "Or any damn time they want to, until the passengers pull the plugs on the valve motors." He shrugged. "That was a risk since Day One, and it hasn't changed."

"So, you counsel to continue as planned?" Morehouse asked.

"Yes, ma'am," Mapes and Mark replied.

"We should at least tell the passengers," Wu said. "They can pull the plugs now."

"No, we don't," Morehouse said.

"Ma'am?" Wu asked.

"Right now, the only card we have left is that the pirates don't know they're being tunnel-fucked," Morehouse said. "Unplugging shit risks giving that away." She stood up—a move tracked by the camera. "What the passengers don't know, they can't tell the pirates." She wagged her fingers.

"As far as I'm concerned, this information"—pointing at her screen—"is need to know, and the only people who need to know are on this call."

After Morehouse broke the connection, Mark pulled up his messaging system. "Personal for Ray Volk," he told the system. After it acknowledged it, Mark said, "So, about your translation problem. I recommend a book called *So your kid's a Marine* by Bill Tracy. You may have to buy it on Amazon Mars but it's well worth the effort." He ended the recording and hit send.

Well, I'm glad Ray got over being rejected by me.

ValuTrip Cardinal

Victoria

Victoria looked at the message from her contact on Earth. "They know—sending a ship to intercept you."

It was expected, but it still put fear in her heart. "Plan B, here we go." She started to compose a message.

Your Royal Highness:

I am returning to be at your side. Could you please arrange for the military reception you most generously offered when we last met? Please confirm via the usual channels.

Your Humble and Obedient Sister,

Victoria Hakken

"It's a pity you're not really a queen, sister," Victoria said once the message was sent. The Syndication that governed Mercury was just that, a collection of nominally-equal entities, of which the Red Kingdom was but one. Unfortunately, the equality was just that, nominal. Victoria either returned with a lot of money or several of the more powerful Syndicate members would gobble up their territories like a dog eating a treat. "But sister, it's time you took some risks as well."

***

At the appointed time, she used the ship's entertainment system to tune to a Mercurian broadcast station. The announcer came on. "We've got a special request from Alexandrina to Victoria, with love." They played "Tie a Yellow Ribbon Round the Ole Oak Tree."

Message received and acted on. She turned off the channel.

Chapter 24

ValuTrip Cardinal

Kelly

"I'm moving, damn it!" Kelly shouted. The guard, one of the few females, gave her another poke in the back with her non-lethal. To avoid a third poke, Kelly broke into a trot.

"Here!" the guard barked as Kelly came to another cabin door. "Your new home."

Kelly stepped inside, her small collection of prisonwear in her arms. She turned and looked at the guard. They were both drenched in sweat—Kelly because she was Martian and not used to heat, the guard because the stab-proof vest she was wearing didn't breathe well, even if the guard was just wearing a bra underneath. "Did I luck out and not get a roommate?"

"Ha!" the guard replied. A mousy woman, white with gray hair, arrived at the door, escorted by another guard. "Here she is."

The prisoner stepped in, and the female guard slid the door closed, saying as she did, "Stay put until breakfast."

"What the actual fuck?" Kelly said. Why had the guards moved everybody to a different cabin?

"Language, young lady," her new roommate said.

"Really?" Kelly asked. She set down her bundle of clothing and offered her hand. "Kelly Rack. You are?"

"Linda Montrose." The lady offered a dead fish of a hand which Kelly took. "And there's no reason to swear."

Well, I can think of a shitload of reasons to swear. "If you say so. So, where are you from?"

"Muskogee, Oklahoma."

"Which country?"

The woman looked a bit surprised. "America, of course." Somehow the woman had scored a paper bag, out of which she took an actual physical book. "Have you heard the Good Word?"

"I'm sure I have," Kelly replied. *There is a God and She's got a mean sense of humor.* There had been a group of missionaries on the ship, notable because they all hung out together. *Like us exchange students.* The seriousness of the missionary group had been the subject of much commentary.

"Good," Linda replied. "Do you mind?"

"Help yourself." Kelly gestured at the beds. "Please, take the bottom bunk."

"Thank you."

Kelly adjourned to the toilet, where she inspected the access panel in the shower. This was not one of the cabins the resistance had been using, so the panel was securely screwed on. Fortunately, the old-style keys worked just fine as screwdrivers.

There was a knock on the door. "Do you mind? I'd like to use the facilities."

"Sure," Kelly said. She stepped out. "Please, take your time."

***

Each of the bunks had a separate fixed alarm clock. Kelly set hers for 23:00, but she didn't need it, rolling out on her own a few minutes before the alarm. Linda, in the bunk below, had been out for some time. Apparently, people from Oklahoma could sleep in the heat, because she was out like a light.

Kelly slid into the toilet, closed the door, and started to work on the access panel. The screws were tight, so between that and the heat she quickly worked up a sweat. *Fuck this,* she thought, taking off her shirt. It helped a little.

"What are you doing?" Linda asked from behind her.

"Ah, I need to meet somebody," Kelly said.

"Who would you need to meet undressed like that?"

Yeah, so I don't like bras. "Ah, a friend."

"What kind of 'friend' do you need to meet in the middle of the night half-naked?"

What do I tell her?

Linda put her hand over her mouth. "Oh dear. Oh dear. I know you."

"You do?"

"Yes," she said, pointing with her other hand, "You...you're with the Green Giant."

Well, that is a good name for Bruno. Not that I'm with him. She looked at Linda. The woman was getting even paler.

"I'm sorry," Linda said. "My mistake." She pointed back toward the cabin. "I'll just go..."

Kelly didn't bother to hide her smile. "Don't wait up."

***

"What happened to your shirt?" Hank asked. Kelly had just crawled through the vent into the wire room where they were keeping the radio. Cody the Cop and Stan the Maintenance Man were there. Both those men could barely fit through the vent, which was just a grate covering a hole in the wall leading to a fan room. They had set up the grate so it was held in place by a pair of tie-wraps at the top, allowing it to hinge open from the bottom.

"It's too fucking hot," Kelly said. She glanced up at the camera. Since her incident with Vicky the Pirate, she'd been very conscious about cameras. This particular camera hadn't been disabled, but rather turned to point to a blank wall. Apparently whatever system monitored cameras wasn't smart enough to report that as a problem.

"It is warm," Cody replied, using the front of his shirt to wipe his face. Like the rest of them, he was sitting on the floor around the captain's radio.

"Has anybody told you that you have a pretty back?" Spider said, crawling in from the vent Kelly had just exited.

"She does, doesn't she," Hank said, ogling shamelessly.

"Down, girl," Kelly said. "You're old enough to be my mother."

"So? Moms like to have sex," Hank said.

"Ladies," Stan said, clearly uncomfortable. "Could we keep our pants on and focus on staying alive?" He glared at Kelly. "And maybe put on a shirt?"

"Didn't bring one," Kelly said.

Spider wordlessly pulled his off and handed it to her.

"Well, now that's settled," Hank said. "Anybody got a guess as to why we got shuffled around?"

"Obviously you've never been in a jail before," Cody said.

"I try to avoid them," Hank said dryly.

"Well, one of the things you do in a jail is periodically move prisoners around," Cody said. "It separates them from their contraband and disrupts both jailbreak attempts and gang activity."

"So, the question is," Hank said, "was this a routine roust or triggered by something?"

"The latter," Spider said. "We're not the only people in the tunnels."

"You're sure?" Hank asked.

"Positive," Spider said. "I found a nest."

"A nest?" the Earthlings asked, more or less in unison.

"A mattress, a pile of blankets, you know, a nest." Spider shrugged.

"Other passengers?" Cody asked.

"Kids," Spider said. "Unless you know an adult who plays with toys."

"I didn't see any kids onboard," Hank said.

Largely because you were just looking to get laid, Kelly thought.

"Helen's kids," Stan said. To the groups' quizzical looks, he added, "Helen Grabowski. The bartender. She smuggled her kids onboard."

"So if they see us they'll go run to Mama Pirate," Kelly said. "This shit gets better and better."

"Well," Hank said. "We'll just have to avoid them. We've got other problems."

***

"There has to be a way," Cody the Cop said for at least the fifth time in the last half hour of going around in circles.

"Face it. It's a bust," Kelly argued. "We can't get past the doors above the first level, and if we did, we still can't get the airlock doors open."

"That's the second time somebody said it's a bust," Hank said, a thoughtful look on her face. "The first time was just before Princess Piano choked me out."

"Well obviously they were wrong," Cody snorted. He gestured around vigorously. "We're here."

"It was that jerk Beale," Hank said, ignoring Cody. "He said Zoren was a bust."

"Zoren?" Stan asked.

"Pretty sure. Why?"

"He's a baggage handler," Stan said. "Which gives me an idea." He stood up stiffly. "Let's take a field trip."

***

Stan led them to a staircase on the first deck. There was a single ladder going up through a round manhole set in a larger hatch which was manually dogged down.

"Hatch is alarmed," Stan said. "Manhole's not."

"Camera is out," Cody said, pointing to a disconnected camera on the wall. A large red tag dangled from the camera.

"Down for maintenance," Stan said. He clucked his tongue. "It's the most maintained camera on the ship."

"Because?" Hank said.

"Because directly above us is where the passenger baggage and any cargo that needs to be pressurized is kept." Stan pointed up. "Lots of opportunities for petty theft."

"So how does this help us?" Hank said.

"Well, we can go up here. There's an emergency door out to both spokes, which leads to the outer airlocks."

"Alarmed?" Cody asked.

"Yes," Stan said. "But not locked or lockable."

"I said there was a way!" Cody exclaimed.

"Yeah," Stan replied, "but this has to be how the pirates hid the people not on the ship's manifest. As soon as they see the alarm, they'll close this hatch."

"And they can still close the airlock doors as soon as we open them. Assuming we can open them." *We're still stuck.*

"We'll get them open," Cody said.

"I hope so," Hank said. "Well, let's call Earth and tell them what we found."

"Aye aye, ma'am," Cody said, tossing a half-assed salute. He looked at Kelly and Spider. "Why don't you two call it a night?"

Why don't you eat shit and die?

Spider tugged at her hand. "Hey, I got to show you something."

"Okay." She nodded and allowed herself to be led away.

A short time later they were in Captain Montoya's cabin. "Look what I found," Spider said, holding up a bottle of booze. "Captain's private store."

Dead man's private store. Well, he's not going to need it anymore. "Glasses?"

He produced two and poured some of the amber liquid. They sat down on the couch. She took a sip, winced at the burn, and asked, "What's the occasion?"

"We might die," he said. "Seemed like a good reason to me."

Yeah. She took another sip. "I have no idea what half-assed plan Earth's going to come up with."

"I'm sure it will be wonderful," he replied. He sipped and winced. "What's in this stuff? It tastes like burnt wood."

Kelly got up and walked over to the table where he'd left the bottle. She picked it up and read the label aloud. "Glenmorangie, aged 10 years," she said, tripping over the unfamiliar name. "Product of Scotland."

"That's Earth, right?"

"I think so."

"Cheers." They each took another sip. His eyes started to water.

"It's not that bad," Kelly said, touching his face. "The booze I mean."

"It's not the booze," Spider said, his voice cracking. "I'm scared." He looked around the dead man's cabin. "I've been scared shitless since the fire alarm went off."

Kelly sat down next to him. *So now he says that.* Admitting that took a lot. "So am I," she said, wrapping her arm around him.

They sat like that for a minute, then he kissed her, on the mouth, tentatively, like she was going to slap him.

"Why'd you do that?" Kelly asked.

"I wanted too," Spider replied.

Kelly kissed him back, not sure why she did so. "Thanks."

"You're welcome." She looked at the other side of the room. "Captains apparently get a full-sized bed."

"They do."

"Come on, damn it, before I change my mind," Kelly said, pulling her shirt off. He sat there, staring at her boobs, and she grabbed one of his hands and clasped it on her breast. *I might not be first in your saddle, but I might be last.* "Come on, cowboy, time to ride."

***

Kelly opened her eyes. Sleep just wasn't happening. She looked and noticed that the light was on in the bathroom. She knocked softly on the door.

"You need to use it?" Spider asked.

"Not really," Kelly said. "I can't sleep."

"Come in," Spider replied.

Kelly did, finding Spider sitting on the floor of the tiny space. He had a length of plastic pipe in his hand, and he was using a piece of sandpaper on it. Sweat dripped off his nose. She sat down on the floor next to him, half-out of the tiny bathroom.

"What are you doing?"

"Trying to make this into a spear."

Kelly looked at the jagged end. It was more-or-less sharp and pointed. "I'd have gone with something heavier."

"Cody's got the pipe wrench."

"You don't have to do this," Kelly said. "Impress me, I mean."

"I'm not trying to impress you. I'm doing my duty."

"We're not in the army."

Spider looked up. "Well, technically we were 'recalled to active duty.'"

He was right. Some high school senior on the other side of the ship, a kid who'd been squad leader in boot, had been appointed "senior Martian military present." Kelly couldn't pick the kid out of a lineup.

"What are they going to do, shoot us?"

"Probably not. Still, I don't think I could look at myself in the mirror if I didn't try." Spider returned to his work. "I'm surprised. You've done a lot."

"It's one thing sneaking around a ship. It's another to take on armed men with a fucking plastic pipe. Fancy way to suicide."

Spider very deliberately put his spear down and looked up. "I'd rather be dead than a slave."

"They won't let the pirates take us off the ship."

"We hope not. But that means the pirates get paid, and that means somebody else will try this. We fix it now or die later."

We fix it now or die later. Words drilled into every Martian's head. You saw a problem with life support, with power, with any critical system, you fixed it now, because you never knew when it was going to fail catastrophically.

Kelly stared at him for a minute, then she punched his shoulder.

"What was that for?" he asked.

"For being so hard-headed. And right, but mostly hard-headed."

"Are all women this confusing?"

"Yes," Kelly said.

Chapter 25

ValuTrip Bluejay

Mark

Mark scowled at his cards. A pair of jacks wasn't much, but it was the best hand he'd seen in a while. Considering that they were playing for peanuts—albeit chocolate-covered ones—in what had to be the most disjointed game he'd ever played, a pair of jacks was good enough. "See you two and raise two."

"I'm in," Peterson replied, pushing in a pair of the bite-sized candies they were playing for. The ship's phone—hardwired to the table next to Captain Brass's chair—rang. Brass answered it.

"Make it so," he said to the person on the other end, then hung up. "POTUS says 'go Sooners.'"

Colonel Wu smiled. "That's the first bet I've been happy to lose." He had rather publicly bet that "no Republican, especially one from her wing of the party" would green light a military operation. Mark had gladly taken the other half of the bet.

"We're transferring you off to *Oklahoma* in three hours," Brass said. "The announcement will be made shortly."

The assault team would leave from *Oklahoma*, as testing with *Bluejay's* identical radar had shown that the relatively stealthy warship could get to within five thousand kilometers of *Cardinal* without being detected. *That is, as long as we can hide dead astern of her while her main engines are running.* Brass looked at Mark. "The General would like you to call her immediately."

"Okay," Mark said, getting up and going to his cabin, where he could call the flagship via the ship's comm system. It was a short walk, and when Mark arrived, he quickly made the connections on his system.

"Morehouse," she said over the secure voice-only link.

"This is Captain Nagata, ma'am. You asked me to call? Over."

"I did. I want you here on *Oklahoma* during the operation. Over."

"May I ask why? Over."

"Tom Wu's going to be in the first wave, so I need somebody here who understands the tactical plan. And frankly, Martians do a lot more training with boarding ops than we do. Over."

And why the hell are you letting Wu play cowboy instead of keeping him in flag plot where he could do some good? But the internal politics of another nation's military were not his problem. And she did have a point—Mars' control of the asteroids meant that they did a lot more of these kind of missions. "Understood. Are you still planning to leave *Bluejay* as a separate task group? Over."

"I was hoping to strip out your tin cans. Over."

I was expecting that. The American force was a bit thin on escorts, and the three Martian destroyers would be useful as a general screen. *Actually more useful than huddled around* Bluejay. "Of course, ma'am. Who will be screen commander? Over."

"Samuels on *Atlanta*. Ricardo should remain TACON of *Bluejay*. Over."

"Very good, ma'am. I'll send the orders immediately. Any other traffic? Over."

"Negative. Out."

ValuTrip Cardinal

Kelly

"Do we have enough people?" Kelly asked.

"A bit late to worry about that," Otarski replied. Kelly bet at least two thirds of the people on the ship had no idea what was about to happen. The pirates had done a damn fine job of keeping passengers and crew separated into small pockets.

"Why is all of this stuff here?" Kelly asked in a low voice. They were standing in what had been billed as the "Kid's Korner" on the sign outside, and it was full of boxes and stacked furniture.

"We were going in for a maintenance period after this run," Otarski said. "We got a deal on carpeting on Mars, so since we had no kids onboard, ownership told us to stash the stuff here."

Her stomach fluttered again. She'd gotten more-or-less used to sneaking around the ship, but the commandos were coming. The time for sneaking around was over. She swallowed with an effort. "Makes sense. Where am I going?"

Otarski pointed to a set of built-in shelves made to look like a growing tree. "Up there, then pop a ceiling tile. Other side of the wall is a maintenance closet."

A closet that had the circuit breakers to turn off the cameras, blinding their captors. The cameras had to stay down long enough for people to run through video-monitored areas without being detected and long enough for them to manually bypass the exterior pressure door controls. *All while the guards were trying to get video back up.* Her stomach fluttered again. *Piece of cake.* "Phone?"

"Next to the door," Otarski said, pointing. "We'll have to unclip it from the wall." He held up a coil of wire. "This should be long enough to splice it back into the system."

***

The maintenance closet was small—maybe two meters wide by three deep. There was a large stand-up yellow pushcart/mobile trash can—of the type used by janitors throughout the universe—in front of the door to the corridor. The door was of the same flimsy fiberglass as most of the non-pressure doors, including the ones to the cabins.

It would offer little to no barrier to entry. But it opened into the closet, creating a pocket behind which Kelly could hide.

She glanced at the phone's time display. Hank would call her when the exact time came to kill the power, but for right now she had several hours to waste. Per the plan, she had to keep the cameras off for at least ten minutes—long enough for teams of passengers and crew to open two pressure-tight doors and get to the ship's outer airlocks.

Hopefully the pirates will take that long to figure out where the problem is. But probably not. That meant she might have to fight off a pirate. She grimaced, her stomach feeling sour. *Fight off a professional gunman with a sharpened screwdriver.* It was a shitty plan and required surprise to work. *Which means ambushing whomever comes in that door from hiding.*

Kelly felt a flash of anger. Hank hadn't asked for volunteers for this mission. *It was "Kelly do this" and "Kelly go there" like I'm her fucking maid.* She wiped the sweat from her face, wondering why the A/C wasn't working. Her anger faded. *And if it weren't for Hank, we'd all be sitting in our rooms sweating our asses off wondering what will happen to us next.*

Enough of the pity-party. She smiled, remembering the sergeant in boot camp who'd used that phrase. *I'm here with a job to do. But more weapons would be nice.*

Back at militia boot camp, her squad's female drill sergeant, a grandmotherly-looking woman with a mean right hook, had taught them hand-to-hand combat. "Remember, ladies," she'd said. "Men outweigh, outreach and out-muscle us. The only way for us to win a fistfight is to end it before he knows it's started."

She looked around the closet, finally settling on a light metal hammer, probably intended to tack down carpet. Now she had a short club. Checking her time again, she made herself as comfortable as possible on the floor.

Victoria

Victoria had just finished her song with a flourish when the PA system crackled. "Mister Beale, please call the pilothouse."

She turned, ready to give Beale a ration of shit for not telling the watch where he was. He waved her off, a ship's phone in his hand. He listened, then said, "I'll be right up," and hung up.

"Yes?"

"We have a contact on radar," Beale replied.

"Shouldn't we be expecting to see radar contacts this close to Mercury?"

"Not on this course," Beale said. "We're just inside the orbit of Mercury and getting ready to approach from sunward. Shouldn't be anything out here."

It was pleasantly warm in the lounge, but Victoria felt a sudden chill. She went to say something, and he held up his hand. "They're how many clicks on our stern? Five thousand?"

Victoria was no spaceship driver but knew enough to realize that was very close, unless you were approaching a dock. *God, I hope this is our welcome party from Alexandrina.*

"Well, put in a turn," Beale said over the phone.

"Change course?" Victoria said.

"Briefly," Beale replied, his hand over the mouthpiece. "Our radar is least effective dead astern of the engines."

Chapter 26

USS Oklahoma

Mark

"Shit!" Mark said. "*Cardinal's* in a turn!"

In Mark's headphones, the bridge announced they were going to try and match *Cardinal's* turn.

Morehouse replied. "Negative, bridge. Kill engines and drift." She cupped her headset mic in her hand. "No way we can match the turn, and everything else is running on our best stealth mode. Any other off-gassing or heat generation will give us away."

"Target is continuing a turn," the bridge officer said over the intercom, concern noticeable in her voice.

"Those antennas have been staring at the sun for a week," Morehouse told the bridge. "Hopefully they'll see us and think we're a radar artifact."

ValuTrip Cardinal

Victoria

"Well?" Victoria asked.

Beale replied by holding up a finger. He listened, then said, "We lost the track."

"It's gone?"

"Nothing on scope," Beale said. "Now."

"False alarm?"

He grimaced. "Maybe. I'm still going up there to take a look."

"Let me know if you see anything." She gestured at the piano. "I'll be here."

"Will do."

USS Oklahoma

Mark

"Our birds are now nine hundred fifty kilometers out," Mark said. "*Cardinal's* turn closed the range a bit. We need to get the passengers moving."

Morehouse nodded. "Make the call."

Mark keyed the radio. "Victor Charlie actual, this is Oscar. Green flag, repeat, green flag. Over."

ValuTrip Cardinal

Kelly

The ship's phone flashed. Kelly started, then grabbed the handset. "Yes?"

"Drop the cameras," Hank said.

"Coming down," Kelly replied, scrambling to her feet. With the receiver still in her hand, she tripped the main breakers for the two circuit boxes. The room went dark, illuminated only by the light from the phone. Supposedly the camera system was down as well. "We're down," Kelly said.

"Good," said Hank. Kelly could hear the two other phone talkers in the background issuing orders to passengers. "We need five minutes, no more, got it? Hold them for five and get gone."

Liar. You need ten and fifteen would be better. "Yes ma'am." In theory, she could just climb up the wall and over into the Kid's Korner. In practice, if somebody came into the room, she was screwed. It wasn't big enough to hide in and she doubted the guards would give her time to escape.

"Good luck. Hanging up."

Kelly took a deep breath and picked up her small hammer. She wedged herself in the corner, her pulse racing. *Damn it's hot.*

Victoria

Victoria had just sat down at the piano when her radio crackled. "This is Eye-in-the-Skye. I've lost all video and lights in security central, over."

"What the fuck now!" Victoria barked.

"Probably just a circuit tripped," Bruno said. "It's so fucking hot on this boat I'm surprised we haven't had more problems."

"I don't want excuses, I want it fixed," Victoria said.

"I'm on it, Your Grace," he said, pushing away from the bar where he'd been eating. He'd taken his stab-proof vest off and hadn't been wearing a shirt underneath it. He waved at Victoria. "Tell her I'm going to check the breakers."

"Okay," she replied.

"So boss," Helen said, picking up Bruno's plate. "One more song?"

"Sure," Victoria said. *It will calm me and everybody else down.* "I got an old one I've been wanting to play. It's called 'The Entertainer.'"

Kelly

There was a vent in the bottom of the door, allowing Kelly to see the sweep of a flashlight. She crouched down low, her hammer in her right hand and her screwdriver in her left. The opening of the door would hide her for a second.

"The only way for a woman to win a fistfight with a man," she whispered, "is to end it before he knows it's started."

Kelly crouched down. The door swung open, and a man started to walk in, holding a white electric lantern in his outstretched arm. Kelly swung her hammer down at his wrist with all her strength. She heard a satisfying crack and the man yowled, dropping his lantern.

She swung her screwdriver at where she thought his chin was, but he'd slammed the door hard at her, deflecting her thrust. She moved, but the door caught her knee painfully, causing her to gasp. She swung to her right, sweeping past the circuit box until she hit a corner.

The man stepped back into the hallway, illuminated by emergency lights and the lantern. Kelly launched herself at the man, aiming to put her shoulder into his gut and the top of the hammer into his throat.

He blocked the hammer with his good hand but took her shoulder in his gut. The momentum carried them both out of the room and they slammed against the far wall of the corridor.

He brought his fist down on her back, hard, bringing tears to her eyes. She dropped the hammer, but still had her screwdriver, which she used to flail at him, stabbing blindly at his bulk. The screwdriver started to get wet and slippery.

The man drove a knee up at her, but his size worked against him as his knee slipped to her side instead of into her gut. The man somehow grabbed her wrist and jerked it sideways. Kelly—more by accident than design—tripped him with her legs and they went down with her on top.

She was able to pass her screwdriver to her other hand and resume stabbing. He blocked with his other arm, but clearly the wrist wasn't working as he couldn't grab her. She finally got a thrust past his arm and into his chest, sinking the screwdriver to the hilt. He stopped moving.

"Fuck you!" Kelly said, wresting her arm free of the dead man. *Green hair. My old buddy Bruno.* His radio crackled, a woman's voice asking where the fuck he was.

"He's dead, you cocksucker," Kelly said. A part of her wondered why she didn't feel anything. *Worry about that later.* "Where's your gun?"

She saw his gun, still on a holster on his belt. She grabbed for it when his right arm came up and locked on her throat. She put both hands on the gun and a foot on his chest then pulled back. Her throat slipped out of his hand, and the gun and holster came off his belt.

She somehow got her finger on the trigger while the gun was still partially covered by the holster and fired two rounds into his chest, shooting through the holster. The shots were painfully loud in the metal-walled room. *I guess we're going to find out just how well this ship's self-sealing hull works.*

Kelly found herself sitting against the door jamb, the pistol, her finger on the trigger, pointing at her toes. She coughed and moved the muzzle in a safe direction. The radio was full of people screaming about shots fired. "No fucking shit," she said.

"Got to get moving," Kelly said, hauling herself to her feet. She saw a spare clip in a pouch attached to Bruno's belt, which she grabbed and started to pocket. She saw more flashlights moving in the main lobby, so she fired another couple of rounds in that general direction as suppressive fire. The corridor she was in was narrow and ended at the Kid's Korner. *Perfect place to hold up and snipe any fucker who comes to reset a breaker.*

Victoria

Victoria stopped playing mid-bar when she heard the shots. She didn't need the five radio reports of shots fired. "Silence on the net!" she barked into the radio.

"We're taking fire!" somebody said on the radio.

"No shit!" Victoria said, standing up. She keyed the radio. "Bridge, sound emergency stations. I'm going to Damage Control Central." As she said that, she started trotting in that direction. By the time she got to the door of the lounge the ship's alarm was sounding.

***

As she walked into DC Central which was just off the crew lounge, she heard more shots. "Report, damn it!" she barked into the radio.

"I think Earl's hit!" came the reply.

What the fuck? Where are they going? DC Central was intended to serve as a command post in the event of fire or other problems.

The far wall was dominated by various displays of ship systems and a schematic, as well as a collection of video monitors with camera feeds. She looked at the schematic, which represented the inhabited area of the ship. It looked like a bicycle tire, which reflected the layout of the passenger and crew areas of their ship. The outside of the tire was deep space, and the inside—connected to various spokes—led to the hub. In reality the tire was spinning, producing gravity, but for simplicity's sake the schematic was fixed.

"Mike, did we ever lock the door to the baggage area?"

"No."

Shit. She keyed the radio. "QRT, secure our bolt hole, now! Green Team, secure the spoke hatches. Any prisoner you see is hostile—shoot to kill!"

"That's money," Mike said.

"They're fucking loose," Victoria said. She turned to the video feed, which was blank. "Skye," Victoria said into her radio. "How do I turn on the video up here?"

"You don't," Skye replied. "The main feed is down here."

Shit. We're blind. She grabbed a microphone which was connected to the ship's PA system. "Attention! We have a passenger revolt! Anybody outside of their cabin will be shot!"

"Central, bridge," an intercom box squawked. She recognized Beale's voice. "I have multiple bandits inbound on radar and exterior video."

"I guess that contact was not a ghost, you fucking idiot," Victoria said. She keyed the intercom. "Keep our pressure doors closed whatever you do."

"On it," he said.

Mike jumped on his radio. "Green team—report status on securing the Blue Line!" The Blue Line, clearly marked on their schematic, was where the inside of the tire was.

She turned and looked at Mike. "Gonna be a bitch doing this blind." She pointed at the dead video monitors.

Mike grunted. "Zack, we need cameras," he said over the radio.

As long as we keep the pressure doors closed, we've got a chance to bargain our way out. She tried to calm herself. *Dear sister, where's our help? I'll let Mike work on that.*

She turned to Beale. "Get those doors closed!"

Kelly

Kelly felt like she was watching herself in a video. Her hand with the gun was shaking, so she went with a two-handed grip. The results were better but still not great. *Breathe now, piss yourself later.*

Bruno's radio crackled. *I should have grabbed his radio.* She was too far away to hear what was said, especially over the din of the alarm. *Six. I've got six bullets left in this clip. Shoot five, dump the clip, and scoot with ten in the new clip and one in the pipe.*

She thought there were two goons in the lobby, judging by flashlight beams. *Let's see if they're smart.*

They were, kind of. Goon One dumped a short burst in her direction from cover on the far side of Bruno's body. She was lying on the floor, and the burst went way high. Goon Two came running, aiming for the open door of the closet like it was the gates of heaven. Kelly fired twice as the goon crossed her field of vision.

Her first round hit the Goon Two in the hip, and he pitched forward and spun to his left. Her second shot was lower than she wanted and caught the goon in the stomach. The goon fired a long burst, lower but still high, as he fell onto his ass facing Kelly. She fired again, catching the goon in the throat. He gurgled as blood fountained out.

"Earl?" Goon One shouted.

Earl's dead, Kelly thought. *Or he will be right quick.*

The alarm thankfully stopped, cutting out in mid-wail.

"Earl!" Goon One shouted again. "I think Earl's hit!"

Ya think? Kelly wondered who Goon One was talking to. *Who cares?* She carefully moved from prone to a crouch. She could barely see the glasses and bottles of the lobby bar. "Goodbye, assholes," she said, firing two rounds at the bar, which sent glass everywhere. She dumped the clip and reloaded, moving to the fan room as she did.

Victoria

"I just lost three airlock doors," Beale said over the intercom.

"Define 'lost,'" Victoria barked back.

"Can't tell if they're open or closed."

"That means they are either open or will be. Try to close them!"

Any reply from Beale was lost to a new radio, the bridge-to-bridge unit. "ValuTrip *Cardinal*, this is the United States Ship *Oklahoma*. I am illuminating you with my main battery lasers. Stop your engines, lower your shields, and prepare to be boarded, over."

"Somehow I don't think they just happened to be in Mercury space," Mike said.

"No shit," Victoria said. "What about the Blue Line? Is the passenger section still secure?"

"We have teams physically at all of them." He pointed at the points on the schematic that represented the pressure doors leading from the central spoke into the main passenger areas. "There's no way that they can get them open now."

"How long does that buy us?" Victoria asked.

"Fifteen, maybe twenty minutes, depending on what kind of cutting gear they brought and who's using it." He tapped again at the schematic. "Then they have to shoot their way past us."

Yeah, it will be armored marines with military rifles against civilian guns and stab-proof vests, and I'm sure they've got super-duper breaching gear. She took a deep breath. *Even cutting Mike's estimate in half that's plenty of time to take out the passengers if we need to.*

The bridge-to-bridge repeated its call.

"Somebody want to talk to the Space Patrol?" Mike said.

"And say what?" somebody else asked. "We surrender?"

"Fuck that," Victoria said. She picked up the handset. "Vessel calling, this is the Mercurian ship *Quicksilver*. I think you've got us confused with somebody else. Over." She looked at the men. "That will buy us a few minutes. Now what are the passengers doing?"

Chapter 27

Mark

"Whoever's driving that thing is an idiot," Mark said, looking at a video feed showing *Cardinal*. The pirated vessel was in a slow turn—not nearly as fast as she could turn and way too slow to dodge the much faster American attack shuttles.

"Vessel calling, this is the Mercurian ship *Quicksilver*. I think you've got us confused with somebody else. Over." Mark glanced up at the radio speaker, which had just emitted that line of bullshit. "Really?" he said.

They had an American Major on the radio, working from the ship's CIC just down the passageway from them. Her voice came over the net. "*Cardinal*, this is *Oklahoma*. Please don't play games with us. Stop your engines and hand over your hostages. Over."

"Time to go bright," General Morehouse said. All the warships had kept their radars off—with radars on, they were too easy to detect, even with crude civilian gear. As her order was relayed, all the warships brought up their radars, and the tactical display filled with contacts.

Humans and computers were busy correlating the new active radar data with what they had passively obtained via telescopic sweeps, which meant contacts were rapidly blinking on and off on the display as the datasets meshed. Two new contacts appeared, on a line from Mercury to *Cardinal*. "New tracks 505 and 506," a watchstander reported. "Standby for IDs."

"That's Samuels' problem for now," Morehouse said, referring to Colonel Samuels on the USS *Atlanta*, commanding the screening warships. "How's our boarding party doing?"

"Bird Two moving now," Mark reported. He was watching a video feed from the attack shuttle.

The problem was that the passengers could get the outer airlock doors open but they couldn't keep them open—the ship's bridge could just command them closed. The solution had been simple but brute force. They had fabricated metal frames and attached them to the noses of the attack shuttles. When a door opened, the shuttle would jam itself in the airlock, frame first. It was the equivalent of putting your foot in a door jamb to hold it open.

As he watched, the attack shuttle jammed the frame into the airlock door as it started to cycle closed. The pilot's timing was good—they caught the frame squarely on the door, wedging it open. "Two's got a breech," Mark relayed. There were a couple of claps of applause in the room. When they'd tried this maneuver on the *Bluejay*, it only worked about half of the time. *But we only need one to succeed.* The other three attack shuttles attempted the same maneuver. Two succeeded, one bounced off. It was more than enough.

"Ma'am," one of Morehouse's aides said, "tracks 505 and 506 appear to be Mercurian cruisers of the *Diligent* class."

"Gee, I wonder what brought them out here?" Morehouse said sarcastically. "Well, Samuels will have to deal with it."

ValuTrip Cardinal

Victoria

"About fucking time," Victoria growled as the video system finally came back online. She'd configured the system to show her a preselected set of cameras. "It's a mixed bag," she said.

Armed people in spacesuits were definitely inside, interacting with groups of hostages in the low-gravity areas of the ship. These areas were normally only used during the embarkation and debarkation process. That was not good.

What was better was that the doors on the Blue Line, granting access to where the bulk of the passengers were still being held, remained closed and her people had set up to defend them. She looked at Mike. "Can we lock the bridge out from controlling the doors?"

"Already did," he said. He pointed at one of the doors in question on the video feed. "It's in full manual. The only way that door opens is from our side."

Or they cut it. "Good. So, Commander Zero, get on the radio. Remind those assholes who are busting into my ship that we can kill the passengers any time we want to." She pointed at a spoke on the schematic. "If I see, or rather if you see, one fucking spacesuit in these corridors, people start to die."

"Copy that."

"In the meantime, some-fucking-body on this ship has a radio and is talking to our attackers. Find them!"

"That can't be!" Mike said. "We had all the radios locked down!"

"Well, either somebody found a radio, or they've got the best fucking Ouija board ever," Victoria said. "The other question is how they are communicating amongst themselves."

"Problem, boss," Skye said over the radio.

"What now?" Victoria replied.

"Check 14-12."

Victoria called up the camera in question. "Blank wall."

"Shouldn't be."

"Hey," somebody on the radio said. "We hear phones ringing in passenger cabins, over."

"Phones?" Mike said. "The prisoners had been locked out of the phone system!"

"Obviously not well enough," Victoria said. Over the radio she asked Skye, "How do we take down the phone system?"

"Central switch is in DC Central, right where you are, under the back counter," Skye said. "Big red on-off toggle. By the way, screen twelve is looking at a data junction room on fourth deck—one deck above you and directly opposite."

And that's where the head of this little resistance is at. "Killing phones," Victoria said, having found the switch in question. She toggled it, and the unit went silent. "That'll fix you!" Victoria said, referring to the prisoners on the phones. "Commander Zero, I think you have some talking to do. Remind the Americans we can kill the hostages." She tapped at the screen. "I'm going to shoot whomever is running this circus."

Mike, in his Commander Zero persona, started working the radios as she left.

USS Oklahoma

Mark

On cue, another voice, American, was heard. "This is the US Space Force destroyer *Grissom*. We are conducting a rescue operation and request you stand clear., Over."

The Mercurian ship captain came back, bleating about how this was Mercurian space. *I don't have time for this. Samuels will have to do his job.* He turned his attention back to the operation on *Cardinal* while the American screening force argued with the Mercurian Navy. Since it was on bridge-to-bridge, anybody, including the pirates on *Cardinal*, could listen to it.

ValuTrip Cardinal

Kelly

"Where do you need me?" Kelly asked, walking into the utility room where they kept the radio.

Hank looked at Kelly, her mouth open. She closed it, then said, "Glad to see you."

More like shocked I'm not dead. "Glad to be seen." *As opposed to being viewed in a funeral home,* which was a saying her grandmother was fond of.

"They'll surely come this way," said Otarski, who was the only other person in the room. He was looking even paler than usual as he pointed at the gun in Kelly's hand. "How'd you get that gun?"

"I took it from Bruno the Green-Haired. He's dead." She looked down at her hands and realized they were bloody. Bruno's blood, from the screwdriver. She felt sick and leaned against the wall. *What was I supposed to do?*

"We heard you blazing away," Hank said dryly. "You save any bullets?"

"Eleven."

"Good." Hank looked at Otarski. "Go to your hole and keep your head down." She pointed at Kelly. "You're with me. We need to be one level up."

They stepped back out into the long and spartan hallway. To their right, an elevator dinged, and Vicky the Piano Lady stepped out. Because of the curve of the ship, the very top of her head wasn't visible.

"Back!" Kelly barked, pulling Hank into the utility room. Vicky fired, her shot going wild. Kelly returned fire as she fell back, not knowing if she hit anything. "Can't go that way."

"What gave you that idea?" Hank said as she pushed the door closed. "Damn that's loud."

"Door's not going to stop a bullet," Kelly said, probably too loudly, as her ears were still ringing from the last shootout.

"Vent, then up," Hank said. More to herself, she added, "I'm too old for this shit."

"Welcome to combat," Kelly said, cambering into the fan room.

"First time for everything."

Victoria

"Son of a bitch!" Victoria said. She'd fallen back into the elevator and the door had closed. She pushed the button and opened the door, staying low and sweeping the hallway with her gun. She advanced toward the equipment room where that damn bitch Hank and Bruno's Martian girlfriend had gone. *I should have figured the Commander would decide to make herself a hero.* They were gone. She debated with herself as to whether she should call more guards and look for them, but the fact of matter was that everybody was busy. She decided to return to DC Central and see if video revealed where they had gone.

She walked into DC Central to hear an argument on the radio. "*Cardinal*, this is *Oklahoma*. If you kill the hostages, any hope you have of surviving is gone. Over."

"Better to be dead than in a cage," Victoria replied under her breath.

"You get our radio people?" Mike asked.

"No. They took a shot at me. Don't know where they went."

"Shot?"

"Shot. With a gun. Presumably Bruno's." *That Martian was a cold bitch.* "Commandos?"

"They have the bridge," he said, while pointing at the video camera feeds. "But they're holding at the central hub."

The relevant cameras showed no activity. Victoria wondered how much she could trust that, given that the Americans surely brought some computer techs along. Given physical access to the camera network and enough time, they could show her anything they wanted to.

"Good, then from the bridge they'll see us drop pressure," Victoria said.

"Dead slaves aren't worth anything," Mike said.

"Not going to kill them," Victoria replied. "Just knock them out." *Run the depressurization for three minutes then run it back up. They'll all be out for a while, giving us a chance to get ahead of this.* She went to the panel they'd jury-rigged to bypass the ship's safeties. "Tell them."

Mike as Commander Zero went out over the radio warning the Americans. *The two biggest fears in a spaceship were fire and depressurization, yet physics meant that to fight one you needed the other.*

If a fire broke out, air pressure would rise because of hot gasses expanding. Too high air pressure meant a risk of hull rupture, so somebody had to be able to vent air. If the fire got too big, the only way to put it out was to vent *all* the air in a space.

Thus, all ships had motorized valves emptying out into vacuum, set up to open on command. Except venting a potentially inhabited space wasn't something one did lightly, thus by design the valves were computer-controlled and only a few people on the ship had the ability to open them. Like the dead captain.

To get around the computer codes, they'd physically rewired the valve motors. Now they were powered by a commercial remote-control transmitter, and completely out of the computer's control. It was a brute-force way to bypass all the bullshit failsafes that prevented depressurization.

She pressed the buttons, and the tell-tale lights went on. As she did, she turned and looked at the main schematic display with a feeling that she'd finally gotten in front of the situation. This feeling faded as the pressure valve indicators stayed resolutely green-for-good, in this case closed, and the pressure gages for the affected spaces did not drop.

"How long is this supposed to take?" Mike asked.

"Faster than this!" Victoria said. "You told me these systems were inspected daily!"

"They were!" he wailed. "I checked them just before dinner!"

"They went back into the damn fan rooms!" Victoria said.

"How many people were in on this?" Mike asked.

"Enough, damn it! Now get your people into them!" Victoria barked.

Suddenly everybody's radio started to squeal. "Jamming!" he said.

"No shit, use the PA!"

Kelly

"I'll need a boost," Kelly said, gesturing at the hatch in the overhead.

"Use this," Hank said, handing over a ladder. "Easier on my back."

Kelly climbed up the ladder just as she heard tapping from the other side. She tapped the response then cranked open the hatch. The muzzle of a gun was pointing at her.

"I've never been happier to have a gun pointed at me," Kelly said.

The spacesuited man grunted and lowered himself into the hatch. He wasn't very big, even in his armored suit. A woman in a Martian Navy suit came down behind him.

"There were supposed to be four of you," Hank said.

"Two of them got stuck," the man said. "That passageway's tighter than a thirteen-year-old's..." he paused, noting his audience. "Well, it's tight."

"So, we gather," the Martian replied. She held out her hand and smiled. "Chief Astronaut Shadout, Martian Marines."

"Tom," the American said.

"He's Delta, and not much of a talker," Shadout said. "They got the Blue Line doors closed."

"I figured," Hank said. "You got silencers and a spare gun?"

"Yes to both," Shadout replied.

"Then let's go get some doors open. Americans spinward and Martians anti?"

Shadout nodded. "Works for me. Lead on."

***

"Security camera other side of this door," Kelly said.

"I know," Shadout replied. "And three meters to the passageway with the door. You open the door, I shoot, then we go."

"Okay," Kelly said.

Shadout quietly counted down from three, and when she got to "go" Kelly pulled the door open. Shadout peeked around the edge with her pistol, popped off two rounds and moved in. They were clearly audible but not the ear-wrecking bangs Kelly had become used to. Kelly hustled down the passageway, gun first and half-a-step behind Shadout.

They were on a landing, industrial-looking, with stairs going up and a pair of hatches, one in the ceiling and one in the floor. As they moved forward, a figure stepped out from behind a support stanchion and fired, catching Shadout in the chest. The Chief gasped but returned fire, dropping the figure.

"You're hit!" Kelly said.

"No shit," Shadout replied. "Armor stopped most of it." Shadout tossed over a rope. "Tie that door closed."

Kelly did as instructed, securing the manual lever which opened the door to an exposed pipe. Shadout had gotten the main pressure door open, and a dozen soldiers streamed down the stairs and into the landing.

"Move down, damn it!" Shadout barked. Two soldiers opened the hatch to the level below, while a third fired a grenade and a burst of automatic weapons fire down the staircase. Thus cleared, the team flowed down. Three soldiers in USSF spacesuits remained.

"We're here to hold this level," one of them said.

"Then let's disperse," Shadout said, "unless you want to end up like those two." She pointed at the pair of dead guards. More firing, a level or two below them, punctuated her remark. One of the guards brought his weapon up.

"Relax," Shadout said. "Those are from the weapons our Marines are carrying." She held a hand up to her helmet, apparently listening to her suit radio. "They found an abandoned checkpoint—pirate guns just sitting on the deck."

"Rats are running," one of the USSF soldiers said.

"Not very far," Shadout replied with a grin. "Now let's spread out in case a rat gets stupid and wants to shoot their way out."

Chapter 28

Victoria

Victoria watched helplessly on the video as her teams of guards were gunned down on the Blue Line. Given that troops immediately flowed into the ship once the doors were opened, the cameras on the other side must have been hacked. She'd turned the phone system back on so they had a way to communicate with the passenger control teams on Deck Five. The news there was no better—two teams had tried to get into fan rooms and been pushed back by passengers. Then her cameras went dead again.

"Well, shit," she said, turning to look at Mike. He'd slipped out of the room, leaving his pistol sitting on a counter. She was alone. "Wonder where he thinks he's going." She went to a cabinet in a corner, which she'd locked with her own padlock. She removed a black box the size of a toaster and patched it into a jack which led to an external antenna. She powered on the device while putting on a headset. When an indicator light went on, she said, "This is Grand Duchess Hakken to the Mercurian Navy. Over."

"Hakken, this is Commodore Michaels. Over."

Well, Alex had gotten their cousin Steve to come get her. "Commodore, I'm glad you're here. It looks like I need a ride. Over."

"Before we proceed, Your Grace," he said. "I'd like to be clear on something. This is a personal favor. It will conclude our family's special relationship. Do you understand? Over."

Yeah. You got me over a barrel and you're going to take advantage of me. "Agreed, Commodore. So, what's the plan? Over."

"Frankly, Your Grace, I'm rather badly outgunned here. Over."

"I doubt the Americans will start a war," she said. "Mars would be very unhappy. Over."

"There are multiple Martian ships in this task force, including a Martian battleship. Over."

Shit. It had been decades since Mars and the Americans had cooperated on a military mission. "Copy. You should have some data from a relative of mine. If so, please look at file Omega Two. Over."

"Stand by. Over." After a gratifyingly brief pause, the reply came back. "I've offered our assistance to the fleet. We will use this to extract you. Over."

Victoria felt a pain in her stomach. Omega Two meant going home in defeat. She looked at the blank video screens. But it meant going home alive instead of in a box or rotting in a cage. "Good. I will be ready. Anything else, cousin? Over."

"Yes. Please destroy the radio immediately. Out."

She took the headset off, set the unit on a sturdy metal desk, and put two bullets into it. The device sparked and gave off a puff of smoke.

Kelly

"Two more, ma'am," Kelly said, gesturing with her pen at the two captured guards that had just arrived. Once the commandos were inside the main passenger area, the pirates had scattered like cockroaches. Kelly had found herself manning a clipboard for Commander America.

"Where'd they find them?" Hank asked.

A Martian Marine answered while saluting Hank. "Sewage treatment room, ma'am."

Hank returned the salute. "Well, if I were a piece of shit trying to hide..."

Kelly grinned, as did the rest of the group. The Marines left, and a Martian Navy four-stripe in a spacesuit walked up. He was followed by another figure in an unfamiliar military suit. Hank and Kelly saluted, which was returned by the man.

"At ease," he said. "Captain First Class Mark Nagata, Martian Navy."

"Commander Henrietta Solis, US Navy, Retired," Hank said.

"You haven't been keeping up with current events," Nagata said, a smile on his face. "Your President recalled you to active duty. He also promoted you to Captain." Nagata looked at Kelly. "As for you, Ms. Rack, you're now a Private First Class, Franklin State Militia."

Well now she really is Captain America. "Thank you, I guess." *And I'm getting out of the military the very instant I can.*

Nagata's face grew serious as he turned to introduce the person accompanying him. "Lieutenant Commander Shah, Mercurian Navy."

"Since this operation is occurring in our space, we're assisting," they said.

Nagata did not look very happy to have that assistance. "Although as this is a US-flagged ship and it was originally hijacked in international space, the United States is retaining jurisdiction. Assisted, of course, by the Martian Navy."

"Of course," Shah replied, a bland look on their face.

A woman in an enlisted USSF spacesuit walked up to the group and displayed a holo of the situation report. "Hostage casualties."

Nagata glanced at it and gestured to Hank. "You know these names."

Hank glanced at it and her face turned white. "Kelly..."

Kelly felt her stomach drop. "Not Spider!"

"I'm sorry..."

Kelly heard her clipboard drop to the floor as she turned on her heels, heading for the infirmary. Spider!

USS Oklahoma

Mark

"Damn," he said, watching Kelly run out.

"A boy her age," Hank said, her eyes watering. "They were sweet on each other."

"He didn't make it?" Mark asked. Her silence was answer enough. Mark put his arm on the woman's shoulder. "You did everything you could."

"If you excuse me," she replied, "I want to go check on our other wounded."

"Of course." She left and Mark turned to Shah. "So, exactly how does the Mercurian Navy want to assist?"

"Well, sir," Shah replied coolly. "We can certainly provide logistical support. Your wounded—"

"Are being transferred to the *USS Boston*, which has excellent medical facilities."

"About *Cardinal* and her passengers?"

"Passengers to *Bluejay*, we're refueling the ship via UNREP from USS *Merrimack* then a skeleton crew will take her back to Earth. And before you ask, pirates will be going to Earth in the *Kentucky's* brig." Mark smiled tightly. "I think we have everything well in hand, Commander."

"There is one other thing, sir," Shah said. "We understand that there are two Mercurian citizens onboard."

"Citizens who were traveling from Mars to Earth and would surely like to complete their journey."

"Actually, no," Shah said. "Or rather, that was not their final destination." He consulted his ocular. "Amy Beach and Henry Vicars. Scheduled to transfer from this ship to the vessel *Sungazer* bound for Mercury."

"There are direct flights from Mars to Mercury," Mark said, wondering where this was going.

"As that may be," Shah replied, "but still..."

"Still what, Commander?"

"Since they were bound for Mercury, and are now here, surely we should take them with us? Don't you think so, sir?"

This stinks to high heaven. Mark looked at the Mercurian. *Well, there had to be somebody here with enough pull to get the locals to look the other way, at least officially, while they brought an unscheduled ship into orbit. I guess we're about to find out who that is.* "I would need to confer with the task force commander," Mark said. He gestured around the ship. "Also, we're a bit discombobulated at the moment. Finding people is going to take a while."

"Of course, sir."

FBI Headquarters, Kansas City

Ray

"Son of a bitch," Ray said, his fingers wrapped around a can of beer. "They did it."

They were watching newsfeeds of the rescue and waiting for the President to make a speech. Ray was still a bit pissed—the Emily Rata woman or whatever her real name was had gotten away—but overall, they'd cracked the case.

His phone pinged with the urgent message tone. He glanced at it and found a text from Mark Nagata.

Who are Alice Beach and Henry Vicars? Mercurian Navy wants to remove them from the ship, and I want to know why.

Ray set down his beer. "Sorry, guys—need to check on something."

***

A few minutes later he found what he was looking for. He dictated a message to Nagata. "Alice Beach and Henry Vicars added by Frank Malan personally *after* the ship departed Mars. No record of them exiting Martian Customs or going through US Immigration Preclearance. Photos look shockingly like Victoria Stevens with different hair and a passenger named Ted Beale. He's the son of our pirate radio operator and a licensed ship's officer. We assume he's also working with the pirates."

ValuTrip Cardinal

Victoria

Damn this shit we bought for the prisoners is cheap, Victoria thought. She'd ditched her regular clothing and put on a wig, then allowed herself to be 'rescued' by an American commando. He was actually quite cute, if a bit short. She'd found a seat in a corner of one of the lounges and was sitting there, interacting as little as possible with the other people.

"Alice Beach?"

Victoria looked up to see an old Martian Chief Astronaut standing in front of her. "I'm Chief Shadout. Could you come with me?"

She was escorted to, of all places, the piano bar of the ship, which had been set up as some kind of headquarters. A Martian Navy Captain and a Mercurian Lieutenant Commander were there, standing by her piano. "I'm Alice Beach," she said.

"I understand you were travelling to Mercury?" the captain asked.

"Yes." Victoria did not have to fake her sadness. "Then this happened."

"Why didn't you go direct?" the captain asked.

"I wanted to visit my sister on Earth," she said. "Emily." As it happened, she did have a sister on Earth and Emily Beach was one of her aliases.

"Ah," the captain said. "And when did you book your cabin?"

"May I ask, sir," the Mercurian Lieutenant Commander asked, "what is the relevance of this? You agree that she's Alice Beach, yes?"

"I know a number of people were on this ship who were travelling under false pretenses," the captain replied tersely. "Such as Bruno Giaberti, ship's electrician and one of the pirates."

"I had nothing to do with any piracy," Victoria said. To the Mercurian, she said, "You can check my passport."

"We did. Captain Nagata, I remind you that it was valid."

"So you have," the captain replied. "Repeatedly. I do find it funny that your little task force just happened to be here."

"We do conduct routine training exercises."

"This is not your routine training area." The captain looked past Victoria. "Captain Solis. Could you join us?"

Victoria looked over her shoulder to see Hank Solis walk up with a shit-eating grin on her face. "Why, Victoria Stevens," she said, grabbing Victoria's wig and pulling it off. "How fitting to see you here."

"I don't know—" Victoria tried.

"Cut the crap, Victoria Stevens," the captain said. He waved to an American in a spacesuit. "Arrest her and read her her rights."

"Devi Shah, are you going to just stand there?" Victoria said.

"How exactly do you know their name?" the captain asked as an American was cuffing her.

"I'm sorry, Your Grace," Shah replied.

"Your Grace?" the captain said, his eyes arching.

"I am the Grand Duke Victoria Hakken, and under the laws of Mercury and the Treaty of Copernicus demand to be transferred to Mercurian soil immediately." Victoria took a step forward but was pulled back by her handcuffs.

"Ship's manifest shows you as a resident of Olathe, Kansas," Hank said.

"I just told you my name," Victoria said. "And under the Treaty of Copernicus—"

"The Treaty only applies to signatories," the captain said. "Mercury is not a signatory. Pretenders to thrones that don't exist are not signatories, especially those that picked their family name out of a book."

"That's a lie!" Victoria shot back. "Our family history—"

"Began on Luna when some bot-fixer made a gun for himself and started shooting," the captain said. "I've got a whole section in my book on the so-called 'Hakken' family." He cocked his head back and looked down at her as if she were some kind of bug.

"Devil!" Victoria heard herself wail.

"I'm sorry, Your Grace," they replied. "We are just here to assist."

"And I think your assistance is no longer needed," the captain said.

"We were looking for another individual..." Shah said as the American arresting her was rattling on about lawyers.

"We captured him on the bridge," the captain said with a smile. "He's already in the brig."

That's not surprising, Victoria thought. Ted Beale was not somebody who thought very quickly on his feet.

The captain's smile faded. "I believe our business here is concluded."

Shah gave her a pained look and walked away. The captain said, "I may have to come over and have a talk with you. I'm working on my next book—*Empire Comes to Space.*"

"Eat shit," Victoria said.

Kelly

Kelly turned down the corridor to the infirmary, which was on the third deck. It was lined with wounded, being treated by a mixed group of military medics, prisoners and civilians. The place stank—reeking of fear, blood, piss and shit.

"Kelly," somebody called. She turned to see Cody, slumped in a chair in a conference room off the corridor. His shoulder was haphazardly wrapped in a bloodstained shirt.

"What happened?" Kelly asked, walking into the room. She looked at the bandage.

"I got shot," he said, grimacing and gesturing with his good hand. "Bullet went through, and they don't think it broke anything, so I'm at the back of the line. At least I got some good pain meds."

Another prisoner slid in front of Kelly and probed the bandage with gloved hands. "You're doing fine," she said. She waved at another woman in a USSF spacesuit. "He's next."

"You a doc?" Cody asked.

"Paramedic," she replied. "Space jockey over there's the doc. We'll have you closed up soon." The prisoner turned to look at Kelly. "Two minutes."

"How'd Spider die?" Kelly asked, feeling suddenly cold for the first time in a week.

Cody frowned. "We were holding the fan room," he said. "When the lead guy came in, I clotheslined him with a wrench. Spider shivved him and grabbed his gun, and they went down in a heap. The next guy on the string coming in got a burst off." Cody paused and took a breath. "I was hit, but our third person got a screwdriver shiv into the shooter's foot. He backed out and I slammed the door shut."

"Then what?"

"Then Spider came up with the first guy's gun. He had some blood on him, but Spider said it wasn't his." Cody took a deep breath. The nurse returned. "Pain pills are fading," he told her.

"You'll be out in a minute," she told him as she started to cut away the excess bandage material.

"Spider?" Kelly asked.

"Pirates sprayed a long burst from outside. Bullets went through the wall but didn't have enough on them to penetrate skin. They blew a couple of fist-sized holes through the door, though. Spider stuck the submachine gun through one of the holes and sprayed a burst back. Then he just passed out."

"He got shot through the door?"

"No, I think he got shot in the initial pass and either didn't realize it or didn't feel it." Cody grimaced, either in pain or recollection. He patted the inside of his leg near his crotch. "Got shot right there."

The nurse looked where Cody was pointing. "Femoral artery's right there. Cut that and you bleed quickly." She looked at Kelly. "I need to take him."

"Just tell me where the bodies are?"

"Sorry to say, kid, but pretty much where they dropped," the nurse said. "We're focusing on the living right now."

Kelly felt her eyes water. "God damn them."

***

Kelly found herself sitting on the floor in the hallway outside of the aid station. The nurse tapped her on the shoulder. "Cody's doing fine."

"Thanks," Kelly said, not trusting herself to say more.

"So, what now."

"Huh?"

"For you. What now?"

"I don't know. Can I see him?"

"Cody? Yeah, he's inside."

"No," Kelly said. "Spider."

The nurse shook her head. "He's not here. We're focused on the living, not the dead."

Kelly found herself standing up. "It's not right leaving our dead just lying around." She dusted off her hands. "I guess we need to organize"—she swallowed hard—"body recovery. And notifications to next of kin."

"Probably," the nurse replied. She waved at somebody who was beckoning from the door to the aid station. "Sorry, I got to—"

"Take care of the living," Kelly said. "I'll get to work on the dead."

Kansas City

Ray Volk

Ray propped his feet up on one of the two deck chairs which dominated the small deck of his condo. He lit a cigar, glad that they had finally been legalized again, and took a deep drag. He waved the cigar at the setting sun, then put it in the antique and hard-to-find ash tray.

"Well done, if I do say so myself," he said.

"Do you always talk to yourself?" Ralph said, walking out on the deck. He was wearing a Martian Marine T-shirt and was sweaty from his jog. Also cute as fuck. He handed Ray a beer. "What were you thinking of for dinner tonight?"

"Burnt tips at Jack Stacks," Ray said.

Ralph flashed his cute smile. "I have no idea what a 'burnt tip' is, but I'll try anything once."

ACKNOWLEDGEMENTS

On the one hand, writing is a solitary pursuit, involving many quiet hours in front of a keyboard, hours stolen from friends, family, and the fun stuff of life. On the other hand, a book does require a surprisingly large number of people to pull off. Here's a partial list of those I need to thank for this book that you (hopefully) enjoyed.

First, my editor and publisher, Bill Tracy, who took a gamble on it, and his lovely spouse Heather, who made my typos and bad grammar into something close to proper English. I'd also like to thank the nice people at Moorbooks who created the wonderful cover. Third, I have to thank my writing group, all of whom provided much useful feedback in telling this story. They are Don Hunt, Wren Roberts, Jason Evans, Lauren Cidell, and Dex Greenbright. Without them this story would have never been born.

Fourth, I would like to thank the folks who put on the Writing Excuses Retreat and Workshop. A very early version of this work was critiqued there, and much value was gained. I would like to especially thank Mary Robinette Kowal, Sandra Taylor, and Howard Taylor. It's also where I met the Tracys, so the Retreat was a two-fer. Speaking of critique groups, I would be remiss in not thanking Rich Chwedyk, who was the prime mover in the Windycon Writers Workshop. Meeting and being critiqued by professional authors is critical in the learning process.

This is my fourth novel. The three previous books, which are a loose trilogy, were published in various formats by Eric T. Reynolds and Charles Sheehan-Miles. I learned a lot from both men. Lastly, I'd like to thank librarians everywhere for instilling in me the love of reading.

ABOUT THE AUTHOR

Chris Gerrib has been an avid fan of science fiction and space exploration since he was a child riding his bicycle to his small town's library where he memorized every book they had on the subject. Since then, he spent a tour in the US Navy, got an MBA, and now has a day job with a multi-national software company as a Project Manager. He lives in the Chicago suburbs and is active in his local Rotary Club. This is his fourth science fiction novel.

You can visit Chris' website at www.privatemarsrocket.net or read his blog at chris-gerrib.dreamwidth.org.

Please take a moment to review this book at your favorite retailer's website, Goodreads, or simply tell your friends!

Made in the USA
Middletown, DE
23 July 2022

69757386R00175